The sheet winches were g   shoulders jerking over   cockpit. The foot of her genoa swept across the foredeck. Bill's yellowish face turned to look at it. He just stood and stared, his mouth open, not even beginning to move. The sail caught him flat in the stomach and swept him into the sea.

'Man overboard!' I yelled at Paul.

Heads turned in the gorilla pit of my boat. But *Castor*'s sails did not shiver. The towering pyramid of sailcloth came on.

'Nobody heard,' said someone.

The pursuit boats were a good half-mile astern. The sea off Sydney is very deep, and there are sharks in it.

'Let's go,' I said. 'Go about, quick!'

The deck surged under my feet as I wound the wheel hard over. We went round with a flap and roar of sails, and the mainsheet man let the sheet whine off the winch as the boom went out, de-powering, slowing down. Our foredeck man said, 'I see him!' I caught a glimpse of a little black head bobbing on the crest of a shining blue wave. Then I heard the hail.

A SPHERE BOOK

First published in Great Britain
by Michael Joseph Limited 1989
Published by Sphere Books Limited 1990

Copyright © Sam Llewellyn 1989

Reproduced, printed and bound in Great Britain by
Cox & Wyman Ltd, Reading

ISBN 0 7474 0189 6

Sphere Books Ltd
A Division of
Macdonald & Co (Publishers) Ltd
Orbit House
1 New Fetter Lane
London EC4A 1AR

A member of Maxwell Macmillan Pergamon Publishing Corporation

1

The voice in my ear shouted, 'Tack now!'

It was thin and tinny, the voice, because it was coming two thousand vertical feet to the VHF receiver in the pocket of my shorts.

'Wait,' I said into the throat mike that constricted my neck but left my hands free for *Pollux*'s leather-covered wheel.

Silence fell, except for the rattle of the helicopter in the blue Australian sky above the glistening white tower of the sails, and the whoosh and plunge of the big aluminium hull. I enjoyed it. There are few silences when you are working a twelve-metre up to the point where it will sail in the elimination races for the America's Cup. Those there are are tense and full of hard thought.

The man beside me broke the silence. 'What about it?' he said.

I glanced astern and to starboard. Across two hundred feet of glittering blue sea, the claret-red bow of *Castor* sliced into a blue wave and kicked water back at her foredeck man, wrestling the head of a sail into the groove of the forestay. The foredeck man was called Bill Rogers, and the sun was shining in the sweat on his face. He did not look well. Before the race, he had told me he had 'flu. But the men who ran the Constellation Challenge did not see 'flu as a reason for staying ashore.

'Wait,' I said. I could feel the tension coming off the men; ten of them, sweating under the Sydney sun in the aluminium box of the hull. A twelve-metre is not the ballerina of the sea that yachting journalists would like you to believe. It has more in common with a tank than a ballerina: twenty-five tons of metal, hugely overpowered, built for battle.

'Go!' screamed the voice in my ear.

I squinted up into the bright sky. The helicopter was flying backwards. It contained Geoffrey Lampson, the coach. He would be creased and red and sweating, gnawing his unlit pipe because far below on the wrinkled metal shield of the water the pawns were not doing as they were told.

'*Pollux*,' squawked the voice again. 'Tack now!'

I looked again. *Castor*'s foredeck was a billowing mass of Mylar sail. Bill Rogers was battering it down. He looked sluggish, off balance. *Now*.

'Go!' I said, and spun the wheel.

Pollux's deck came level under my feet as her nose turned through the wind. The fat aluminium boom clanked across, the genoa slid smoothly round the front of the mast, and a spatter of spray sailed aft as she leaned again, to starboard this time, and shot across *Castor*'s bows. I saw Rogers's mouth open, a dark O in his yellowish, sweating face. Then he flung himself flat on the deck, into the billows of the unset sail, as *Castor* turned after us and the genoa swept across the foredeck like a great Mylar squeegee.

'Caught him on the hop,' said the tactician with a grin.

'Good,' squawked Lampson's voice in my ear, claiming the credit for my timing. 'Worked very well. Keep her on that tack.'

I was sweating with heat, and tension, and anger at the chittering from the mechanical insect hovering above me. 'Let's tack,' I said.

The winches jingled and we tacked again, back on to starboard. The gap of water between the boats was three hundred feet now. Lampson's voice yammered in my ear. I tried not to listen. Paul Welsh, *Castor*'s helmsman, was shouting. He sounded nervous, which was fine. I kept my eye on the gap between our transom and *Castor*'s bow. We had won the

2

start, and kept him covered. Now, inch by inch, we were moving away.

Castor and *Pollux* were owned by the Constellation Challenge. For six weeks now, we had been trial-horsing against each other out here in the blue Tasman Sea. And for six weeks, I had been getting more and more depressed.

To put together a twelve-metre challenge, you need to find a lot of money, and some managers who know how to organise the spending of the money on a couple of boats, and some people who will sail the boats fast. In a good syndicate, making the boat go is the object of the exercise, and there will be no nasty little secrets.

But the Constellation Challenge was being run by his Lordship of Honiton, a pillar of the ludicrously smart Pall Mall Yacht Club, who would not have recognised democracy if it had turned up at luncheon on a bed of rice. Honiton ran an international management consultancy and a medium-sized property empire; nasty secrets were as essential to him as oxygen. He had appointed Geoffrey Lampson as coach, and Lampson had gone out and hired the crews. I had been doubtful about joining up. On the other hand, even if you are winning a lot of races, invitations to helm a potential America's Cup challenger do not land on the mat every day. I had been regretting it ever since, and so had plenty of other people in the crews.

The voice in my ear had been shouting for a couple of minutes now. I had stopped listening.

In the boat astern, Paul Welsh was squinting up at his sails. I saw him nod to the trimmers. He was going to have a try at tacking away.

'Tacking,' I said, and wound the big leather-bound wheel.

We tacked simultaneously.

I saw Paul's black eyebrows draw together in a scowl. He hated losing, particularly to me. He always had, ever since we had been children. He tacked again. We followed suit.

A puff of wind got under the sail stacked on *Castor*'s foredeck. It jumped and billowed. Paul shouted, 'Kill that!' His voice was raw and angry.

3

Bill went up on to the deck after it. I had been watching him work for three months, and I could see that he was groggy, travelling at half speed.

'Tacking!' shouted Paul.

Myself, I would have waited till Bill had done his stuff. But Paul was completely ruthless when it came to winning, on or off the water. In his book, what happened to Bill was Bill's problem.

The sheet winches were going, the grinders' meaty shoulders jerking over the big handles in the cockpit. The foot of her genoa swept across the foredeck. Bill's yellowish face turned to look at it. He just stood and stared, his mouth open, not even beginning to move. The sail caught him flat in the stomach and swept him into the sea.

'Man overboard!' I yelled at Paul.

Heads turned in the gorilla pit of my boat. But *Castor*'s sails did not shiver. The towering pyramid of sailcloth came on.

'Nobody heard,' said someone.

The pursuit boats were a good half-mile astern. The sea off Sydney is very big, and deep, and there are sharks in it.

'Let's go,' I said. 'Go about, quick!'

The deck surged under my feet as I wound the wheel hard over. We went round with a flap and roar of sails, and the mainsheet man let the sheet whine off the winch as the boom went out, de-powering, slowing down. Our foredeck man said, 'I see him!' I caught a glimpse of a little black head bobbing on the crest of a shining blue wave.

Then I heard the hail.

I knew what I was going to see before I saw it. Paul had assumed that Bill had dropped flat and let the sail go over his back. The idiot must be thinking I was tacking across his bows. The rules only allowed me to do that if I had clear water. What I saw was his bow, a sharp red blade tearing down an ink-blue slope of water, chopping straight at *Pollux*'s mid-section.

I spun the wheel, paying off. *Castor* held her course; with Paul Welsh at the helm, she would. The gibbering in my ear was climbing the octave. He was screaming about the rules of racing. But when a man has fallen overboard, race rules yield

4

to common sense, and no sane race committee will hold you to blame for saving life.

I roared again, 'Man overboard!'

Castor's bow came on. But *Pollux* was turning hard.

There was a moment in which everything became still. I could see the faces of *Pollux*'s grinders, the whites of their eyes showing all the way round the irises as they realised what was going to happen too. They started to shout.

It happened.

That sharp claret-coloured bow with its moustache of white water caught *Pollux* on the slope of her retroussé transom with a noise half-way between a crunch and a clang. The deck lurched under my feet, flinging me on to the mainsheet man. The hulls wallowed together, *Castor*'s nose buried in *Pollux*'s tail. Metal grated on metal with a long, wrenching groan. For a second, I thought: it's all right, it's not the rudder, it's not a vital spot.

Then I saw the runner.

The runner is the bit of rigging that runs from close to the boat's stern to halfway up the mast. It has a big block at its bottom, which you use to tension the runner and support the mast. The stay is under four tons of load, and all the load is held on the titanium pin that secures the backstay to the deck.

As *Castor*'s bow wrenched out of the gash it had cloven in our stern, the block moved.

I had time to shout, 'Look out!'

Then the block tore out of its mounting. Something walloped my right forearm, hard. The mast, unflexing, flung the block at the sky like a bait on the end of a fishing line. I watched that black lump fly up, up into the blue. Everything seemed to move very slowly. The middle of the mast flexed forwards. The genoa was full. Someone was shouting about easing sheets, taking the load out of the mast. I recognised the voice. It was my own.

Too late.

There was a heavy *crack*, and the top fifty feet of the mast bulged forward and collapsed. Sails roared and drummed and

5

tore. The hull became heavy and sluggish in the water. The shouting stopped for a horrorstruck second, and started again.

In the eye of the storm, everything seemed quiet. It was the pain that kept the noise out. Big pain, in my right forearm. I found I was bending forward over it. I wanted to put my head on the cool metal deck, but I could see Bill in the blue water thirty feet downwind. He was jerking his head around nervously. Looking for sharks, I thought. With my good hand I yanked a horseshoe lifebelt out of its clips on the lifelines and tossed it at him. I did not see if he caught it. The pain in my arm was growing until I was wanting to shout out loud. The VHF was screaming in my ear. I yelled, 'Shut up,' into the throat mike. Then I clawed it off my neck with my left hand, snatched the earphone out of my ear, and tossed the whole rig clumsily overboard. I found I was crouching on the deck. It was wet; there was water in the bottom of the boat. A lot of water. When I squinted up, the tangle of mast and rigging and sails was leaning wearily over the waves. Four grinders were helping Bill up over the side. They were having an easy job of it, because *Pollux*'s freeboard had become very low. I thought with a jolt: she's sinking.

Castor came alongside. My crew scrambled over. They had a dazed look under the bright sun. I waited till last, partly because that is what captains are supposed to do, but also because by now I was having trouble moving. The pain was a hard ball of agony above my right wrist. Every time my heart beat, the pulses banged like red-hot gongs.

'Give us your hand!' yelled a grinder, high above me on *Castor*'s claret-coloured side.

My right hand was hurting so much that I needed my left to hold it still. So they leaned over and grabbed the back of my shirt and dragged me aboard. Paul Welsh was looking at me, deeply tanned, his broad forehead creased over his movie star's nose.

'What the *hell*,' he said. 'You tacked in my water. You – ' His eyes had flicked down my arm. 'Jesus,' he said, and his brown skin turned the colour of putty.

He was establishing his alibi, but my arm hurt too much for me to argue. I held it tenderly and looked overboard at *Pollux*.

One of the pursuit boats, a big ChrisCraft, was coming to take her in tow. But I could tell from the way the white bubbles spattered out of the jagged hole in her back end that it was going to be too late.

Paul said, 'You didn't have to do that. The pursuit boat would have picked him up.' His eyes were flicking from *Pollux* to me, and he looked as if he was going to be sick. I had not wanted to look down at my arm, but now my eyes followed his. It was the same old arm as ever, with one difference. Just above the wrist, there was a new elbow under the Australia-brown skin.

'Ugh,' I said, and my stomach churned with the sort of vertigo you get when you know something bad and permanent has happened to your body.

'Let's get you home,' said Paul, solicitously. Even through the pain, I knew he was saying it for the crew's benefit, not mine. One of your publicity-conscious self-aware nice guys, that was Paul.

But nobody listened. Instead, we watched *Pollux* spew a last pile of silver bubbles, and slide away like a porpoise into the deep.

The wind bit, and the boat heeled, and I hung on to my arm and watched the bits of debris that floated on the blue waves where half a million pounds' worth of boat was falling slowly towards the bottom of the Tasman Sea.

2

The hospital was clean and cool, full of little palm trees and reporters shouting questions about sunk boats, and was this another of Martin Devereux's displays of aggression. I kept my mouth shut in case I threw up all over them. They clustered round the door of the room where the doctor was. The doctor shut it in their faces and did nasty things under bright lights. Then he told me I was very lucky. Something had hit my radius and ulna a hell of a whack, three inches above the wrist. The wrist joint was unaffected. I looked at the plaster and the frozen fingers sticking out of the end, numb with local anaesthetic, and said yes. I did not feel very lucky. The nurse asked for my autograph, and I could not give it to her because I am right-handed and I could not write. So she signed hers on the plaster, and put her telephone number there too, and winked at me. She had a red mouth and hot black eyes, but all I wanted to do then was go home and lie down until my arm had lost its sense of outrage. Besides, there was Camilla.

The Constellation Challenge looked after its helmsmen well, according to its lights. It did not believe in its crews living hugger mugger, all in one big house. It liked (as Honiton put it) to separate the officers from the ratings. It had rented me an apartment in the top back of a big wooden house in Rush-cutters Bay.

Each step of the outside stairway felt six feet high. There was a big window in the living room, with a balcony. The glass was cool on my forehead. The view was of blue water and bluish gum trees, with heavy suburban houses crouching shoulder deep in the greenery. I was tired of its foreignness. I wanted to see the grey sky and sharp horizons of Marshcote, my home on the south coast of England. Back there the pubs would be noisy, full of the smell of salt and wet jerseys and smoke. Henry and Mary would be stumping round the yard, dealing out the pay packets and swearing at the rain which would undoubtedly be drifting across the marshes on the eternal wind, rattling the corrugated iron of the sheds and pocking the oily water in the corners of the marina basin.

But this was Sydney, and there was going to be hell to pay.

The bathroom smelt of Camilla's scent. She only stayed the occasional night, but there was a spare of everything. Her unguents were arranged with military precision on the glass shelf above the bath: oil for before, after, during and while thinking about sunbathing, and other bottles of stuff whose uses I would never know. The local anaesthetic was wearing off, and my arm was throbbing angrily. I did not want to dope myself with the strong painkillers the hospital had given me. So I rummaged in the cabinet for paracetamol. There were eye drops and lipsticks and vitamin pills. No paracetamol.

I glowered at myself in the mirror. I have got a big, roundish face, blue eyes and a large nose. My chin sticks out, which is part of the reason people think I am aggressive. My hair is yellowish brown, and needed cutting.

Tonight, I was by no means a pretty picture.

The sun had got at my nose, which was peeling. Otherwise, I was greenish-grey. The collar of my team shirt carried an advertisement for Three Stars Scotch whisky. The chest bore the logo of Green Parrot Homes, a building company.

You look ridiculous, I thought. As ridiculous as a bathroom with six kinds of sun oil and no paracetamol. But then the bathroom was Camilla's territory, and Camilla never got hangovers, because hangovers give you wrinkles under your eyes and the process which generates them makes you lose control.

I struggled out of my clothes and into the shower, and let the water go to work on the salt. I held my plaster up and out of the water, which helped the throbbing, but not much. Then I got dry and went into the bedroom, and lay down on the bed and wished I was elsewhere.

After a bit, the arm got so bad that I ate the hospital painkillers, and got drowsy.

I thought about Henry and Mary. I wanted to see them. It was not just that I had a broken arm that hurt, and that the Constellation Challenge was getting up my nose. Mary had been writing me letters; and what was in the letters was worrying.

I heard the front door slam. That would be Camilla. She said, 'Oh, *really*!' That would be the clothes on the floor.

I said, 'I'm in here.'

'Super,' she said. 'Only I wish you'd clean up after yourself.'

'Ah,' I said. 'Sorry.'

She did not come in. She stayed out there, tidying up. The telephone rang. 'Hello?' she said. Then her voice became soft and lovely. 'Oh,' she said. 'I'll tell him. Hang on.' Then to me, 'It's Jack Halpern, of the *Sydney Morning News*.'

'I don't want to talk to him,' I said.

'*Martin!*' There was a hint of the whiplash in her voice.

I said, 'I'm feeling a bit rough. I've broken my arm.'

'My poor *sweet*,' she said. I heard her make an excuse and put the telephone down. Immediately, it rang again. She answered it. 'Could you ring back?' she said. Then she said, 'Oh *George*,' in a new, reverent voice. '*Lovely* to see you at the Taits last night.' There was only one person called George she used that voice with. I lay and ached and waited for it. 'Darling!' she cooed. 'It's Georgie Honiton.'

I sat up on the bed. The door opened. Camilla was tall, with endless brown legs and one of those short-nosed, wide-mouthed model's faces. She was wearing a turquoise one-piece bathing suit that fitted her with breathtaking exactness. Her eyes matched the bathing suit. As usual, they were slightly suspicious.

I walked stiffly to the telephone. The voice at the other end did not bother with hellos. 'Devereux,' it said. 'Where were you?'

'I've been to the hospital,' I said. 'I've broken my arm.'

'Ah,' said Honiton. 'Sorry to hear that.' His voice was warm as baked Alaska. 'Have you got a minute? We want to debrief.'

'I'm on my way,' I said, and hung up.

Camilla said, 'You can't drive with that arm.'

'I'll get a taxi.'

She smiled, sweetly. She had small white teeth, very sharp. 'No you don't,' she said. 'I'll take you. Georgie'll never forgive me if I let you go wandering the streets in this state.' She kissed me on the cheek. 'So up you get, and off we pop.'

I grinned at her, as best I could. 'Thank you, Nanny,' I said.

She pouted. You lived with Camilla on the understanding that you sailed glamorous races in glamorous boats, and won. Off the water, Camilla took care of things. Neither of us was supposed to have any illusions about the way things were.

As she drove across town I slumped among the cushions and hugged my arm and thought about the pure glamour of the America's Cup, and tried to remember when I had last spent time with real friends and worn shirts without whisky advertisements on them, and sailed a race without Geoffrey Lampson's voice squawking in my ear.

The Challenge office was tacked on to the sheds by the dock in the inner harbour. The sheds housed a big workshop, where between outings the fitters tore the boats' hulls apart and put them together again. Camilla kissed me goodbye, and drove off to a cocktail party. I wiped off the lipstick and went in.

The office contained two palm trees, three desks, six telephones and two pictures: one of a naked girl doing something lewd with the boom of a one-tonner, the other a photograph of *Endeavour II* losing the America's Cup in 1934. It was a small, sweaty room. This evening, it contained some powerful people.

There was Geoffrey Lampson, his heavy red jowls hanging over his white collar, his narrow eyes fixed on the naked lady.

11

There was Georgie Honiton, tanned and spruce in a blazer, smiling his urbane smile as he chatted with plump Mr Morton from the Constellation Bank, the Challenge's main sponsors. Honiton's cunning amber eyes flicked across, acknowledged my presence, and flicked back to Mr Morton, whose red lips were pursed, as if he was about to refuse someone an over-draft.

Paul had brought two trimmers and a tactician. They all sailed with him when he was match racing, and presumably came in for a share of his prize money, so he could count on their loyalty. Politics have never been my strong point. Paul was looking faintly smug. I began to feel uneasy, the way you feel when you lose the initiative at a race start. I should have brought some people.

Paul grinned at me with his white movie star's teeth. I grinned back, shoving the ugly banging in my arm to the back of my mind, trying to grab the advantage back. He had very little to grin about. The ramming had been his fault. He was still wearing his shorts and Three Stars shirt, but he had put on a tie.

'Patched you up, eh?' said Honiton. His cynical eyes were not on my cast, but on where my tie should have been. He might not know a lot about boats, but he was an authority on etiquette. As far as he was concerned, Challenge crews wore Challenge ties on Challenge occasions.

My arm throbbed. I had blundered.

'So we're all here,' he said. 'Good evening, everyone. Perhaps you'd like to start, Geoffrey?'

Lampson's thick red hands lay like cuts of meat on the desk. 'All right,' he said. 'Martin, sorry you hurt yourself. But I might as well tell you straight. I was giving you instructions from the chopper. You ignored them.'

'That's nothing to do with it,' I said, caught off balance. The collision had self-evidently been Paul's fault.

'And then, God knows why, you tacked slap across Paul's bow,' said Geoffrey.

Somebody slammed a fork-lift truck into a container on the

quay outside. But as far as I was concerned, the world had gone as quiet as when you fall down a well.

'Could you repeat that?' I said. There was an unpleasant smell in the room: fear, and anger, and something else less definable.

'You tacked across his bow,' said Geoffrey.

'In order to pick up Bill Rogers. He'd gone overboard.' I kept my voice calm and level. Martin Devereux was well known for saying what he thought, but this was no place for it. Paul's face did not move.

'We know,' said Geoffrey, breathing heavily. 'We have eyes. There were support boats. They would have pulled him out.' His voice was getting heavier, gaining momentum. 'But instead, you put your boat about a length in front of Paul – '

'Four lengths,' I said. 'Easily.'

'That is not what Paul says,' said Geoffrey. 'That's not what I saw.' I stared at him. He was lying. Why?

The explanation swam up through the painkillers. A helmsman with a broken arm was out of action for at least a fortnight. And if that helmsman was reckoned by Honiton to be dangerously independent, and liable to speak his mind to anyone who would listen, who better to parade in front of the sponsors as the man who had sunk their investment, and never mind that he was the best helmsman on the quay.

Suddenly I recognised the smell in the room. It was the smell of scapegoats.

I said, 'You know damned well that is not true. The pursuit boats were half a mile astern. There are sharks in that sea. Paul didn't alter course, so it was a fair assumption he hadn't seen Bill. I was obliged to go back for him, and Paul was obliged to keep clear of me.'

Honiton's jaw was thrust forward, and he looked grave; but the gravity could not hide a glimmer of pleasure. 'Kindly moderate your language,' he said. 'Paul maintains that you tacked in his water immediately before the collision.'

'I'm afraid the guys in the crew will back me up,' said Paul, with a boyish flash of the white teeth.

'Not Bill,' I said.

'Ah,' said Paul. 'But he was overboard, wasn't he?'

I looked at him, and at Geoffrey and Honiton, and knew there was nothing else I could say. They had put the dotted line around my neck, and written CUT HERE.

I said, 'You left Bill for the support boat because you were well behind, and I was slowing down for him, and you wanted to catch up. And when you saw you could foul me too, you came in to ram. You sank *Pollux*. Now you're trying to stick me with it.'

There was a deep, deadly silence. I stood there and felt ill, and knew I had done it again. Tact and diplomacy, I thought. The soft answer that turneth away wrath. Scapegoats are meant to have better manners.

'I think you'd better withdraw that,' said Honiton.

His eyes were hooded like a toad's. Paul stood there looking like a surly Greek god with whisky advertisements all over his shirt.

I was damned if I was going to sit there and be Martin Devereux the mad Anglo-Irishman, who said what he thought and took the consequences without a blink. So I said, 'That's enough of this rubbish. I am resigning, as of now.'

Their faces became stiff – not with surprise, I realised; they were holding their breath, hoping I would not unsay what I had just said and make them do their own dirty work.

Honiton said, 'You are not behaving very well, Martin.'

Paul was watching me closely. I could see the sly triumph in his nice brown eyes. I remembered a school sailing match on the Thames at Bourne End in Firefly dinghies. Paul was at Eton, and I was at a school near Reading with a name he pretended he could not remember. I had beaten him good and proper. And he had stood there afterwards, with that look in his eye, and said, 'No wonder he's good. He works in the yard that looks after my father's boat.'

His team-mates had sniggered. He had not succeeded in shaming me. But I had knocked him into the river anyway, while his friends stood there with their jaws hanging. We had never looked back, Paul and I.

14

'In fact,' said Honiton, 'I shall make it my business to tell . . . those whose job it is to know . . . how you have conducted yourself.'

Resignation accepted, with extreme prejudice. 'I may get over it,' I said.

Honiton permitted himself a thin stretch of the lips. The sweat of relief broke out on Lampson's brow. The gods had accepted the sacrifice.

'Watch yourself, Paul,' I said. 'They'll have you next.'

Then I walked out of the room through the reporters yelling questions, and put my throbbing arm into a taxi.

Camilla came home at half past eight.

'Darling,' she said. 'I've heard. I'm so sad for you.'

I said, 'Don't worry yourself.' Her eyes were not worried. They were shifting round the room. My heart sank. She had come home not to show her sympathy but to look for her address book.

The telephone rang. As soon as Camilla walked into a house, the telephones all started ringing. I heard her in the hall.

'*Paulie!*' she said. 'Look, it's a bit awkward.' She did not sound awkward. I got up, feeling sick. Her voice became lower. I heard her say 'Tomorrow.' Then she rang off, and came back into the room.

I had already pulled my suitcase off the wardrobe.

'What are you doing?' she said.

'Packing,' I said. 'I'm going home.' I took a deep breath. 'Are you coming?' I held my breath, but I knew the answer already.

'Home?' she said, staring at me with her huge turquoise eyes. 'Home where?'

'Home,' I said. 'England.'

Her nostrils were wide and delicate. They made me think of thoroughbred horses. Now, they were flared with scorn.

'*England?*' she said. 'In *March*? You must be *joking*.'

I nodded. 'Yes,' I said. 'I was.' I began to drag shirts out of the chest of drawers, using my wrong hand. 'So that's it.'

'That's what?' She had a way of opening her eyes extra wide that made them blank and obtuse.

15

'Us. Over.'

'Oh, don't be so *boring*,' she said. The eyes flicked at her watch.

'You'd better go,' I said. 'You'll be later for dinner.'

She nodded. The blonde hair fell on either side of her face. For a moment I thought she looked sad, but it was only the shadow. 'I'd better get my things,' she said. 'Tomorrow.'

'Yes,' I said.

The door slammed. Her heels clicked down the stairs, heading for tomorrow, and Paulie, now the Constellation Challenge's star helmsman. I sat on the bed in the big white room which felt empty and desolate, and thought: that is what you get for getting involved with a racer chaser.

Eventually, slowly and painfully, I got up and started to pack my shirts.

The telephone rang all night, and from time to time people hammered on the door. I lay and let my arm throb and my head ache, and did not answer.

Next day, on the morning plane to London, the stewardess brought the papers round. 'Oh,' she said. 'It's Dev, right?' She smiled, a nice red lipsticky Australian smile. I admitted I was, and she winked, and I smiled back, feeling hollow. Then I started on the papers.

The front page of the *Sydney Herald* summed it up neatly. DEV SINKS BOAT, BREAKS ARM, WALKS OUT, it said. The story was full of conventional regrets from Honiton. It would have been full of quotes from me, too, if I had spoken to anybody last night.

Instead, it gave a quick and mostly accurate résumé of my life and habits. It pointed out that I was among the top sixteen match racers in the world, and among the three most outspoken. It wondered whether what it called my notorious propensity for plain speaking had led to my resignation. And it speculated on the possible effect of said plain speaking on my future career.

I was beginning to speculate about the same thing. Paul was

16

a sly and polished performer in committee; that is what Eton and a red-brick palazzo in Hampshire will do for you. Myself, I came from a wreck of a house in County Waterford and a by-no-means smart boatyard on the south coast of England, places where hiding what you thought was not regarded as much of a virtue.

I threw the paper away, eased my bad arm in its sling, and looked out of the window at the coast of New South Wales down there in the dawn.

Getting slung off the Constellation Challenge was not, in theory, a disaster. Having dropped out of the year's match racing competitions, I could in theory drop back in. In practice, it was not as easy as that. You compete in match racing by invitation. Most of the invitations for the summer's racing had already gone out. And Honiton, from what he said at our last meeting, was going to do his best to make sure that what invitations were still to come went to anybody but Martin Devereux. Honiton was a powerful man.

It looked as if Martin Devereux had better settle down to being a junior partner in the South Creek Boatyard, and forget about match racing for a year or so.

By this time the businessmen in Club Class had read the front pages, too, and were beginning to stare. I did my best to look like somebody else, and pulled Mary's letter out of my brief-case, and put my cast on it to stop it fluttering away in the forced draught, and read it for the tenth time.

Hope it's all going well, the letter said. *We've been having non-stop gales, as you can imagine.* I could. I had grown up with Mary and Henry, in their red-brick house by the harbour where the wind howled across the marshes. *Henry is working too hard. Everybody wants fitting-out and they all want it done by Easter at the latest, and Henry's damned if he's going to let any of them down.* I could imagine that, too. Henry had his eccentricities. But he had commanded a destroyer escort on the Murmansk convoys, and he was strongly attached to the notion that a gentleman's word is his bond.

Actually, I'm getting worried about the old brute. We're losing a lot of customers, and I'm afraid it's because he's getting too old for it.

There was a terrible pile-up this last gale, two boats written off. The insurance premiums are up through the roof, and he's muttering about enemy action.

I folded the letter and shoved it back into the briefcase. Henry was getting old, all right; he was seventy-one. But the sting of the letter was in the last sentence. He belonged to a tradition that said you neither made nor accepted excuses. If he was muttering about enemy action, then the chances were that enemy action was taking place.

Furthermore, Mary had been married to Henry while he had been thrashing his way through the U-boats in the Barents Sea, and in the way of Navy wives, she had developed an upper lip as stiff as a plank. For her to mention that she was worried was the equivalent of anyone else hoisting the Ensign upside down and shooting off every flare in the locker.

I took one of the hospital's painkillers, and settled back. By the sound of things, there was going to be so much to do at South Creek that there would be very little time for match racing, even if someone did ask.

3

There are many parts of the south coast of England more beautiful than Marshcote. It is a sprawling town of red brick that appeared in the 1850s, when the Great Western Railway took one of its branch lines near the then fishing port of Wyke. Wyke had vanished under red-brick terraces. The terraces had filled with dockers and pilots and hauliers and the town had, briefly, prospered. For forty years, the railway carried the goods that landed in the harbour up to the main line, and away to Bristol and the manufacturing districts of the Midlands and the Home Counties. But prosperity was short-lived.

The Creek silted up, and a restricted channel was kept open only by dint of expensive dredging. The ships that could use the harbour became smaller and smaller, until all that remained was a smattering of inshore fishing boats, whose owners were to be found leaning in a state of alcoholic gloom over the mahogany bar of the Burnett Arms.

Marshcote, having submerged Wyke's cob and thatch with a grim thoroughness that daunted the least selective of tourists, had set about crumbling gracelessly into its surrounding salt marshes, unloved either by its inhabitants or its visitors.

Twenty-six hours after take-off from Sydney, I got off the Fish Train. Actually what fish there was nowadays went by road, but some fossil instinct of British Rail's shot a train out of

Paddington in the small hours, and deposited its contents at Marshcote Junction at 5.12 a.m.

The station yard was dark and wet with a thin rain that tasted of the sea. My arm was aching and my jet lag was screaming for coffee, but there is no coffee in Marshcote at five in the morning. The rain found its way down the back of my neck. There were no taxis. At this time on an Australian morning, the breeze would be warm and gum-scented from the woods, and the boats would be stirring at the dock like beautiful weapons. For a moment, I breathed bitter regret with the rain. Then I hoisted my bag on to my good shoulder and walked through the soaking streets towards the Creek.

South Creek Boats is a mile and a half to the south-east of Marshcote. The darkness was as thick as wet velvet, but I could have found my way there with my head in a paper bag. Down to the bank of the creek, turn left; follow the track across three rickety wooden bridges across gulleys in the marshes until it forked. Take the left-hand fork through a reedbed that hissed under the lash of the wind. It slammed rain into the face like bullets, that wind. It should have doubled my longing for the warm breath of Australia. But as I slogged across the flats I was grinning, because I was nearly home.

The wind faltered to let through the long, bubbling yell of a curlew. The rain slackened. The sky was grey now, and on the edges of the world ghostly shapes were coming into being. Over to the right was the long, dark rampart of the sea wall. Ahead, silhouetted against the red stripe the dawn made between the edge of the cloud and the black horizon, was a clump of Scotch firs and a huddle of buildings, with beyond them a bristle of masts. South Creek.

There are few trees in Marshcote, and most of them are at South Creek. It also possesses the highest ground for miles, in the form of a bank of gravel which rises some twenty feet above the marshes. Some time in the seventeenth century, someone built a red-brick house on the rise. Then at the turn of this century an enterprising ship repairer bought a steam dredger and deepened the natural basin where South Creek entered the sea. Henry MacFarlane had bought the house on his return from the war, and in 1948 built three long, low, corrugated-iron sheds beside the basin.

As I leaned into the wind for the last quarter-mile, I got a sudden whiff of diesel exhaust. Straining my eyes into the murk, I saw a car, a boxy four-wheel-drive affair, heading slowly down the road that ran along the causeway towards Marshcote. It had no lights on. Probably some early-season hard nut coming back from an all-night flog in the Channel, anxious to get home to a hot bath.

The idea of hot baths brought thoughts of hot kitchens and strong coffee. I accelerated. Five minutes later I was in the car park by the side of the basin where eighty people kept their yachts at pontoons Henry had laid, next to his own collection of boats.

There were perhaps forty chocked yachts in the car park, and no cars. Overhead, a couple of herring gulls whipped sideways through the wail of wind in rigging and the clang of halyards. At the pontoons in the basin, the masts stood in orderly rows.

One of the masts moved.

It was over on the outside jetty, near the wooden spars of *Aldebaran*, Henry's Baltic trader. It was a tall mast, and it carried no sail. There was no sound of an engine. It was gathering speed, sliding behind the other masts, rotating a little. It was behaving like the mast of a boat adrift.

I dropped my bag and started to run along the jetty.

The mast was moving straight downwind, and there was plenty of wind for it to move down. It belonged to a Moody Grenadier, a fat cruising yacht with a big deckhouse that caught as much wind as a medium-size sail. It had come off E, the outside pontoon, and it was wallowing towards the end of D, the next one in, moving briskly across the harbour. There were no lights, and nobody on board that I could see.

My feet slammed on the duckboards of the pontoon. The Moody was bearing down on a Seadog ketch moored at the end. It was going to hit the Seadog's stern beam-on. It must have been making a good three knots. Seadogs are very, very solid, Moodys less so, but much more expensive. There was going to be a crunch that would cost someone a lot of money.

I heaved myself over the Seadog's lifelines and ran along the narrow side-deck. The boat was rocking to the little black waves the wind kicked out of the basin. The Moody looked like a block of flats, ten feet away, closing fast.

A careful owner had left fenders down the seaward side of the Seadog. I untied a big one clumsily, left-handed, and dangled it over the stern. The waves made drumming noises on the Moody's plastic sides, and the wind was howling in its shrouds. It hit the fender with the side of its cockpit. The Seadog lurched forward on its springs. The fender squashed like a marshmallow, but did not burst. The Moody hung for a moment, the wind pressing its starboard side on to the Seadog's stern. Then the bow paid off, and it began to scrape downwind with a horrible grating sound. I saw a mooring line hanging overboard from the after cleat. There was no time to wonder how it came to be dangling like that. I grabbed the boathook out of its clips on the Seadog's coachroof. As the Moody sailed past I reached out and twitched the line out of the water, wrenched my right arm out of its sling and clipped the line between my fingers while I threw the boathook away. Then I hauled the line in and wrapped it three times round the Seadog's port after mooring cleat.

The mooring line tautened. The Seadog lurched outwards on its warps as the bigger boat tried to tow it into open water. Everything creaked and groaned, and I thought, that's it, we're all going ashore now. But the Moody stopped, six feet out there in the water off the end of the pontoon, held like a great pendulum by a single line.

I made the line fast, and tried to get back up the side with the fender before the Moody could swing alongside. This time, I was too late.

She hit with a crash that knocked me off my feet. I jarred my arm on the coachroof, and shouted, a loud, nasty shout the wind whipped away. When I lifted my head again, she was lying quietly alongside. I crawled to the rail, and peered over.

There was an ugly tear in the Moody's rubbing strake, and at least one of the fenders had burst under the impact. But that was no great disaster. On the far side of the basin the wall was a pile of concrete boulders studded with the rusting stumps of reinforcing bars. The wind was kicking up a fair-sized sea, and the waves were grinding sullenly on the concrete. It looked as if I had saved the Moody's owner an expensive rebuild.

I lay there for a minute. Across the harbour the diamond-paned windows of the house reflected the dirty orange of the dawn. There were no lights, and no smoke from the spindly chimneys.

A voice from the jetty said, 'All right, you bastard.'

My heart walloped in my chest. I turned, and saw four eyes. Two of them belonged to the stocky, grey-haired man who was standing on the end of the jetty. The other two were in the end of the barrels of the twelve-bore shot-gun he was pointing at my face. It was hard to say which were the most sympathetic.

'Good morning,' I said, and walked down the Seadog's side deck into the barrels of the gun.

4

'Good Lord,' said Henry MacFarlane, lowering the gun. 'What the hell are you doing here?'

I said, 'Some idiot forgot to tie a boat up.'

Henry's grizzled head moved on his thick neck. His eyes rested on the Moody, measured the course she would have taken out of her berth and on to the lumps of concrete. 'Lucky you came,' he said. His square hand came up, awkwardly, and thumped me on the back.

In the growing light, he looked as if he had been carved from stone. He had always been like that: hard as granite, legs planted apart so nothing short of a railway engine could knock him down. But the skin under his eyes had a whiteness now, and there was a sag to the flesh of his jaw that had not been there last time I had seen him.

'Let's put her away,' I said.

'Men'll do that,' he said.

We made the Moody fast alongside the Seadog. Then we walked back along the jetty and round to the empty berth on E. The rings for the mooring lines were empty.

'Didn't break,' said Henry, contemplating the rings. 'Weren't cut. Came untied.'

I said, 'There was a car leaving as I came.'

He looked across at me as if he was going to say something. Then he said, 'Oh, balls. Let's get some breakfast.'

The kitchen felt hot as a blast furnace after the raw wind outside. It was a bare room, with six wooden chairs, an enamel-topped table and a catalogue from a firm of winch-makers on the wall. On the ceiling, cracks like the canals of Mars linked places where the distemper had flaked away into Mary's saucepans.

In my youth, the South Creek kitchen had always been as tidy as the bridge of a destroyer. Over the years, that had changed. Now there were piles of letters and bills on every horizontal surface, and someone had left a pat of butter to ooze into the works of an old manual typewriter.

Getting too old for it, the letter had said.

Henry put the tin coffee pot on the Rayburn, and said, 'Mary's not up. What the hell have you been doing to your arm?'

It was typical of him that with a hundred and fifty thousand pounds' worth of boat recently adrift in his marina, he should be more interested in my life than his own. I told him what had happened in Australia.

'Silly buggers,' he said. 'If they want you to sail those things like that, they ought to armour-plate them.'

I laughed. Henry was a great devotee of armour plate. Then I said, 'Who is coming in here and setting boats adrift?'

'I don't know,' he said. 'I don't know.'

He took a cigarette out of his gunmetal case, and lit it. It was an old trick, to avoid looking me in the eye. He said, 'I'll take you round later. See what you think.' He got up too quickly and poured out the coffee before it was brewed. I suddenly realised that Mary was not the only one who was worried about whether he could cope any more.

'Probably an accident,' he said. 'The car you saw. Probably the milkman.' He slammed the thick white mug down in front of me and stumped over to the fridge. Yanking the door open, he said, 'Milk. Where is the blasted stuff?'

'The milkman doesn't come till eight,' said a voice from the door. It was Mary, big as a tree, in a blue dressing gown and sheepskin slippers.

'Oh,' said Henry, avoiding her eye. 'Is that it?'

Hugging Mary was like hugging a full-grown oak.

'Jolly nice to see you,' she said. Her face was as weather-beaten as Henry's, her eyes blue and humorous, like a whale's. There were lines around them I did not remember. She got a cup of coffee and sucked down a mouthful.

I looked across at Henry. As he lifted his mug to his lips, his hand was shaking.

The South Creek morning started up. Mary took a well-whittled lump of boiling bacon from the larder, and we talked about who had done what to whom in the town. I knew Mary better than anyone else in the world. She was a big, determined woman, who said exactly what she thought, and had little time for anyone who did not do likewise. She could no more lie than play the harpsichord. This morning, she was obviously as glad to see me as I was to see her. But I thought there was something artificial about her cheerfulness.

Henry nodded and grinned from time to time. But mostly he kept his eyes on his cup. Half-a-dozen men in overalls came in, said good morning, and left. There was Tony Fulton, the yard foreman, a large, brown, indispensable man with an adolescent's grin and huge shoulders in a blue denim workshirt. When I was not around he did most of the serious work, and ran the yard's charter fleet of eight 25-foot cruising yachts. Then there was Dick Hammer, small and dark and (although he had not yet started work) extremely dirty, who was in charge of the moorings; the mechanic, the fitter, and a couple of dogsbodies. Hammer did not look surprised when Henry told him the Moody had gone adrift, but then it was always hard to detect his facial expressions under his coating of grime. He went out to check all the lines.

'Come on,' said Henry, when we had eaten. 'Let's go and look round.'

We walked round the fuel dock, and the sheds, and the pontoons. Hammer was puttering about in a filthy old punt with rope fenders. 'They're all all right,' he said. 'Bugger left it untied, I reckon.'

'You should have bloody checked,' said Henry.

'I did bloody check.' His propellor churned greyish-white whorls in the black water as he powered away.

Henry stared at the Moody, his head sunk between his shoulders. Then he nodded, and walked on to the corner of the car park where the chocked yachts stood.

'What's this?' I said.

In the corner, two of the charter boats were lying on their sides, or what was left of their sides. They looked as if they had been attacked with road drills.

'Pretty horrible, eh?' said Henry grimly.

'What happened?' I said.

'We'd chocked 'em up for the winter. Over there.' He pointed to the coping stones where the car park ran along the water. 'Storm of wind. They came off their chocks. Down into the water, bump, bump, bump.'

We went to the edge and looked over. It was the tangle of concrete lumps and steel girders the Moody would have hit if I had not caught her. There were still bits of fibreglass among the boulders, like shreds of meat in a lion's teeth.

'Write-offs,' he said. 'Insurance man not pleased.'

It had turned into a grey, dingy morning. The kitchen window of the house was a yellow square of light. As we walked across the yard I saw Mary sitting at the table inside. She was not looking cheerful any more. She was sitting with her wrists on the table, her face grey, staring straight ahead of her at nothing. And I knew that something was very wrong.

The office was full of the smoke of the men's first roll-ups. The telephone was ringing. Henry got involved. I went back to the house. Mary smiled with genuine pleasure when she saw me.

'So,' she said. 'Are you back for long?'

It would not be encouraging to tell her that Lord Honiton of the Pall Mall Yacht Club was about to do his best to blight my sailing career. 'I thought there'd be work to do here.'

'Oh, *yes*,' she said. I could hear the relief in her voice. 'That would be wonderful.' The pink came back into her cheeks.

I said, 'Henry showed me the boats that went over in the gale.'

27

Mary's face looked suddenly tired and grey again. 'Yes,' she said.

'You don't often get a northerly that strong.'

'It wasn't a northerly,' said Mary. Her voice was far away, and very small.

'What?' I said. I did not understand. The boats had been on the northern lip of the basin; a southerly would have blown them inland, not on to the concrete.

'The gale,' she said. 'It was blowing from the south.'

And her big grey head went down on to her hands, and the tears stared to run between her big red fingers.

I had known Mary since she had taken over my care and management when I had been eleven. But I had never seen her cry before. I stood beside her and patted her wide, solid back with my good hand, and felt inadequate. I poured her some coffee and waited for the crying to stop, which it did soon. Then I said, 'What's going on?'

'You know Henry,' she said. 'He won't tell me.'

'You've asked him?'

'Of course I've asked him,' she said, with heat. 'You'd bloody ask if someone was doing their best to wreck your business.'

I did not point out that it was my business as well, because she was well aware of that. Henry owned the land and took the big decisions, as senior partner. As junior partner I came and went as I pleased, organised the year's work, and helped when racing permitted. It was a good arrangement. Henry and Mary took pleasure in watching me win, and I brought the marina some publicity from time to time.

'It's all getting out of control,' she said. 'I don't know what the hell he's up to. You know what he's like.'

I knew. When I had been twelve, during my school holidays, he had taken off for six weeks without telling anyone where he was going, to pursue the master of a Dutch oil tanker he had seen rinsing out his tanks off Oar Head. He had caught the master, but there had not been enough evidence to prosecute. So he had made the unfortunate man drink half a gallon of the water he had polluted. Henry believed in fighting his own battles.

'He'd talk to you,' she said. 'Would you try?'

'Of course,' I said.

The door slammed open. 'Come on,' said Henry. 'Let's go and haul the pots, if you're not too disabled.'

'Of course not,' I said. Jet lag and broken limbs must not stand in the way of the central tenet of Henry's life. *The pots must be hauled.*

His square face cracked in a big yellow grin. 'Good boy,' he said. 'Bloody nice to have you back.'

As I stood up, the telephone rang. Mary answered, then gave me the receiver.

The voice on the other end said, 'Dev! How's tricks? Eddie Silk here.' It was a bluff, friendly voice. I was not deceived; Silk worked for an English rag called *This Week*, and liked stories about sport that involved spite, and money, and as little sport as possible.

Silk said, 'Hear you had a bit of a barney with old Honiton. Sorry to hear about it. Takes a bit of doing, to resign from an America's Cup squad.'

I said, 'I broke my arm.'

'And sank a boat. Right. Right. But a couple of guys I was talking to said you might have, well, lost your bottle. I mean arms heal. But you resigned.'

'Tell them they are wrong,' I said, keeping my voice calm with an effort.

Silk did not seem to notice that I had spoken. 'Because the theory was that Paul Welsh was sailing better than you, and you jumped before the coaches could push you. So what I wanted to know was, will you be sailing in match racing events this spring, to get back in the running? Because now you're out of the America's Cup, you'll want to stay in top class match racing, right? Like the Senator's. You'll want an invitation for that. But will you get one?'

'No decision yet,' I said.

The Senator's Cup is the Everest of match racing. It is a series of events that carries a huge cash prize, and the promise that anyone asked to compete is one of the world's eight best helmsmen. The American Yacht Federation, who issue the invitations, are very sensitive to the opinions of people like Honiton. As Silk said, now that I was out of the America's Cup, I needed to get into the Senator's, or my career was on the skids.

He said, 'I hear Welsh got your bird as well. You must be pretty upset.'

That did it. I said, 'If you roll around in gutters, you get your ears full of sewage.' Then I banged the telephone down, and followed Henry out into the sun and the clean salt wind.

5

Out in the creek, the last of the ebb tugged at the keel of Henry's potting boat, and the wash slapped the mud beaches of South Creek as we headed for the deep water of the estuary that ran out into the Channel.

We motored in silence, except for the heavy chug of the diesel and the cry of the gulls. The masts and roofs of the yard sank behind the sea wall.

'Bit slow compared to what you're used to,' he said.

'Quieter,' I said.

A flock of black-and-white Brent geese planed over the sea-grass beds of the mudflats. Eddie Silk began to fade. It was always like that out here, where the sandbars spread their white fingers under the pale green water and the waves thundered on the margins of the land. It had been like that the first time I had come here, a few days before my twelfth birthday. My father had died three months previously; my mother had left him long before. Tappamore, the grey Georgian ruin by the side of the Blackwater, had succumbed to ivy and creditors. And I had been a small, aggressive boy with a lot of blond hair, a suitcase, and a letter addressed to Henry in my father's writing.

Henry had told me about the letter afterwards. They had met in the war, and become friends. My father had formed such an admiration for Henry that he had decided that Henry would be

31

the best person to look after a twelve-year-old, minor public school education paid for, pending his entry into the adult world. To pay for my keep there was ten thousand pounds, which Henry had invested in South Creek on my behalf. There had been some truth in Paul's crack at Bourne End; even at the age of fifteen, I had been a non-voting partner in the yard that looked after his father's boat.

The estuary widened on either side. Oystercatchers glided over the beaches, and a couple of cormorants floated hull-down in an eddy. After two miles the shore suddenly fell away. We jinked round the breakers on the end of the bar at the estuary's mouth and were shot by the ebb into the open sea.

I said, 'What exactly is going on, Henry?'

He pretended not to hear. I knew I would have to wait.

Henry's pots were set just outside the suck of the waves at the base of the black cliffs of Oar Head. I brought the boat up to the yellow buoy with MacF stencilled on it. He caught it on the boathook, looped the tail-line on the winch, and began to haul.

There were six pots on the first string. Between them, they contained no lobsters at all. I pulled out the crabs left-handed, and rebaited with stinking mackerel.

'No bloody fish left in the sea,' said Henry. We moved on to the next buoy.

We caught two lobsters. One was in the second string. The other was in the sixth and last. Baiting one-handed was tricky, and I was getting tired. So I was relieved to see the buoy winking under the crags of Oar Head, and even more so when the last-but-one pot glimmered from the black depths as I stooped to the bait bin.

'Ah, ye brute!' cried Henry, behind me.

I turned. There was a huge lobster in his hand, waving blue claws the size of a child's boxing gloves.

'Seven pounds if he's an ounce!' said Henry. He snapped elastic bands on to the claws and laid the lobster reverently in the fish-box. As he re-shot the pots, he sang 'Hearts of Oak', loudly. When the last one had gone, I brought the bows round on to the red-and-white daymark at the end of Crimmer Point.

The sun glittered on blue sea and green land as I leaned against the water's weight on the tiller.

'Seven pounds. Eight,' said Henry. His eyes were glittering. 'I didn't think they made 'em like that any more.' He punched me on my good arm. 'Marvellous,' he said.

I knew Henry's moods. This was one of his triumphant phases, in which he would talk. I said, 'Who's been knocking over your boats?'

The lines around his eyes were black crevasses as he gazed at where the sun rode above the little stud of the mast. 'Sea Horse Land,' he said. 'Property company from London.'

I stared at him. '*What?*'

'Bloke came down a couple of months ago,' said Henry. His face was grim, his eyes narrow. 'Horrible little ponce in a shiny suit, Jaguar car. Left me his card. Offered to buy the whole place, lock, stock. I told him to go to hell.' He rammed tobacco into his pipe with his thumb, as if crushing someone in a shiny suit. 'He rang the next week. I said the same thing. Then he asked me about my insurance. I told him it was none of his business.'

'Insurance?' I said.

'He asked me if I had enough.'

'I see.' Henry loathed talking about money, and thought the world was run by gentlemen. 'But property companies don't usually go around wrecking businesses.'

'This one does,' said Henry.

'Did you tell the police?'

Henry bent down behind the coaming to light a cigarette from the gunmetal case. 'Of course I did,' he said. 'I told them I thought those yachts didn't fall, they were pushed. They came and had a look and told me it was a disgruntled former employee, or maybe the wind.' Smoke veiled his face and whipped across the blue bight of the bay. 'The wind was in the wrong direction. And I haven't *got* any disgruntled former employees,' he said.

That was true. Henry inspired loyalty and affection in his workforce. I said, 'What are you going to do about it?'

Henry's eye rested on the seven-pound lobster in the box. It was no longer a bright, enthusiastic eye. It was narrow and cold and reflective, and if I had been a U-boat commander it would have brought me to the surface, displaying the white flag. 'I rang the chap. Told him I wanted to come and see him, but he wouldn't give me the address. But that's all right,' he said. 'I've got a bit of a scheme.'

'What sort of scheme?'

'A scheme,' said Henry. His face had closed up again. And I knew that what we had here was a Henry who was resolved to show the world he was not losing his grip.

It was on the tip of my tongue to remind him that I was his partner, and that Mary was his wife. But Henry worked on strict need-to-know principles. I knew that unless he was ready to talk, a nudge from the junior partner would only deepen the silence. So I cranked up the throttle a notch, and we chugged in silence back to South Creek.

That night I slept in the Point House, a small brick cottage that sits on a grassy knoll in the dunes a mile to seaward of South Creek. I had bought it ten years ago for less than a second-hand car. The living room has two pictures of Brent geese on the walls, a fine grit of sand on the flagstone floors, and a wood stove in the corner. It is a place far removed from twelve-metre yachts and the gloss of Sydney; an excellent place to go if you do not want to think about people like Camilla, or Honiton.

I awoke early, made double-strength coffee, and listened to the scream of the gulls over the wide yellow sickle of the beach. Then I went outside, fired up my old grey short wheelbase Land Rover, and drove to the yard.

The office was empty. The battered electric clock on the wall said 7.40. I sat down at Henry's desk and looked through his black address book. There were names, and telephone numbers, and business cards stuck in next to the names and telephone numbers. The one I was looking for was printed in black and blue. There was a stylised picture of a sailing boat and a palm tree. SEA HORSE LAND, it said, in capitals. In the bottom left-hand corner, it said *Terrence Raistrick*. On the lower right-hand side was a telephone number. There was no address.

I picked up the old bakelite telephone and dialled a number in London. The voice on the other end sounded sleepy.

'Harry?' I said.

'Oh, God,' said the voice. 'What do you want, at this hour?'

Harry Chase and I had been at school together. He was a crime reporter on the *Guardian*, with a powerful appetite for Carlsberg Special Brew and Tom Thumb cigars. He got preferential holiday rates from South Creek Charter. We had dinner together in London sometimes. On these occasions he told me stories about criminals.

I told him I wanted to know about Sea Horse Land.

'Never heard of it,' he said. 'Story?'

'Couldn't say,' I said. 'Yet. Have you still got friends in the police force?'

'Do you ever go sailing?'

I read him the telephone number on the card. 'Can you get me an address for that?'

'Car phone.'

'Then how about an owner and an owner's address?'

He groaned. 'Must I?'

'Going boating this summer?'

'Call you later,' he said, and put the phone down.

For the next hour, the phone rang. Mostly, it was owners, fussing about their boats. Then at nine o'clock, just as I was about to make my second cup of coffee, I picked it up and heard a smooth, confident voice.

'Martin?' it said. 'Jack Archer here. Ringing for the Pulteney Yacht Club.'

'Yes,' I said. Jack Archer was a small, pink man, a director of Padmore and Bayliss, Britain's biggest production boatbuilder. Recently, he had got on to the committee of the Pulteney Yacht Club, a smart but recently formed outfit in a village seventy miles down the coast. He was clever and ambitious, and I was pretty sure I knew what he wanted.

'The Iceberg Cup,' he said. 'I . . . that is, we at the Club . . . would very much like you to sail.'

The Iceberg Cup was also a recent invention, and by no means one of your top match racing events. In fact, it was distinctly second-rate. I said, 'I'm not sure I'm fit.'

'Broken arm, I heard,' said Archer. Archer heard everything. He would certainly have heard about my row with Honiton. 'But, well, I know we're a bit below your standard, but you should walk it, eh? And of course it won't do you any harm with selection for the Senator's, will it?'

'What are we sailing?' I said.

'Bayliss 34s,' he said.

I reflected. Archer was asking a newsworthy, if shaky, skipper to compete in a second-rate event, in boats his company produced. It all added up to publicity for him.

'Seven and a half grand for the winner,' said Archer.

The boatyard could do with seven and a half grand, and I could do with a race to sail. Because a race was a race, even the Iceberg Cup.

'All right,' I said. 'Thanks. I'd like to.'

'Great,' said Archer, full of small, pink man's enthusiasm. '*Great.*'

I called Charlie Agutter and asked if he could organise himself and a crew at short notice. Charlie was a friend from the days we had both sailed on *Sorcerer* in the British Captain's Cup team. Also, he had designed the Bayliss 34, so he would be a useful man to have aboard. Charlie said he could. As I rang off, Tony stuck his head round the door, looking for Henry. I said, 'Hang about a minute.' He sat down. He was big enough to dwarf his chair.

'Tony,' I said. 'What's going on?'

'Every bloody thing's turning to ratshit,' said Tony. He laid a pinch of Old Holborn in a cigarette paper. The anchor tattooed on the back of his right hand moved across his face as he licked the cigarette shut.

'Such as?'

His lips disappeared as he drew on the thin cigarette. 'You saw them boats,' he said. 'The ones that went over the edge. There was them.'

36

I nodded. His grey eyes were remote, thinking. 'Then there was the diesel. Somebody let a lot of water into the diesel holding tank down the fuel dock. Bloody awful mess, seven hundred gallons spoilt. And there's been a lot of little things. That boat you caught this morning. It's not the first. There was two last week slipped their lines. One of 'em's up on the hard with a bloody great hole in its bow.'

'And you reckon someone's doing it.'

His leathery face was impassive. 'We tie good knots, and we keep water out of diesel, and we don't bung expensive boats on to the stones for fun.'

That was true. During the five years he had been yard foreman, the yard's efficiency had brought the customers in droves.

'Have you seen anything? Anyone hanging around the yard?'

He shrugged. One of the things the customers liked was that Tony was in the habit of telling the truth, never glossing over disaster, but without undue pessimism either. 'There's a lot of ways in, and a lot of work to do in the daytimes. Short of hiring Securicor, there's not a lot you can do at nights. Particularly when you're Henry's age.'

The office door opened. A thin man with a grey moustache came in. ''Scuse me, gents,' he said. 'Come to look at a Baltic ketch called *Aldebaran*.' He pulled a packet of Rothmans from the pocket of his suede jacket, lit one. 'Bit lonely out here, innit?'

I said, 'What part of *Aldebaran* do you want to look at?'

'The lot,' he said. 'My card.' The card said MATES & BUSHELL – Surveyors – Sheerness.

'Who's asked for a survey?' I said.

'Bloke called Paul Welsh,' said the thin man. 'For a client. 'E rung me from Australia.'

I stood there until I realised that my mouth was hanging open.

'I'll pop into my overalls,' said the surveyor. 'Can you get 'er on the hoist?'

I said, 'What the hell has Paul Welsh got to do with this?'

37

Tony's wide brown forehead creased with worry. 'You ought to hear it from Henry,' he said. 'I've got to see the boat.'

I went over to the house to find Henry.

He was sitting at the partner's desk in his office. Behind him, box files rose to the ceiling. The desk itself was covered with papers.

'A surveyor's come to look at *Aldebaran*,' I said. 'He said Paul Welsh had sent him.'

'Ah,' said Henry. He rubbed his jaw. 'Yes. That makes sense.'

'What has Paul Welsh to do with *Aldebaran*?'

'He's selling her,' said Henry. 'Look, Martin. We've been very short of money. You know I used to run a sort of brokerage here. Well, Paul Welsh wrote to me six weeks ago, made me an offer for the goodwill. I took it.'

'Just like that,' I said.

Like Tony, Henry was looking worried. 'Look,' he said. 'He only wanted to use the name. He said he wouldn't be coming near the place. I knew you wouldn't like it. But we needed the money. So I sold it to him. If I'd have asked you, what would you have said?'

'Find the money somewhere else,' I said.

Henry said, 'Exactly. Well, there isn't any money anywhere else. Paul saved our bacon.'

I stood and looked at the face that was losing its hardness at the edges. The eyes had a pleading expression that did not belong there. He had done what was best, according to his lights. And when Henry had done that, those around him had to put up with it.

'Fifty thousand quid,' he said. 'That's what he paid. And if he can sell *Aldebaran* before she falls to bits, that'll be more money. Let's have a look at that surveyor.'

It was no good asking him why Paul Welsh would want the goodwill of a brokerage as small as South Creek. Henry was not the kind of man to wonder about secret motives.

But I was. Paul was rich, but he did not go around laying out fifty thousands in simple charity. I had spent a lifetime Paul-watching. There was more to it than that.

I followed Henry along the breakwater to where *Aldebaran*

hung dripping in the travel hoist, her rotten white hull fat as the belly of a whale. The surveyor was walking round with a bradawl, digging at planks. 'Long job,' he said. 'Very long job. Nice boat, though.'

Henry gave him the kind of smile he would have given a madman, and went to haul his pots. I returned to the office.

At quarter past twelve, Harry Chase rang.

'Your number,' he said. 'Total bastard to find out. You owe me a free charter.'

'We'll see,' I said.

'Belongs to a company called Sea Horse Land,' he said.

'I know.'

'Registered in the Isle of Man. Directors, a bank manager and a solicitor, the usual. Nothing else traceable. Except an address where the phone company sends the bills.'

'Which is?'

'22, Upper Tier, Waterfront, Southampton.'

'Thank you,' I said. 'Send us your dates, and we'll see what we can do.'

6

I found Tony in the Burnett Arms, a gloomy red-brick building in a gloomy red-brick street. He was sitting on a stool in his usual corner, sipping a pint and talking to a crab fisherman. When he saw me, he grinned, and bought me a half.

I said, 'We're off to Southampton.'

'What for?' he said.

'Visiting Sea Horse Land. I want to ask them some questions about people who untie other people's boats and put water in other people's fuel.'

His glass stopped halfway to his lips. 'You sure?' he said.

'I'm not sure about anything,' I said.

'Hell of a way to go,' he said.

'So we'd better start now.'

He stared at me for a moment, then sighed. 'Waste of time,' he said. 'There's a yardful of boats to fit out.'

'We'll take your car,' I said.

His Adam's apple bobbed in his thick neck as he finished his pint. Then he said, 'Sometimes I am amazed that you're not blood-related to Henry.'

'Oh?'

'You're as stubborn as he is. And nearly as thick-headed.'

'Thank you,' I said.

We left the pub, and climbed into his car, and drove more or less in silence to Southampton.

Waterfront was one of those new developments that property developers put up in an attempt to make money by bringing maritime glamour to derelict reaches of Southampton Water. The bollards in the car park were fibreglass cannon barrels, and there were two World War Two anti-aircraft guns in the empty plaza in front of the shopping arcade. The arcade itself resembled a vast glass barrel half-sunk in concrete, overlooking a marina gap-toothed with empty berths. Rain made pockmarks in the pools of water on the paving slabs, and crawled down the glass of the arcade. Inside, the only humans in sight were some dispirited-looking shopkeepers, waiting for customers who would not be appearing for two months, if ever.

'Gives you the shivers,' said Tony.

Tier 2 was a gallery of offices that ran round the roof of the arcade. No. 22 was between a travel agent and a yacht broker. It had a plate glass front, with a model of a marina in it. Inside, a girl was sitting at a green desk. Behind her was a door.

'Can I help you?' said the girl. Her voice was American.

'Looking for Mr Raistrick,' I said. 'Of Sea Horse Land.'

'Have you an appointment?' she said. She was pretty, with grey-green eyes, a delicately arched nose, and short blonde hair.

'No,' I said. 'It concerns South Creek Boatyard.'

The grey-green eyes seemed to sharpen suddenly. 'Who shall I say is calling?'

I told her. She pressed a button on her desk, and said, 'Mr Devereux and Mr Fulton of South Creek Boats to see you, Mr Raistrick.'

There was no answer. Somewhere behind the back wall of the office, a door slammed. 'I'm sorry,' said the girl. 'Mr Raistrick doesn't appear to be — '

I took two steps forward and pulled the door open. The girl said, 'Hey!' But by that time, I was already in the back office.

The outside walls were all glass. Beyond the glass, a catwalk ran along the outside of the building. There was a door on to the catwalk. It was open, because a dark-haired man had gone out on to the catwalk, and was running.

I went out into the rain. The man's feet were hammering on the steel deck. He was dressed in a dark suit. He turned his head. I caught a glimpse of a white, suety face with a heavy black moustache.

It is not easy to run when you have a heavy cast on your arm. I yelled 'Tony!' I heard his feet pounding the catwalk behind me. 'Catch him!' I said.

Tony began to run. He was fast. They went out of sight, down a spiral staircase that dived off the end of the catwalk and into a Victorian shot tower at the corner of the building.

The girl was beside me. She said, 'I guess he went out for coffee.'

I looked at her quickly. Her face was solemn. I said, 'He's in a big hurry,' and followed them along the catwalk.

The entrance to the shot tower was a dark arch. It stank of urine. A spiral staircase descended into shadow. My footsteps rang in the central well.

Down below, someone groaned.

Out in the car park, a starter motor whinnied and rubber squealed. On the next-but-two curve of the stairway, a dark shape was hanging through the banisters.

I ran down. It was Tony. I grabbed him by his shirt, pulled him back on to the steps. His big face was pale. Blood covered its right-hand side. The left eye was clear. It was half-open. He said, 'Little bastard tripped me.' He rolled on to his hands and knees. I helped him up the stairs.

It was still raining, but the daylight seemed dazzlingly bright. Tony had a long, ragged cut above his eye. I took him back to the office. The girl was waiting outside.

She looked white. There was enough blood to make anyone feel white. We went into the inner office, and she brought water and we cleaned Tony up. When she went down the landing to the lavatory to empty the bowl, I followed her, to make sure she did not do a Raistrick. She watched me ironically as I leaned against the washbasin.

I said, 'I want a home number for Mr Raistrick.'

She said, 'He didn't give me his home number.' Her eyes

42

were steady. 'I've only worked here a week.' We walked back to the office. She wrote a London number on a piece of paper. 'I guess I won't be working here much longer. This is a company Mr Raistrick used to call a lot. I know he took instructions from them. They might be able to help you with your problem. Maybe it would be best if you didn't say I gave you the number.'

I gave her the South Creek number. I said, 'Perhaps you could call if Mr Raistrick comes back.'

She smiled. Her colour had returned, and it was an attractive smile, but it did not give anything away.

I fetched Tony from the inner office and drove back to South Creek. His eye was swelling. 'If I catch that bastard, I'll kill him,' he said. His face was heavy and sullen with pain, the big jaw thrust forward like the ram of a battleship. He lapsed into silence, watching the tedious suburbs of Solent City drone past the window.

I stopped at a call-box and dialled the number the girl had given me. A woman's voice said, 'Marine Investments.'

I said, 'I'd like to speak to one of the directors.'

'What is it concerning?'

I hesitated. If I gave the wrong answer, I would be fobbed off. But there was a right answer. I said, 'I'd like to discuss the sale of the South Creek Boatyard.'

'Who shall I say is calling?'

I gave her my name.

There was a pause. Then a man's voice came on the line.

'Hello?' it said. 'And what can we do for you, this afternoon?' The voice was rich and plummy.

'Who's that?' I said.

'James,' said the voice. 'Your cousin James.'

I stood there for a moment with my brain whirring. James de Groot was my second cousin. He was a director of dozens of companies, and his name was seldom absent from the financial pages of the nation's press.

'Well?' he said. 'What do you want?'

I said, 'You have been dealing with an Isle of Man company called Sea Horse Land.'

'Have I?' he said. An edge of wariness had come into his voice.

It was beginning to add up. I said, 'It wouldn't surprise me if it was you that told your friends at Sea Horse Land about a nice bit of beachfront called South Creek, ripe for development. You can tell them from me that it isn't for sale. You can also tell them that there are laws against extortion and damage to private property. I will be giving your name and the name of your friend Terrence Raistrick to the police tomorrow.'

'I am not at all sure I know what you are talking about,' said James. 'And I think you would have difficulty proving these allegations, if allegations is what they are.'

'I'll manage,' I said. 'Tell your friends.' I put the telephone down, and got back into the car.

Tony said, 'What happened?'

'Peace has broken out,' I said.

I could not face Mary or Henry, so when Tony dropped me off I drove straight to the Point House, walked out on to the flats and watched a chequered flock of Brent geese feeding on the seagrass. James had made a lot of money on the dodgy edge of the money world, and Harry Chase occasionally passed on rumours that the Fraud Squad were taking an interest in him. It was faintly puzzling, though; the Sea Horse Land campaign against South Creek was more violent than his usual style.

I turned away from the geese, and walked back through the dunes to the house. After this afternoon, he would be going back to good clean fraud.

7

My bed in the Point House was under the slope of the roof. The wind prised at the window and rattled the plank door, and the roof timbers cracked like knuckles. I shoved James and Raistrick out of my mind, and slept like a brick.

Someone was hammering. I opened an eye. There was shouting mixed with the hammering.

'All right!' I yelled, stumbled out of bed and opened the door.

It was Tony Fulton. There was a long plaster above his eye. He looked pale and haggard, as if he had slept badly too. He walked in, looked around at the rough walls, the driftwood stove, the shelves of books. His own tastes ran towards patterned wallpaper and solid comfort.

'What time is it?' I said.

'Nine.'

I went to the sink in the corner and splashed cold water from the jerry can over my head.

'You'd better come,' he said. 'Henry's gone.'

'Gone?' I said.

'He went out to haul his pots round about six. He came back on the tide, brought the pots home. Mary says he packed a case before he went. He took his motorbike. I've got to get back. They're going mad down there.'

I pulled on a pair of jeans, a jersey and a pair of Docksiders, fumbling with my bad hand. The Land Rover coughed, then fired and began its tank-like rattle. I aimed it across the rabbit-cropped turf and into the dunes.

Henry's theory was that if you did not tell anybody when and where you were going they would not waste time making preparations, or worry about you when you had gone. While this might have been a useful cast of mind for a destroyer captain, it was no way to run a marriage.

The sun was up and the wind was down. The marsh smelt green as I jumped down from the Land Rover and walked beside the basin to the house. Mary was in the garden, on her hands and knees, grubbing the year's first grass from between the paving stones with the broken blade of a table knife. She hated weeding, but when things went badly wrong she was subject to sudden orgies of it, as if by tidying up the garden she could tidy up her life.

'Oh,' she said. 'Hello.' She did not look up.

'I hear Henry's gone,' I said. There did not seem to be any point in trying to put it gently.

'That's right.' Her voice was harsh and clipped. 'Nothing to worry about. He's done it before.' That was true: this was not the first time Henry had left me to look after her – not that she needed any looking after. She was levering at the roots of a tuft of grass. The knife-blade broke. The jagged shard stuck in the ground scored the back of her knuckles. She rocked back on her big haunches, staring down at the bright blood that welled from the gash. 'Oh,' she said. 'Oh, *bother*.' And she kept saying it, as if the words were the only ones in the world that held any meaning for her.

There was something obscene about a strong woman like Mary bereft and helpless. For a moment, I felt a fierce anger at Henry. I took her unwounded hand, and pulled her up, and led her to a teak bench mouldering in the sun under a tangle of roses. She kept saying 'Oh, *bother*.'

'It's all right,' I said. 'I've been to talk to some people. There won't be any more accidents. Tony and I can run things.'

She looked up. Her hair was hanging across her face in grey ropes, and her blue eyes had a stunned look. 'It's not the yard,' she said. 'It's him. He's not young any more. He's got a weak heart.'

There was a hail from the gate. It was Emily Johnson, a plump niece of Mary's who flew Tiger Moth biplanes, and frequently came to drink tea with her and argue about roses.

I got up. Mary liked Emily, and Emily had the knack of cheering her up. 'He'll be all right,' I said. And because I had cleared things up with James, I was confident that I was telling the truth.

Then.

It was a hard week. The Iceberg Cup started on the following Tuesday, and I had to plan the last of the refitting by then. There was no word from Henry. On the Saturday morning, Tony came in. The lump on his forehead had subsided. He sat down, rolled himself a cigarette, and frowned at his lighter while he fired it up.

'Well?' I said.

'That surveyor,' he said. 'The one who looked at *Aldebaran*. He's turned in a good report.'

'He must be blind,' I said.

'Boat's sold,' said Tony. 'That's what matters.'

I nodded. It was very good news indeed, for Henry and Mary. It was less good news for the purchaser, but that was the surveyor's problem. 'I'll buy us a drink later,' I said. He grinned at me, the wide, conspiratorial grin that had been worth a fortune to the yard during the past five years. Then he went out, leaving on the table the newspaper he brought up from Marshcote every morning. I turned to the back pages, as usual, to check who had done what in the world of fast boats.

The story was in the top right-hand corner. As I read it, the sweat came to my palms. The person who had done things in the world of fast boats was Martin Devereux, and according to the story, what he had done was nothing to be proud of.

CONSTELLATION PULLS OUT, it said. The story was simple enough. The burden of it was that Martin Devereux, a helmsman whose aggressive instincts had got the better of his common sense, had sunk half a million pounds' worth of twelve-metre, damaged another and resigned. The sponsors had lost the will to continue, and the syndicate had fallen apart. It was not the kind of press notice you put on the title page of your cuttings book.

I read it twice. That was enough. Then I sat and gazed at Enid who did the typing. Enid had a pale face, lank hair and a red nose. She was sniffing into a handkerchief because of her cold, which lasted all year. And I thought of Camilla's endless brown legs, and of the blue skies of Sydney, and the ice-white triangles of twelve-metre sails, racing. And I thought: you have really cocked it up this time, Devereux. Trading the America's Cup for Pulteney in April is the act of a lunatic. And a lot of people are going to be most unhappy that you have caused this to happen.

Enid sniffed and re-folded her wad of handkerchief, looking for a dry spot. The telephone rang.

'Good morning, good morning,' said Jack Archer's voice on the other end, brisk as a faceful of wave. 'All right for next week? Arm and everything?'

'In plaster, but fine,' I said, and waited: Jack Archer was a busy man, unlikely to waste telephone time inquiring about my health.

'Read the papers?' said Archer. 'Yes. Just thought I'd tell you that we're expanding the numbers to ten, next week. OK?'

'Fine,' I said. There was not much else I could say. 'Who else?'

'Jacques LeBreton,' he said. 'And Paul Welsh. He's free, now.'

I took two deep breaths. Then I said, 'Archer, you are a crafty little sod.'

'I know,' said Archer. 'The sponsors are very pleased. Wonderful needle match, you and Paul. Devereux wrecks Welsh's chances. Not that Welsh had a hope. Everyone's doing a story. Reporters will ring. Make it good, would you?'

'Naturally,' I said, and rang off.

Archer had been right about the reporters. The telephones did not stop for the rest of the morning. I told them that I was greatly looking forward to the Iceberg Cup, implied that I loved

Paul Welsh like a brother, and made plans to spend a long lunchtime in the Burnett Arms to wash the taste of lies out of my mouth.

I was on my way out the door when Archer rang again. 'By the way,' he said. 'Since you were so nice to those hacks, I thought I'd tell you something you will like to know. Senator's Cup Committee are interested in you.'

'I don't believe you,' I said. 'Not after this morning.'

'Wait a minute,' said Archer. 'They're also interested in Paul Welsh. And I can tell you that whichever of you looks shiniest in the Iceberg and the Marbella is getting a ticket to the States.'

I paused to absorb some oxygen. 'The Marbella,' I said.

'That's right,' said Archer. 'Six weeks away, of course. Honiton's on the committee, but they're inviting you. Plenty of time.'

'And sailed in Bayliss 34s.'

'Very perceptive.'

The oxygen was penetrating to the brain. I said, 'You are a big authority on my career, all of a sudden.'

'I take an interest,' said Archer. 'So does your stuffy pal Honiton. I've been fighting for you, Martin. We have great faith.'

'Yes,' I said.

'Lovely boy,' said Archer blandly, and rang off.

I sat down in the office chair, and watched a big Westerly float out above the water on the crane, and thought about Archer and Honiton, fighting over Devereux and Welsh. A nice, clean sporting game, match racing.

The door opened, and Mary came in. She looked better than she had for a week. 'Look at that,' she said, and tossed a postcard on the desk.

It had a picture of a punk with a lime green Mohican haircut. On the other side was the address, a Gatwick postmark, and a message in Henry's neat navigator's handwriting. *Off to Spain*, it said. *Taking pills. All love, H.*

'So he's all right,' she said. 'Silly old fool. Why won't he tell me before he goes? I could do with a bit of sun myself. Goodness, it's a relief.'

I put my arm round her shoulders, happy that Henry had thought to end her worries. But he had told me in the boat that he had got a scheme. That did not sound like a holiday. I had an uneasy feeling that Henry was sending cards to keep Mary happy. And if that was the case, it was possible I knew less about what was going on than I thought.

8

Pulteney is one of your great British fishing villages, only slightly spoilt by progress. Not many people there go fishing any more, because there are not many fish left in the English Channel. But it has a good horseshoe-shaped harbour, with grey stone quays and a lifeboat station. It is a better place to run a boatyard than Marshcote, because the steep streets of little stone houses where the fishermen used to live are now inhabited by rich people who love yachts and gin and tonic, not necessarily in that order. Neville Spearman, who ran the yard a mile or so down the coast at New Pulteney, could get away with charging more for his pontoon berths than anyone else west of the Solent. And the warehouses fronting the quay now housed not fish and nets, but yacht brokers and chandlers, and Charlie Agutter.

Charlie Agutter was about thirty-five, a thin man with a face composed largely of hollows, and dark hair that stuck out in spikes like a sea urchin's spines. In his time, he had been a very good helmsman. Nowadays, he was a sought-after tactician, and one of the best yacht designers in the world.

I dug him out of his office, and we walked on to the quay. It was early in the year for Pulteney, a grey day, with a force five-to-six westerly knocking off the tops of a dirty-looking sea outside the harbour mouth. The flags on the mast of the brown cedar Yacht Club building stood out stiff as boards.

'We're meeting in the pub,' I said.

Charlie looked at the Yacht Club with dislike. 'Good,' he said. We went into the Mermaid, at the other end of the quay. The bar had stained tables and a nicotine-bronzed ceiling. Charlie said hello to four or five old men at a table in the corner. He ordered pints. We drank.

Three big men came into the bar. The biggest of them all was Scotto Scott, a New Zealander who looked after Charlie's boats for him. Then there were Noddy and Slicer, mastman and foredeckman respectively. I ordered them lagers, and we chatted. But my mind was not on it. My mind was on the pure pleasure of getting a go at Paul Welsh.

After lunch, I wrapped waterproof tape round my cast, and we went down to Spearman's. They had the race boats over in the Pits, the berths on the outer pontoon that Neville rented at concessionary rates to anyone who was likely to get him some publicity. Jack Archer was waiting by the boats, pink and dapper in a blazer and grey flannel trousers. He came forward and distributed plump, dry handshakes. He had small, bright blue eyes. 'Good to see you. Glad you could come.' He winked. 'Welsh isn't here yet.'

The boats lined up at the pontoon were long and flat and sharp, with the evil grace of spearheads. We let go the lines and backed off the dock. A cold-looking TV cameraman filmed us past the snout of the breakwater and into the river.

'Nice boat,' I said. Charlie nodded without false modesty. He had designed the 34 fast and agile. Its waterline length of thirty feet gave it a theoretical maximum speed of about eight knots. But like most of Charlie's quicker boats, it could get up and rattle across the water at nearly double that speed.

The banks of the Poult fell away on either side. We climbed into our wet gear and got the sails up. The boat heeled, and the tiller came alive. I turned off the engine. In sudden silence, we soared into the open sea.

It had all gone now: cousin James, Paul and Honiton, Henry and his postcards. What was left was the rudder's bite, and the lift of the cockpit sole underfoot, and the flutter of the tell-tales in the slot between the mainsail and the genoa. Match races are sailed one against one, in identical boats. In most other forms of racing, skippers can tweak their boats to get an edge over the opposition. In match racing, there are no technical advantages. You win if you get your boat going as fast as it will go, and you use the rules and anything else you can get to fight for the edge.

So we took the Bayliss, and we worked on it. We did sail changes till Noddy and Slicer poured sweat. We hung dead in the water, looking for the tiny no-man's-land between steerage way and wallowing. We analysed the polar diagrams that told us how close to the wind it would deliver its best speed. We took it out into the big seas where the tide ripped round the end of Danglas Head, and watched what happened when you jammed its nose into a head sea and set its stern to a following sea. We poked, and pried, and tinkered, took the boat's performance apart, and looked at it through a microscope, and put it together again. Charlie noted it all down on a clipboard. We came up the river at low water on a dead run, spinnaker up. There were twenty or thirty people waiting on the breakwater. Some of them were filming.

'We'll sail in,' I said.

It is usual to go into a marine berth on the engine. It is more impressive but much more difficult to go in under sail. Charlie looked at me, then at the film crews, and grinned his mischievous grin. Scotto, who spent a lot of time mending boats that people had been showing off in, looked less enthusiastic.

The wind was blowing upriver, across the entrance. We came out of the river on a reach, heeled well over to starboard.

'Kite,' I said.

The iron sheathing on the breakwater whizzed by as Noddy and Slicer pulled the spinnaker in under the boom.

'Gibing,' I said.

A long lane of brown water had opened out down to starboard, lined with boats. It looked very tight. It was very tight. I pointed the bow down the lane. Scotto pulled in the mainsheet to centre up the boom as the wind came dead astern.

'Genoa,' I said.

The genoa collapsed on the foredeck.

'Mainsheet,' I said. We were turning in the lane now. The slot where the boat fitted was opening ahead. 'Tweak.'

Scotto pulled in enough sheet to fill the sail for a split second. The boat eased forward.

'Let go,' I said.

The sail roared, unsheeted. Very slowly, we moved into the slot between the pontoon and the next-door boat. The bow came to a halt a foot away from the jetty. The mainsail came rustling down. The boat lay stock-still, exactly central in its little dock. There was no sound, except for the whirr of the cameras on the quay.

We sat there for perhaps ten seconds, posing. Then Noddy and Slicer went ashore with the lines.

'Mad bloody Irishman,' said Charlie.

When Devereux sailed, mad bloody Irishman was what they wanted, and mad bloody Irishman was what they got.

We spent the next two hours going through Charlie's check-list, taping anything that might fray or catch, sticking tell-tales to the sails, working out positions for sheet leads. When we had finished it was half past five, getting dark. We walked down the breakwaters together, in a clump, talking. Coming into the berth under sail had been a stupid trick. But it had brought the team together, and made us confident, expecting to win.

There was a party that night at the Yacht Club. Normally I would have thought twice about going. But it was also the draw for the races, so I put on clean trousers, and a Constellation Challenge blazer to show that I had nothing to be ashamed of, and went along.

The room was full. As I went in, the buzz of conversation stopped. Charlie was over by the bar, a glass of whisky at his elbow. With him was Paul Welsh.

I took a deep breath and went straight over.

'I hear you're a yacht broker nowadays,' I said.

He smiled, his languid Etonian smile that did not mask the heat in his brown eyes. 'One has to make a living.'

'But why South Creek?'

He said, 'It has a lot of potential.' He paused, sipping his whisky. 'Unrealised potential.'

'And you're going to realise it.'

'Who knows?' said Paul. 'It's been a bloody pig's breakfast for years, so it's time somebody did.'

I could feel the expression on my face freezing as the anger rose. A flashgun went off somewhere alongside my head. Calm down, I thought. Getting angry doesn't work. I forced a smile into his surly Greek god's face. I said, 'I am looking forward to working with you, because I will be able to wash your mouth out with soap and water on a daily basis.'

Charlie pulled me away. He said, 'Save it for tomorrow, would you?'

That was why Charlie would never be a match racer. Tonight was an extension of tomorrow. It is never too early to begin heading for the line.

9

They made the draw that night. The heats were sailed all against all, nine races per boat. The four skippers with the highest scores were to go through to the semi-finals. We won all our races but one, when the clew pulled out of the jib. We beat Paul by two minutes, about which he was not happy. We were at the top of the points, and he was equal second.

On Friday night there was another bunfight in the Yacht Club, and they drew for which semi-finalist would race against which. Archer rummaged in the hat with his hard pink fingers. His eyes came up from the ticket blue and twinkling, and he smiled the smile of a fulfilled publicist.

'First semi-final,' he said. 'Welsh against . . . Devereux.'

There was a rustle in the room. Heads ducked to whisper, and two or three reporters sidled away for the telephones. It looked as if the sponsors were going to get their money's worth.

We spent a quiet evening in the Mermaid, and ate dinner cooked by Georgia, Scotto's Trinidadian wife, in their cottage on Quay Street. Then I went up through flurries of warm Atlantic rain to the white house half-way up the hill and Charlie's spare room.

The bed was comfortable, and I was tired. But I could not sleep. For twenty-five years Paul had hated my guts. But that had not been common knowledge. Now the spotlight was on us; not on the racing, but on the personalities. And despite all my good resolutions, I was nervous.

Next morning, the forecast said southwesterlies force five to six, gusting seven. Charlie and I drank black coffee, ate ham and eggs and a lot of toast and marmalade. The cobbles of Quay Street were shiny with rain, and the wind dashed it in our faces hard enough to make us squint.

There was a lot of wind for match racing. On the quay, we looked up at the Yacht Club's mast for the blue-and-white chequered 'N' flag that would mean racing had been abandoned. But there was only the blue ensign and the sponsor's house flag, crackling in the breeze.

I said 'Here we go' through a throat that was suddenly tight. The race boats had been brought round from the marina and were moored in rafts of two alongside the quay. As we went down the ladder and into the cockpit, a gust moaned in the shrouds. I had a nasty jumpy feeling in the pit of my stomach, and my head felt gluey and slow. Two boats down, Paul Welsh was lounging in the back end of his cockpit, dressed in dove-grey and white wet gear. I could hear his voice again, talking about everything Henry and Mary had built up at South Creek. *It's been a pig's breakfast for years.* The water among the lobster boats in the harbour was black and restless with little sharp-edged ripples.

'Rough,' said Charlie.

'We're off,' I said.

We peeled away from the wall and went for the entrance. In the grey frame of the quayheads, the horizon was jagged, like the teeth of a hacksaw. The sails were up by the time we hit the entrance. A gust whizzed across the water, laying the boat far over. Water came green down the lee deck, and the stanchions trailed white plumes of spray.

Pulteney is shielded from the worst of the Channel seas by the Teeth, a long wall of rocks to the southward, so the water was relatively flat. But a line of rocks does nothing to abate the wind, and there was plenty of that.

Astern, the triangle of Paul's sails moved behind the quays.

White spray broke over his bow as he hit the first of the waves outside the harbour. My mouth was dry. I had a cup of tea from the thermos, but it made no difference.

The VHF yammered. The committee said two reefs in the mainsail. We took in the reefs. The boat felt more comfortable now, less inclined to stand on its ear when the gusts came tearing in from the south-west.

Charlie sat huddled over his watch, the red hood of his oilskins hiding his face. 'Two minutes to first gun,' he said.

There are two guns, in a match race. The first is eight minutes before the start. It signals that the competitors can enter the start area, the funnel whose mouth is the start line, and that hostilities can commence. Most match races are won or lost at the start. The idea is that by hard manoeuvring and pushing the right-of-way rules till they squeak, you can get ahead of your competitor, and into a position where you can frustrate his intentions all the way round the course. On a calm day in a sensible breeze, a match race start is somewhere between a sea battle and a game of chess.

Today, with wind ripping the tops off the seas and the grey sky sitting on the horizon, it was going to be all war and no calculation.

I watched Paul's white sails dip as a gust caught him. The first gun went. Cautiously, I edged into the starting area. He hung back, waiting, his sails rattling like machine guns to the gusts dragging trails of white horses out of the south-west.

'We'll stay clear,' I said.

Charlie nodded. The wind was blasting his hair flat against his head. Getting in amongst the opposition on a day like this was asking for trouble. Paul knew it, too. So we stayed apart, head-to-wind, the boats pitching in the short, nasty chop.

'Three minutes,' said Charlie.

'Sheets,' I said.

The winches jingled. The sails came in, became hard white wings. The boat picked up speed, bore off the wind on to the right-hand side of the course, half-planing on the flat sections forward of the keel. We went out in a wide loop, tacked, and came back very fast, heading for the right-hand end of the line.

'He's going left,' said Charlie.

I kept half an eye on Paul. I was on starboard now, close-hauled, and I had right of way. Paul had no option but to keep clear. The bow chopped at the waves, the impacts booming in the hollows of the hull. On the starboard bow, the big inflatable buoy marking the right-hand end of the start line bore down.

'Ten,' said Charlie. 'Nine. Eight.'

The buoy was fifty yards away. The boat heeled as a gust battered the sails down at the jumping grey sea.

'One. Zero,' said Charlie.

Over the committee boat, the wind ripped grey smoke from the barrel of the starting gun. The bow smashed a wave to white spume. We hammered out on to the course. Paul was level now, on the other tack. The two boats heaved out on to the grey sea, converging.

'He'll duck under,' said Charlies. We had right of way. 'Watch the slam dunk.'

I nodded. The slam dunk is when the port-tack boat goes under the stern of the right-of-way boat, and uses its speed and momentum to tack up and under. It is a useful manoeuvre, but there are countermanoeuvres.

'He's coming,' said Charlie.

Out of the corner of my eye I could see Paul bearing away, picking up the speed off the wind that would shoot him under our stern and give him the momentum to round up on to our starboard bow. The sound of his passage over the waves was a hard rattle, and white water spewed from his lee rail. He was a long way off the wind, his nose pointing far astern.

'Tacking,' I said quietly.

The boat heaved on a wave, the boom clacked over, and we were on the port tack. Paul's face was dark with anger under the peak of his hood. His eyes flicked up at his sails, shivering in the eddies of dirty wind from our main. Charlie hid a grin behind his hand. Paul had missed his slam dunk, and he had gone so far off the wind to build up speed that he had lost ground. Now, we were between him and the windward mark, covering him tight, and there was nothing he could do about it.

We led him up to the windward mark, and rounded the buoy clean as a whistle. On the first downwind leg, he trailed us by a hundred yards of hard grey waves.

'Got him,' said Scotto.

I did not answer. I was concentrating. No race is finished until you get the gun. There was another round to be sailed. And after that, there were another two possible races to complete the semi-final. There was too much wind to make any assumptions.

'Gibing,' I said, and leaned on the tiller.

We passed the buoy on starboard, and moved up on to the windward leg.

'Leaving him for dead,' said Noddy.

I sailed hard up to the windward mark. Spray lashed back over the deck. He's right, I thought; it's not a race, it's a procession.

Then I saw the patch. It was long, and it stretched fifty yards from side to side, a slab of water where something smoothed the sandpaper ripples to an oily gloss. My arm moved before my mind gave it conscious orders, heaving the tiller towards me. But by that time we were in the middle of the patch, passing among brown skeins of weed, and through.

'Jesus,' said Scotto. 'That was close.'

I pushed the tiller away again. And I knew from the feel of it that it had been more than close.

Charlie said, 'Boatspeed's down.'

The figures on the log read, 6.1, 6.5, 6.1. The boat felt sluggish in the water. When I glanced over my shoulder, I could see Paul's bow, growing.

'Weed on the rudder,' I said.

Scotto craned his head over the wildly thrashing back end. 'Bloody clogged,' he said.

We did everything we could think of. We sailed backwards, prodded with oars and boathooks. The weed stayed put. We trailed in a full five minutes after Paul.

Scotto went overboard into the freezing water, and pulled

handfuls of slim brown fronds off the rudder. We drank tea, and I watched Paul. Two more races, I thought. Two more races, and I can win both of them.

But there was something wrong. I told myself the weed had been mere bad luck; but it had lost us the initiative. There was a bad, sick feeling in my stomach. Paul had the South Creek brokerage, and he had the luck. I could not keep the anger down. It was not easy to believe that I could beat those kind of odds.

But I had to try.

We reached out beyond the left-hand end of the line. We were clear of weed, going well. The wake roared aft in white fans. It would have been an exhilarating ride, if we had been thinking about such matters. But I was not. Instead, I was plotting the track that would get us a start on the far end of the line, where the puffs were now coming with a gentle curve that would lift us on to the windward mark.

Charlie said, 'One minute.'

We hard-tacked from one reach on to the opposite reach, 180 degrees. The boom came over with a bang. Now the forestay was lined up on the left-hand buoy of the start line, and beyond it, Paul Welsh. We were hurtling together on a collision course, us on port tack, Paul on starboard, parallel with the line, the flat-sectioned hulls hammering white chips out of the sea. The spray came down the deck like buckets of pebbles.

'Gun,' said Charlie.

There was too much wind to hear the gun's thump. This time, we were going manoeuvring, never mind how much wind there was. The buoy whipped past to port. I kept swallowing nothing, waiting for the calm to come, the icy lens that would make everything clear, so I knew what the other man was going to do before he did it.

It did not come.

'I'm going down to starboard,' I said. My throat was so tight I could hardly speak. We had to bear off downwind, accelerate, tack on to his tail. Water came across the deck, splattered my face. I could hear the *boom* of Paul's hull as it bounced on to a wave.

'Now.'

I pulled the tiller. The nose swung downwind. Paul was coming level now. I was sweating. As we went down, I saw his boom coming in at eye level. I hauled the tiller. But my boat came upright on the front of a wave. We were in the trough, and he was on the crest. The heavy alloy tube of his boom whacked into the taut wire of our port Shroud. He began to shout.

My stomach felt as if I had swallowed something cold and heavy. He had a right to. He had been the right-of-way boat. I had collided with him.

They were all shouting now. The shroud slid down to the end of the boom. It caught in the tongue of metal that holds the topping lift, and stuck. The deck underfoot said *twang*. Sails were roaring. I could see their foredeck man watching as their bow slewed round. His eyes were wide open. Like Bill Rogers, I thought. Just like Bill Rogers. And I set my teeth, and pressed my broken arm against my chest, waiting for the crash as their bow came into our stern.

It did not come. Instead there was another *twang*. And suddenly Paul's boat was away, sliding astern. Sweat was running down my body. I looked up.

The shroud should have been a tight line from the masthead, over the tip of the spreader, and into the chainplate. Instead, it had a slack, ugly curve that flopped in the wind.

'It's off the spreader!' yelled Noddy.

There was a sudden, small *bang*. The mast bent at the spreaders and slapped down to leeward. The boat lay dead in the water, rolling.

'Screw that,' said Scotto.

Below, the VHF said, 'Protest upheld. Devereux disqualified. Second race to Welsh.'

'Now he tells us,' I said. And we began to clear up the mess.

A spectator boat towed us back to the harbour. It was an ignominious procession. I looked up at the pierhead. There were a lot of people clustered at the base of the little lighthouse.

They were all watching. Among the eyes were many camera lenses. I tried to look as if I was enjoying myself.

'It was bad luck,' said Charlie. 'They shouldn't have sailed the race.'

I shook my head. It had not been bad luck. It had been sheer bloody bad judgement. I had gone out for the second race nervous as a kitten, expecting to be attacked. And I had got what I had expected, and reacted too fast, and it had lost us the mast.

Paul was on the quay, flashing his teeth and looking cool and dashing. He had a right to.

I dodged the journalists, went back to Charlie's house and had a shower. There was a reception in the Yacht Club. I was strongly inclined not to go. We sat in his living room sipping whisky, with John Coltrane on the stereo, *On a misty night*. He said, 'You'd better go and be a diplomat, Devereux.'

I was about to argue. But there is no sense in arguing when you know the other man is right, any more than there is in cursing dumb luck when it loses you a semi-final.

Eddie Silk was there, imposing his greasy fingerprints on a glass of the Yacht Club's whisky. He was not one to let me forget my problems. 'Lucky nobody was killed,' he said.

'No chance,' I said, looking over the greasy dome of his head.

A public relations man was talking into a microphone. '. . . the Managing Director of Iceberg Vodka,' they said. A pale man in a beige suit climbed on to the dais at the end of the room, and started tapping the microphone. But I was not looking at the pale man. I was looking at a girl with dark eyebrows, a delicately arched nose, and short blonde hair. The girl who had sat behind the receptionist's desk in the office in the Waterfront building. And she was looking at me.

I started to elbow through the crowd. The speaker was making the link between vodka and the sporting spirit. The girl's eyes were grey-green and impenetrable. She said, 'I hoped you would be here. I'll meet you outside.'

Outside the clouds had split, and beams of late sun were

gilding the puddles in the worn granite coping-stones of the quay. She was wearing a white silk shirt and a tailored jacket with brass buttons that showed off the sharp curve of her waist. There was an RNLI badge on her lapel. She looked very proper, very sailing club. We stepped over the mooring lines of a couple of trawlers and into the door of the Mermaid.

Away from the cocktail party, she looked nervous and uncertain. I said, 'What's your name?'

'Helen Gallagher.'

I bought drinks. We sat down at a scuffed pine table in the corner. I said, 'I didn't expect to meet you again.'

She said, 'I came looking for you. I wanted to ask you some questions.'

'Go ahead.'

'Why did you come to Southampton?' she said.

'Because your Mr Raistrick had made an offer for South Creek, a boatyard in which I have a share,' I said. 'And when we refused it, accidents started to happen.'

Again she nodded. She looked unhappy, staring at the scarred surface of the table.

'But I called the number you gave me,' I said. 'And I've stopped the trouble.'

She looked at me with her grey-green eyes. They were sceptical enough to make me feel uneasy. She said, 'How much do you know about Sea Horse Land?'

There was something about this woman that did not add up. I had very little reason to trust her, but it was difficult not to. I said, 'I know the guy who runs the company whose number you gave me. He likes to make money, but he doesn't want to go to jail. I've spoken to him. He's stopped.'

She nodded. She looked relieved. I did not understand why. She finished her drink, and stood up.

'Is that all?' I said.

'That's all. I'll go back by myself, OK?'

I opened the door for her, and watched her pick her way straight-backed across the mooring lines and disappear into the club door. Beside the rusty upperworks of the trawlers she looked small, and delicate, and oddly lonely.

I drank another half-pint. Our interview had left a peculiar taste in my mouth. She had come all the way to Pulteney to ask me a couple of questions. What was odd was the way she had taken their answers. I was pretty sure that she had not been interested in the facts about Sea Horse Land, but in finding out how much I knew. I had the distinct impression that I was being checked up on.

I left the Mermaid, said my goodbyes to Charlie, and heaved the Land Rover out of the car park and up Fore Street. If she had thought she was going to allay my curiosity, she had another think coming. All of a sudden I was very curious indeed. And it seemed that the person who could best satisfy my curiosity was my cousin James.

James lived in Compton Hall, a large and beautiful Queen Anne house in Somerset. It was a quarter to ten when I hauled the Land Rover's snub nose between the brick lodges of the main gate. The house was blazing with lights; there were five expensive cars in the drive. I climbed down from the Land Rover, combed my hair with my fingers, and trotted up the steps under the portico.

The hall had a marble floor and a couple of Hellenistic statues with no heads or arms. It was all very tasteful; the interior designers had seen to that. A murmur of voices came from behind the double doors on the right. The doors opened, and a servant in a black jacket and striped trousers came out, carrying a tray of pudding plates. He started to say something. I said, 'It's all right,' and went past him.

There was a long mahogany table, with silver candlesticks down the centre and sleek men and women round the edge. James was at the far end, smiling and bonhomous, his red jowls bulging over the collar of his dress shirt, sitting under a second-rate Reynolds he had bought because he thought it looked like him. His eyes chilled when they saw me, and his smile slipped a fraction. He said to his guests, 'Excuse me a moment.'

He took me by the upper arm and led me out of the room before I could pollute the atmosphere of good wine and big money with my sailor's oaths. He led me to a library, with a log

65

fire and whisky and soda on a tray. He closed the door, and turned on me. The bonhomie had vanished. His face was heavy with anger. There was drink on his breath. 'What the hell do you mean by barging in here like this?'

'I want to know your exact relationship with Sea Horse Land,' I said.

His face did not flicker; but then it never did. 'Mind your own damn business,' he said.

He went to a box of Monte Cristos and took out a cigar. The box stood among mounted photographs on the shelf above the folios. 'Want one?' he said. I said I did. He stood for a moment with his broad back to me, fiddling with cutters and bands, and brought it over.

'Sea Horse is finished,' he said, when he had the cigars burning. 'It got out of control.'

I looked at his thick red lips, puffing smoke. He never, ever, offered me his good cigars.

I walked over to the box, picked up the cutters and snipped a little more off the end. The servants had ranged the photographs with military precision, side by side, the spaces between them correct to the millimetre. One had slid back behind its neighbours. Gently, I slid it out and looked at it.

It was a group photograph, in colour. There were four men. In the centre, red and smug, was James. By his side was a dark man with a gold chain on his shoulders, and two other men, one in a dark suit, the other in a blazer and flannel trousers with creases like knives. In the background were new-looking apartment buildings, and a crane standing among palm trees with a red-and-yellow Spanish flag flying from its jib. Strung between two of the palm trees was a banner that said 126 APARTAMENTOS A PUERTO LAS BRISAS. Another man, broad-shouldered and dressed in a beige safari suit, was standing under the banner, looking away from the camera. There was something about the way he was standing that gave me the impression that he might be looking away deliberately, so as not to be recognised.

But I was not interested in people in safari suits. I was looking at the figures in the foreground.

The third face from the right was pale and suety, with a heavy black moustache, smiling a conventional smile above a white collar and a non-Old School tie. I had seen it glancing over its shoulder as it pounded along the iron catwalk of the Waterfront building. It was the face of Mr Terrence Raistrick. Next to him, thin and immaculate and narrow-eyed, was Lord Honiton.

I picked up the photograph and turned round. James said, 'Now if you wouldn't mind, I must get back to my guests.'

I held out the photograph. 'There you are,' I said. 'You and old Raistrick. And dear old Lord Honiton and all.'

James snatched the photograph out of my hand. His face was very close to mine. Its fine, beefy colour was gone, and it had turned a nasty yellowish grey. 'That's a very old photograph,' he said. The fear was rolling off him in waves.

'All Sea Horse Land boys?' I said.

James said, 'I am no longer involved with Sea Horse Land. Nor is Lord Honiton.'

'So who is?'

'There may still be a certain amount of activity in Spain,' he said. 'I really couldn't say.'

I said, 'Where's Raistrick?'

He said, 'I have no idea.' I could believe that. 'And if I were you, I shouldn't go asking a lot of stupid questions. Honiton's been gone for months. I'll show you the correspondence, if you want.'

I looked at him. His colour was returning, and anger was flooding in to replace the fear. I believed him, about Honiton. When Honiton washed his hands, he washed them surgically clean. I was not so sure about James.

I said, 'You don't have to show me any letters. But I don't want to hear from Sea Horse Land again.'

As I pulled the Land Rover's heavy steering through the Somerset lanes, my mind chewed over James's behaviour. He had been discreet, by his lights.

But why had he been so frightened?

Honiton was a powerful man, ill-disposed to anyone who crossed him. But he was too careful of his reputation to get entangled with anything really nasty. Which was more than could be said for James.

I thought about it for the whole of the weary slog back to South Creek. In the end, I decided that the odds were that James was telling the truth about Honiton, and that he had backed off sharply himself when Sea Horse Land started getting into hot water. It would not be the first time he had stood back from a company that was going bad on him. And the reason he had been frightened was because he did not want a lot of fuss.

All the same, it sounded as if Sea Horse Land still existed, at least in its Spanish incarnation. And if it existed in a form too hot for James to touch, I did not like the sound of it at all.

All at once, I was worrying about the people Henry was going to be meeting on holiday.

10

The feeling of menace was still with me when I woke the next morning. I went straight down to the office, and rang James. He did not sound pleased to hear me. I said, 'I want to know what's left of Sea Horse Land in Spain. Names and addresses.'

He cleared his throat. 'Don't know,' he said. 'Man's moved. Haven't seen him.'

I said, 'You know my friend Harry Chase, the journalist. Do you want him to start asking?'

'He can ask,' said James. 'But I can't tell him what I don't know.'

I said, 'Wait and see,' and hung up, and stared at the chart of the basin thumbtacked to the wall. If James was not knuckling under to threats of journalists, either he had nothing to tell, or he was very frightened.

Whichever the case, Henry was on his own.

I was clipping the slings under the fresh antifouling of a Westerly Centaur when I head someone shouting my name.

I held the steadying line as the hull went up and away on the crane. The voice was Mary's.

She was standing at the garden gate with her hands curled like a wrestler's. Her cheekbones were flushed.

'Come here,' she said. She did not wait for me to answer, but stumped into the house and stopped outside Henry's office.

'Now,' she snapped. 'Would you please tell this man that it is time to leave?'

Past her blue woollen shoulder, I saw Paul Welsh sitting at Henry's desk. Behind him a cliff of books and box files rose to the cobwebs on the ceiling. He looked up from the file he was studying. 'What?' he said.

Mary jerked a thick red thumb over her shoulder. 'Out,' she said.

'I'm inquiring into the state of the brokerage,' said Paul. 'As is my right.'

He had a point. When a match racer threatens you with the rule book, he will usually have a point. I said, 'Paul. If you wouldn't mind,' and pushed past Mary into the room. I turned, winked at her purple, speechless face, and shut the door.

'I said I'm busy,' said Paul. His well-kept brown hands were moving along the contents of a box file.

I said, mildly, 'You could have made an appointment.'

He said with heavy irony, 'As I believe you know, I own the brokerage here. And God knows there is enough to put straight.'

I could feel the anger mounting. It was the same anger that had wrecked my concentration in the semi-finals of the Iceberg Cup. Very slowly, and very quietly, I said 'You should have bought some manners at the same time.' I was itching to grab him by the scruff of his immaculate guernsey and toss him out the door. Instead, I took a deep breath. 'Henry's away,' I said. 'It would be . . . more convenient for you to come back when he is here.'

'It's not convenient for me,' he said, without looking up.

'All right,' I said. 'Words of one syllable. Leave. Now.'

He turned over another page. 'So call the police,' he said.

That did it. Suddenly it was Martin Devereux from a school near Reading whose name nobody could remember, and Paul Welsh who went to Eton and whose father kept his yacht at some horrid little yard on the south coast. I went across the room and got his ear between my thumb and forefinger, and pulled. He said 'Ow!' in a shocked falsetto, and tried to pull free.

I said, 'Get out before I throw you out.'

He twisted his head free, tried the superior smile. It was a pathetic, watery thing. He said, 'I have always thought there was something terribly *second rate* about you, Martin.'

'Out,' I said.

'I was going,' he said. He was pale, and his mouth was pressed into a line. As he passed me, his foot went back, then forward again, at my groin. It was a petulant, clumsy move. I dodged aside, caught his ankle with my good hand. We stood there for a moment, eye to eye, him hopping to keep his balance.

'Then go,' I said, and heaved him over on to his back.

He slid into the doorway, picked himself up, white with anger. But he would not meet my eye. Instead he looked back at the room, the chaos of box files, the yellowing paint, the scuffed old partner's desk. 'Christ, what a *dump*,' he said, and left.

That evening, I had an argument with Mary.

'I don't want that man back,' she said. I was in the study, going through a pile of bills.

I said, 'He's got a perfect right to see the brokerage records.'

She stuck out her chin. 'Not in my house.' She paused, frowning. 'Maybe he's been pinching things already. Something's missing.'

'Missing?'

She looked at my face with her pale blue eyes, and said, 'I've laid siege to this bloody room for thirty years. Every time Henry went out, I leapt in and cleaned it before he could come back and turf me out. Something's missing, all right.'

'And you think he swiped it.'

She shook her head. 'On second thoughts, I don't think so. It was something biggish. He wasn't carrying anything when he left.'

'And you can't remember what it was?'

She shook her head. 'I can hardly remember my own name, nowadays.' I looked at her big, weary face, her heavy arms laid on the chipped enamel of the table. Mary had looked after me when I had been turned loose at the age of twelve. Now she needed looking after herself.

'Tell you what,' I said. 'I can't be bothered to go out to the Point House. I'll stay the night.'

Her head came up. She was going to tell me not to be ridiculous. Then I saw her change her mind, and the lines of worry that ran from her nostrils to her mouth smoothed. 'If you insist,' she said.

That night, I lay in the familiar night sounds of South Creek, and dozed. Outside the wind was blowing, the halyards rattling, the sea thundering on the beach beyond the sea wall.

Suddenly I was fully awake. My room was immediately over Henry's office. Above the racket from the basin, I could hear another noise. It was a cautious slithering and knocking that came up through the floor and into the bedstead. I closed my eyes. Rats, I thought; the marshes were infested with rats, and there was no way of keeping them out of a house as old as South Creek. But it was too big a noise for rats, and the things sliding and bumping were too heavy.

I swung my feet out of bed on to the cold floorboards and pulled on my trousers and a jersey. Then I opened the door and started to walk downstairs.

Mary was a war bride. Her views on fuel economy had been founded during the blackout, and she would have bathed in champagne before she would have left a light on all night.

But there was a faint stripe of yellow coming from under Henry's office door.

I was half-way down the stairs. My right foot came down, feeling its way along the skirting board to the next step, close to the wall to prevent the creak. Slowly, I shifted my weight.

The stair creaked like a full-rigged ship taking a squall. The light in the office went out.

I covered the rest of the stairs in one jump, twisted the doorhandle and barged in. I got the fleeting impression of black, with a square of lighter grey which was the window. And a smell; the smell of drink. Then something collided with the side of my head, and my ears rang as I crashed down into a pile of box files. *Police*, I thought; *the aggressive Mr Devereux fails to call the police.*

72

A shape crossed the window: wide shoulders, a thick body struggling with the sash. I got my left hand up and swept down the light switch. Nothing happened. Bulb out, I thought.

When I put my left hand on the floor to push myself up, it found metal. I knew it well; it was a heavy bronze shackle Henry used as a doorstop. I came to my feet with it in my hand just as the man at the window got the sash up. I saw his leg come up against the pale grey square of sky. Swinging the shackle back, I threw.

It was a clumsy throw, executed with the wrong hand. But the shackle thumped, and the figure in the window lurched outwards. There was a distinct crackle as he fell into the flowerbed. I went after him feet first, and landed on something that must have been a body, because it grunted and rolled away. The blood was pounding in my ears. I could see him now, a dark, bulky shape crawling out of a tangle of vegetation. 'Stop right there,' I yelled. 'You're nicked.' He did not stop. I lowered my head and went in at him. We grappled for a moment, there on the lawn, and I tried to get my foot behind his ankles to throw him. But his body was wide and thick, and the plaster cast made it impossible to lock my hands behind him. He wrenched free, and I hit him on the side of the face with my left hand. I felt his fingers groping at my right arm.

Panic bells began to ring. *Oh no, not that,* I thought, and tried to wrench it away. But I was too slow, and he caught hold of my arm and pulled it back, and I cringed at the knowledge of what would come next, because we were up against the wall of the house, which was made of hard, hard brick.

He pulled the cast back and slammed it against the corner of the wall.

My stomach heaved, and the thudding in my ears became a roaring. There was something wrong with my knees, which were as weak as wet paper. I sank down on to the wet grass and folded over my arm.

From above, Mary's voice said, 'Who's that?' and a light came on.

The man's footsteps thumped across the lawn. I tried to go after him, but my knees were still not working and by the time I

73

was at the low brick wall that separates the garden from the yard, a starter was whinnying out in the car park. I leaned against a laburnum trunk and watched the headlights scythe a long swathe of darkness as the wheels juddered across the grit and settled for the road inland. It had a high, boxy silhouette. It was too far away for me to see the number plate. Out in the car park, the exhaust smelt of diesel.

I staggered back into the house, hugging my right arm to my body as if it was a baby.

Mary said, 'What the hell's going on?'

'Burglars,' I said. She looked pale, still half-asleep. 'I don't think they got anything. Ring the police. Tell them it's a four-wheel drive car, Toyota Land Cruiser type. They'll pick it up.' There was a crack in my plaster where it had hit the wall. I held my arm tight, and hoped she could not see my knees shaking under my pyjamas.

The office floor was knee-deep in papers and box files. She pawed at them, not knowing where to start, and I stood and looked at the open window and thought of overweight burglars whose breath smelt of drink and who would have the instincts to smash the plaster cast of a man with a broken arm. Suddenly my stomach turned. I went into the garden and was horribly sick.

The policemen came. There was Sergeant Hone from Marshcote and three CID men from Exeter. They had not picked up the car. It could be anywhere by now, they said, being as how it was four-wheel-drive.

I nodded, and thought of the high, boxy car with the diesel exhaust I had seen leaving the morning I had arrived from Australia. They asked if anything was missing, and Mary told him their guess was as good as hers. Then I described the man, which was no help. 'You was lucky,' said Hone, a thickset man with a freckled face and ginger moustache. The CID men puffed fingerprint powder about. 'There's been a spate of burglaries.' He took a mouthful of whisky and rolled it round his tongue. 'A right spate. Videos, you name it.'

'We haven't got a video,' said Mary.

'Ah,' said Hone. 'But he wasn't to know, was he? You were lucky.'

'You want to ask James de Groot what he knows about it,' I said. I gave him the number.

We sat at the kitchen table in silence while Hone rang Compton Hall. I kept my arm very still in the cracked cast.

He came back, frowning. 'Mr de Groot's in America on business,' he said. 'Left at noon.'

Next morning, I went to Casualty in Exeter. They X-rayed my arm, told me it was mending nicely despite the jolt. Then they put on a new plaster and sent me away.

When I got back to South Creek, the police were back. There had been no fingerprints. Nobody had noticed a car. They wanted to know if there was anything missing. Mary said there was not. They left.

When they had gone, she said, 'Do you think it was Paul Welsh?'

'Too fat,' I said.

'It seems odd,' she said. 'Somebody comes in the dead of night, rummages about, doesn't pinch anything.' She paused. 'Maybe he was after the same thing as Paul.'

Whatever was in Henry's study was certainly of consuming interest to Paul and the burglar. But the burglar had been too big, too bulky for Paul. He had been much more the size and shape of James. James knew I had broken my arm, and it would have been right up his alley to disable me by trying to re-break it.

But James had been on an aeroplane to America.

It was light, now. I went to the office to sign some letters. When Tony arrived, I called him in. 'We need a man on the gate,' I said. 'All night. Every night.'

'Bloody hell,' he said.

'With a radio,' I said. 'I'll have the other end in the Point House.'

'They won't like it,' he said.

'They'll have to put up with it,' I said.

'Can you see our Dick deterring criminals?' he said.

'Yes,' I said. 'Long as he's got a radio.'

Tony shrugged his enormous shoulders. 'If you say so,' he said.

I worked until the sun was a big orange ball dropping behind the masts in the basin. Then I went out into the car park. Tony was there, grinning all over his brown face. 'Dick's on duty,' he said. 'Got two copies of *Penthouse*, half a gallon of tea and an ounce of Old Holborn. No bloody thief'll get past him.'

'And the radio,' I said.

'And the radio.'

'Thanks.' I climbed into the Land Rover, waved to Dick, and headed for the Point House.

I was tired. I heated up a steak and kidney pie and ate it. When I had washed up I banked the fire, tested the VHF receiver, and turned up the volume so I would hear Dick if he tried to make contact in the night.

Then I sat and stared at my chessboard. But I could not concentrate on the game, because Henry kept butting in, away in Spain, doing God knew what with dangerous people. The pieces on the board kept assuming new formations in my mind: James and Helen and Raistrick, and the burglar, rotating around South Creek, prowling. I could see the yard in miniature, the basin with the pontoons, the corrugated iron sheds, the red-brick house on its bank of gravel. Then the focus changed, and they were pirouetting round something else; but the something else was shadowy, draped in grey curtains –

A log crashed on the fire. My head jerked up. Slowly, I got out of the chair and made my way up the narrow stairs.

When I opened my eyes it was still dark. The moon was coming in at the window, printing silver squares across the white candlewick bedspread. My watch said 4:38. I lay for a few seconds, listening to the moan of the wind, trying to work out what it was that had woken me.

Then the voice came again. 'Martin!' it shouted. There was fear in it. More than fear: panic. I went to the window.

The glade in the dunes lay flat and grey under the moon. A car was parked at the far end, its headlights skewed at the sky.

Across the glade was running a big, lumpy figure in a long robe that flapped about its legs. Mary.

I pulled on trousers, jersey and boots, and ran downstairs as she came through the front door. Her hair was wild from the wind. Her blue dressing gown was covered in sand, and her face was streaked with tears. 'Bloody pontoon,' she panted. 'Bloody pontoon. My car's stuck. Come on.'

We ran outside. I started the Land Rover. Her Volkswagen estate car was off the track, its wheels sunk to the hubs in sand.

'Pontoon's adrift,' she said, and then no more, because she was too busy hanging on to her seat as I flung the Land Rover at the bumps.

As we came across the marsh and down to the basin, I could see that there was something wrong by the way the masts stuck up against the paling of the eastern sky. Normally, they stood in orderly ranks. Now, there was an ugly bunch of them down by the car park.

We roared round the basin. I jumped down, shouted, 'Ring Tony!'

'I already have,' she said.

'Where's Dick?'

'Haven't seen him,' she said.

I ran to the edge of the basin. The masts were like a pinewood after a gale. The pontoon, a heavy wood-and-galvanised-iron float fifty feet long, had come all the way across the harbour on the wind. The boats moored to it bow-on had preceded it. The whole mess had hit the concrete boulders, and now it sat there, rocking on the eighteen-inch chop. The noise was horrible; the noise of the dock grinding half-a-million pounds' worth of boats to glass dust.

I looked around for Dick's punt. It was not in its usual place, tied up by the fuel dock. I ran back to the Land Rover, pulled a flashlight out of the glove rack. The beam played over black water and splintered fibreglass.

'What can I do?' said Mary. Her voice was thin and tremulous.

I said, 'Put some clothes on.'

The yellow disc of the flashlight settled on the outside of the dock. Dick's boat was over there, long and black. I went down the wall, climbed over the shattered transom of a big Westerly and on to the dock. Dick's boat was not moored. It was sitting there, held on its fenders by the pressure of the wind.

I jumped in, steadying myself on the engine cover.

The engine was still warm.

I stood for a second, listening. Halyards rang, water lapped, and boats ground on rock. Nothing else.

'Dick!' I shouted.

No reply.

There was no time to wonder why. I hit the starter button. The 120 horsepower diesel started with a deep, heavy chug. I got one of the long warps out of the locker and bent an end of the warp to a ringbolt at each end of the pontoon. Then I took the middle of the warp to the samson post on the stern, made it fast, kicked the gear lever *ahead*, and eased the throttle forward.

The engine roared. As the bridle tightened, the boat became the apex of a triangle with the pontoon as its base. Foam churned silver under the stern. I sat there. There was nothing else to do. Ropes groaned. Astern, the masts shifted uneasily as the weight of the pontoon came off them. Very slowly, I hauled the pontoon out into the open water. The boats came after, still moored, hanging from their warps like battered peapods.

There were lights on the shore now, and cars. A squat vehicle drove out on the far breakwater: the winch truck. A boat came from upwind.

'Got a cable,' said the dark shape in the stern in Tony's voice. 'It's on the winch. Bend it on.' He passed me the eye of a heavy wire hawser. I tied the loop of the bridle on to the eye, went astern to make some slack, knocked the knot off the samson post, and got out of the way so the winch could take the strain. As I laid the punt alongside the fuel dock, the winch was roaring, and the mass of the pontoon was moving back across the basin.

I tied up and ran round to the winch truck. Tony was there. The light was growing. The winch truck was roaring and wheezing, the hawser stretching bar-taut across the water to the shattered hulks that had once been five elegant yachts.

Tony said, 'Lucky you caught it.' There were hollows under his eyes in the truck's headlamps.

'Have you seen Dick?' I said.

'No,' he said. 'Probably asleep in the shed.'

The light had grown enough for the figures on the far side of the basin to be clear. There were two yard hands, and Mary. The yard hands had climbed down the wall of boulders, and were prodding with a boathook at the debris that lined the water's edge. They were bent and concentrated, as if they had found something interesting.

Cold prickled under my jersey. I ran round the outside of the basin. Mary was standing on the wall, looking down. She was saying 'Oh, no. Oh, no.'

The reason was at the bottom of the wall, where the yard men had pulled him out of the water. It was Dick Power. In the early dawn he looked perfectly clean, for the first time since I had known him. That was because he had been under the water for an hour or more, and he was dead.

We pulled him up to the top of the wall. He was stone cold. The light grew; the police arrived, and the ambulance, and their blue flashes swept over the ugly mess in the dark water. A policewoman took Mary inside, and made her tea. I walked back round to the winch truck.

The pontoon was alongside. It was almost as if it had never been gone, except that the boats tied up to it had a lot of damage around their rails and gunwales and transoms. There would be a good twenty or thirty thousand pounds' worth there.

But that could wait.

I went to the first mooring point of the pontoon. It should have been secured by heavy galvanised chain to iron rings on ringbolts set four feet into the concrete of the breakwater. In the light of my torch, the chain hung straight down into the harbour. The galvanising had rust flecks, but no more than you would have expected.

'That chain was new this season,' said Tony. He bent, and

79

pulled up the end that was dangling in the water. 'Must have been a dodgy link.'

'Two dodgy links,' I said. 'One for each end of the pontoon.' You practically never get a dodgy link in a forged galvanised chain. You never, ever, get two at once.'

'Oh, yeah?' Tony looked at me steadily.

'Somebody cut the bloody things,' I said. Poor Dick, I was thinking. Poor bloke, with his *Penthouse* and his sandwiches and his tea.

'We'll dredge up those links,' said Tony. 'They'll be there, if they was cut. And we'll find out who bloody killed Dick.' His voice was cold and angry.

I knew exactly how he felt.

11

The divers went down. They found the remains of two links. One looked as if it had been ground away little by little, on the concrete. The other looked as if it had twisted and snapped as one end of the pontoon blew downwind. Two TV crews filmed from the breakwater.

'Frankly,' said Detective Sergeant Hone, 'it looks like a problem of maintenance.'

'Or sabotage,' I said.

Hone said, 'Or sabotage. We'll have to wait for the inquest. Meanwhile, I wonder if we could have a little chat in the office?'

I took the telephone off the hook and we had a little chat. I told him that it looked to me as if South Creek had been subjected to a continuous campaign of sabotage. He nodded. Neither of us had had much sleep. There were black circles under his eyes. 'I've been making inquiries,' he said. 'I hear that South Creek's got a bit of a reputation for disasters.'

'That's the rumour,' I said. 'It's not the truth. A company called Sea Horse Land is trying to buy the yard cheap. They're wrecking boats to drive the customers away.'

'So you keep saying,' said Hone. 'So you keep saying.' He sighed, and his eyes strayed out of the window to the wreckage in the corner of the hard standing. 'But just say you were wrong,' he said. 'Just say the yard was being run by . . . untidy minds. I understand you're away a lot. And Commander MacFarlane is . . . well, he's not as young as he used to be.' He got up. 'Now if you don't mind I'll have a word with your other people.'

The notices on the wall fluttered as he went through the door. I put the telephone back on the hook. It started ringing immediately. Four owners had seen the carnage on the local breakfast-time news, and wanted to know what we were going to do about it. I told them to get in touch with their insurance companies, and sat back and waited for the insurance companies to get in touch with me.

The telephone rang again. I took a deep breath and picked it up.

The line sounded hollow and distant. A little voice said, through a storm of crackles, 'Hello? Who's that?'

It was a dreadful line. But it was unmistakably the voice of Henry MacFarlane.

'Henry,' I said. 'Thank God you rang – '

'Is anyone hurt?' he said.

'Dick. Dead. Drowned.'

There was a silence. Then the voice said, 'Poor Dick. Poor Dick.'

I said, 'How did you know?'

'Someone out here,' he said.

'Where are you?' I said.

'Spain.' Even through the crackles on the line, he sounded distracted. 'Now look here. It's taking longer than I thought. I can't come back just yet. There are some things you've got to do. For a start, you can keep an eye on that chap Paul Welsh.'

I had been up most of the night. My head was numb. 'Why?'

'Never mind why. Don't let the bugger out of your sight.'

The line crackled. '. . . *Aldebaran*.'

'What about *Aldebaran*?'

'Find out who's bringing her out. Come with the boat. Don't trust that bugger Paul. I'm going to need help.'

I said, 'Henry, what's going on?'

'No time to chatter,' said Henry. 'You're sailing in the Marbella Cup, aren't you? So you can come out in *Aldebaran*.

Now. The next thing. Haul the pots.' I got the impression that he was trying not to be overheard. 'And take it to the bank. It's bloody important. Got to go. All love to Mary. Tell her I'm taking the pills. Poor old Dick. Look here, I'll get in touch later.'

'Where are you?' I said. 'Take what to the bank?'

But the line had gone dead.

I sat and wondered what was taking longer than he thought, and how the hell Henry knew what had happened at South Creek last night, if he was in Spain.

The secretary arrived. I told her to collect telephone numbers. Then I went over to the house to see Mary.

She was in the garden, weeding the paving, stabbing furiously with her bone-handled stub of knife at the grass in the cracks between the stones. I said, 'Henry rang. He's still in Spain. He's taking his pills. He sent his love.'

Her face lit up for a moment, then dulled. 'Well,' she said. 'That's something.'

'He had to get off the line,' I said. 'Otherwise I would have put him through.'

She shrugged. Blast you, Henry, I thought. Why didn't you ring her instead of me?

'Did you tell him about Dick?' she said.

'He already knew.'

She frowned. 'How?'

'He wouldn't say.'

She stood up, easing her back, hands on knees. 'Let's go in. I want a drink.'

She poured herself three fingers of whisky into a glass. I told her exactly what Henry had said. 'So,' she said, when I had finished. 'He's worried about bloody Paul Welsh. That makes three of us. And he wants you to haul the pots. He's raving. He hauled them before he left. Better have a look.' She squeezed my hand, and smiled, her pale blue eyes blurred with a mixture of whisky and tears.

We walked across the hard to the jetty, trying not to look at the hideous mess out on the pontoon. Henry's pots were stacked neatly against the black corrugated-iron end of the shed.

'How many did he set?' I said.

'Forty-eight,' she said. 'I worked it out once. About a ton of the things. Just him and that little winch on *Hellcat*. Every bloody day. At his age.'

I looked at the stack. Eight rows, stacked six high —

There were only seven rows.

I said, 'It's six short.'

'Is it?' she said.

'He said "Haul the pots",' I said. 'Where would he drop them?'

'The Eel Hole,' she said. 'He always put a string in there because nobody else ever did. No lobsters there, of course. Just congers.' She put a hand on my arm. 'I'm feeling a bit feeble,' she said. 'I'm going to go and lie down.'

I watched her go, her shoulders bowed, as if she was carrying a heavy weight, and thought: whatever you are up to, Henry, it had better be worth this. Then I went down to the pot boat, started the engine and cast off.

A dozen or so pot buoys bobbed in the water under Oar Head, winking fluorescent orange and lime-green against the brown bladderwrack. A green hill of water rose to starboard, crashed white, sank again. In front of the nose a black lump of rock shouldered out of a green wave, roaring and streaming white water. I shoved the tiller to port, and swept round the dog-leg between the two fences of rock that guarded the Eel Hole.

Inside the ring of rocks was a quarter of an acre of clear green water, laced with the foam of smashed waves. In the middle of the patch was a yellow pot buoy with MacF stencilled on it. I pushed the boathook under it, caught the tail-rope, looped it on to the winch and began to haul.

The first two pots came up empty. My pulse was hammering now, and not only because of the exertion of hauling with one-and-a-half hands. The third pot had a big conger in it. I tipped it overboard and kept hauling.

The fourth pot was empty. So was the fifth.

As the sixth came up through the clear water, I could see a

shape swimming in the curved wicker; something squat and square.

I heaved the pot aboard, and put my left hand in the hole. I drew out the enamel cash box that Henry had carefully fitted in before slinging it into the sea. Then I pushed the tiller hard over, and headed for the exit.

12

The cash box sat on the study desk, gleaming in the ripples the sun reflected off the water outside. Henry liked things about him that were solid. You could have shot this one through the *Ark Royal* without denting anything but the *Ark Royal*. The day had turned warm and muggy; gulls' screams floated in through the open window, and there was the distant bang of Enid's typewriter from the office.

Mary said, 'That's what it was. He used to keep it on the shelf by the window. I must be mad.' She shook her head. 'But why did he take so much trouble to hide it?'

I said, 'He wants it taken to the bank.'

'The bank's shut,' said Mary.

We both stood and looked at it. Mary said, 'If we knew what was inside, we might know what the old fool was up to.'

I had been thinking the same thing.

'We ought to take it out of his hands,' she said. Her voice was weary. 'I'm tired of him swanning off like this.' She paused. 'Perhaps that's what your burglar wanted. Perhaps that's what Welsh wanted, too.' She walked over to the desk. 'So where's the key?'

There were whole boxes of keys in Henry's desk. None of them fitted the cash box.

'Hacksaw,' she said.

I took out my knife, scratched the side. The paint came off all right; but the metal remained unscored. 'Case hardened,' I said.

'What about one of those welding torch things?'

'If what's inside is paper, it'll burn it up.'

'So how do we do it?'

'Take it to a locksmith tomorrow.'

'Blast,' she said. 'I want to know.' She paused. 'And I don't want it in the house overnight.'

I said, 'I'll take it to the Point House.'

She gave me a suitcase to put it in. I lugged it out to the Land Rover, dumped it in the passenger seat.

The car park was full. It always filled up on a good day in spring, and there is nothing like being on television to raise the profile. Down in the basin, a couple of owners were following surveyors over the wreckage of their boats.

While I felt deeply sympathetic to them, I had too much on my mind to be sure of staying tactful. So I ducked into the big shed before anyone could catch me. It was cool and dim in there, with the soothing dinosaur shapes of chocked boats. There was a telephone extension in the corner. I picked up the receiver, and dialled Paul Welsh's number.

'Hello,' he said, in his smooth Etonian voice.

I said, 'Who's delivering *Aldebaran* to Marbella?'

'Is it any business of yours?' The voice was still smooth, but cold and hostile.

'Yes,' I said. 'It's Henry's boat, and he's asked me to check up for him.'

'Very well,' said Paul. 'I'm delivering her myself.'

'Yourself?' I said. It was as surprising as if he had suddenly told me he was giving up racing and joining the Merchant Navy. 'What's wrong with a professional deliverer?'

'Insurance problems.'

'They won't accept your surveyor's report?'

'The purchaser's surveyor's report.'

I said, 'Have you got any insurance at all?'

He said, 'All you have to know is that I am being paid for this boat F.O.B. Marbella, and I am delivering her myself, on my own responsibility.'

'Ah,' I said. I was beginning to understand Henry's worries. The purchaser was going to hand over the money on the quay at Marbella – a shrewd move, if Paul had twisted the surveyor's arm to give a glowing report. If *Aldebaran* did not survive the delivery trip, the purchaser would save his money, and Henry would lose his.

Watch the bugger like a hawk, Henry had said.

I sighed. 'Got a crew yet?' I said.

'I'll take a couple of guys from the yard.'

'Which yard?'

'South Creek, of course.'

I said, as mildly as I could, 'I'm afraid I can only let you have one.'

'Well then,' he said. 'That'll have to do. Who is it?'

'Me,' I said.

'Now wait a minute,' he said.

'As crew,' I said. 'And owner's representative.'

There was a long, long pause. Finally, he said, 'Well, why not?'

I said 'Goodbye, skipper' and walked out to the Land Rover.

One of the sliding windows on the driver's side was open. I frowned. I was tired enough to do something stupid like that. I unlocked the door, climbed in. The suitcase was still on the passenger seat. Leaning over, I gave it a shove, to feel the weight.

It rocked on the metal floor, light as a feather.

Suddenly I was sweating. It was easy to lift on to the knee: too easy. I flicked the catch.

The suitcase was empty. The cash box had gone.

The car park was emptying out. The ice cream vans had gone, and there were only half as many cars as there had been.

I ran down to the office. Tony was drinking tea and smoking a roll-up. I said, 'Did you see anyone near the Land Rover?'

He said, 'The whole bloody place has been crawling all day.'

I ran back to the house. Mary was sitting in the garden, reading the *Spectator*. She had been drinking. It was hard to blame her.

I said to Mary, 'The box. It's gone.'

'Gone?' she said. Her eyes were pale and haunted. She stared out of the window at South Creek, her home for forty years, where people had started to wreck boats, and steal things, and die. Then she sat down, and began to cry.

I felt like crying myself.

13

Aldebaran was a seventy-foot ketch, built for the Baltic timber trade in the 1920s. Timber ships do not have to worry too much about sinking, because their cargo keeps them afloat. When they had brought her off the Baltic run, she would have had the positive buoyancy of a fencer's mask. Since that time, a lot of caulking had been done by a succession of despairing owners, to little effect.

She had two masts, gaff-rigged. Forward of the mizzen was a brass-bound wheel in a cockpit, with a companionway to the saloon. The saloon itself was panelled with wormy pine. The settees had worn buttoned-leather upholstery. Smells eddied like fog in the chasms belowdecks: bilge water, skinned paint pots, spilt paraffin. Her engine was an antique Perkins that started best when you rammed blazing rags against the air intake, and her steering gear was operated by a system of chains and pulleys that clanked like the family ghost.

From a distance, she was a vision. Close up, she was a bad dream.

The best the yard had been able to do by way of refit was install two heavy-duty electric bilge pumps and a petrol generator to run them. Then we had bolted a couple of big winches to the deck to give us control over her vast sail area and ponderous fir spars, and crossed our fingers.

On the morning of the sixth day after my telephone call to Paul, I had bacon and eggs and coffee with Mary at the stone table on the south side of the house. We had heard no more from Henry. All around, bare grooves of earth between the paving stones bore witness to the amount of weeding she had been doing. She put her hand on my arm. 'Bring him home,' she said.

We got up, and walked round the basin to the pontoon. With her booms trussed dead central and a shiny new liferaft lashed in its canister under the mizzen boom, *Aldebaran* looked almost purposeful.

Paul arrived in his BMW with his gardener, sent the gardener home with the car, and told off two of the yard hands to help stow gear. There were better things for the yard hands to be doing, but I kept my mouth shut. It would be good practice for the weeks ahead. Mary helped, too, and her Tiger Moth-flying niece Emily Johnson, who had a knack of turning up to give moral support on harrowing occasions. I noticed that Paul stayed out of Mary's way.

At noon, I stowed the last case of Paul's Perrier water in the settee locker in the saloon. Then I started the diesel and came up on deck.

Mary kissed me goodbye, and walked down the gangplank slowly and stiffly, like an old woman.

Paul was at the wheel, lean and immaculate in guernsey and sharply-pressed O.M. Watts canvas trousers. 'Cast off fore and aft,' he shouted. 'Get 'em in, get 'em in!' Tony winked across the widening gap of dirty water, and tossed me the line. Emily waved.

I coiled the lines down and carried them aft to the lazarette. Tony and Emily were standing protectively one either side of Mary. Mary was waving. *Aldebaran*'s nose eased out of her berth. There was a rush of white water under her counter as Paul put the helm hard over to kick her stern round. Then her long bowsprit was easing out between the breakwaters.

They came on to the sea wall to wave. The diesel drove *Aldebaran*'s fat sides down the brimful creek towards the glitter of the sun on the southern horizon. The figures on the breakwater shrank, became tiny. They lifted their arms in a final wave, and went away. South Creek's masts vanished in the great sweep of marsh and sky.

'Sail, please,' said Paul.

I went forward, got the main halyard on the winch, and ground up the main, throat first, then the peak. It was hard work; Paul made no effort to help. Then I pulled up the jib and the foresail. My arm had come out of plaster at the beginning of the week, and it was not up to strength. I was sweating as I went aft to the mizzen.

When the mizzen was up, he stopped the engine. *Aldebaran*'s sails bulged like dirty white wings, and the wake made a white railway line on the blue water.

The weather forecast said winds southerly, four to five. There was a depression heading north three hundred miles west of Ireland, which meant that we should have a comfortable close reach down to Ushant, by which time we would be in a new weather system. After that, we had to tiptoe across the Bay of Biscay and run down the Portuguese Trades. Then it was a matter of taking our chance through the Straits of Gibraltar, and on to Marbella. It was about 1100 miles – two weeks with a fair wind, and any time you liked without. To start the Marbella Cup, we had to get there in three.

Over the weather-grey teak rail on the starboard quarter, Oar Head was sinking into the sea. I went and sat with my back to the nice new liferaft and let the April sun shine on my face, and listened to the creak and boom of a big wooden ship in a long, even sea. I had sailed wooden boats out of South Creek ever since I had been thirteen; Henry had seen to that. Lately, of course, the boats had been made of ultra-light plastics, braced with man-made fibres filched from the American space programme and British Aerospace. In theory, I should have been pleased to get back on a wooden boat.

In practice, what I felt was apprehensive.

I had sailed these waters with Paul before. We had both been nineteen. His father had been alive; a small, aggressive man, who had dragged himself up from a Hackney garage to a chain of car dealerships, and acquired a taste for offshore racing and high society on the way. Paul and I had been delivering *Cortina*, his father's boat, for Cowes Week. He had kept the helm all the way. I had done the navigating, and changed the sails, and made the tea. *Cortina* was a fast thirty-eight-foot sloop. In those days we did not get many like her at South Creek. I had already made my mark in dinghy races, and I was hoping with a desperate nineteen-year-old hope that as a reward for helping in the delivery I would be asked to stay aboard and race. I dropped hints. Paul gave me his handsome Etonian smile and said he would see what he could do. After we had pulled into the Medina, the crew had come aboard. And Paul had given me an envelope. Inside was a five-pound note, and a second-class single ticket to South Creek.

'Thank you for your help,' said Paul.

I stared at him. 'What about the racing?' I said.

'*Terribly* sorry,' said Paul. 'No room.' And he laughed, as if the idea was ridiculous.

The first few days went smoothly enough. We fell into a sort of routine, Paul and I; six hours on, six hours off. *Aldebaran* plugged doggedly south-south-west, demanding little attention. All we had to do was listen to the weather forecast, run the engine for three hours a day to charge the batteries that ran the autopilot and the rest of the electronics, keep the bilges pumped dry, and try to stay civil when we met. At least, I tried to stay civil. Paul did not trouble himself. At the end of my watches, I cooked spaghetti or stew for both of us. At the end of Paul's, he ate corned beef sandwiches, without offering me any.

It is easy to get angry on a boat, and my temper is not of the most even. But he was so obviously trying to needle me that it was easy to make my own sandwiches, and do the washing-up in the galley, and grin at him when he scowled. Whenever the strain began to tell, I thought about the Marbella Cup. In a way we were already sailing the Cup, out there on the heaving blue swells of Biscay. Every time I refused to get the needle, I won a little.

We were a week out, a hundred miles off the north-western corner of Spain, when the trouble began. I turned in at midnight, caught the shipping forecast; westerly, five to six. When I woke up for the early watch, the ship's motion had changed. Gone was the long, smooth corkscrew, steadied by the press of the wind in the sails. Now the motion was edgier, a sharp pitching with from time to time a heavy *crunch* as the bow dug in.

I rolled out of my sleeping bag and into my boots, and stumbled forward into the dark cavern of the hold to start the generator. The pumps whined, labouring heavily; pressed as hard as this her seams were working, and she was taking water. Then I pulled on oilskin trousers and coat, and went on deck.

Before I had gone below, the moon had been shining on waves smooth and black as whales' backs. Now they were the colour of slate in the bleak morning light, and the westerly wind wailing in *Aldebaran*'s old shrouds ripped off their crests and drooled trails of dirty scum into their troughs. Paul was at the wheel. I gave him his tea, keeping my body between it and the wind to stop it blowing out of the mug.

He turned his head and nodded at me. There were exhausted hollows under his eyes. I was tired myself. Even in fair weather, seventy feet is a lot of boat to sail with two men.

'Autopilot won't hold her,' he said. 'Old bitch.'

'She wants a reef,' I said. 'She's not a racing boat.'

He turned abruptly. 'I want to get there,' he said.

A frosty shadow rushed over the water to starboard. The wail of the rigging became a shriek. The deck tilted steeply underfoot. Paul struggled with the wheel, to stop her paying off. I grabbed a spoke and heaved. Slowly her nose came up. Below, the bilge pumps screamed, chewing air as the water ran far over to leeward.

'It's going to get worse,' I said. 'Shall we take the main off?'

He looked at the main, then at me. His upper lip twitched faintly. 'Better safe than sorry,' he said, with irony.

I did not tell him that nobody was getting any points for looking like a hero. Instead I clipped my safety harness to the jackstay running along the deck, and took the main off. It was hard work, winches or no winches. Without Paul's help, it took half an hour.

When I had finished, *Aldebaran* was moving more easily, one sail at each end: jib forward, and mizzen aft. The feeling of pressure had eased. She stopped going over on her ear in the gusts, and the autopilot held her again.

'Bloody slow,' said Paul, hands in pockets as I returned sweating to the cockpit.

'Better safe than sorry,' I said.

The sky was bleak and hazy, the sun surrounded by a dirty halo. Down in the saloon, the radio crackled. *Warnings of gales in Sole, Biscay, Finisterre*. We were bang in the middle of Finistère. *Westerly severe gale force nine imminent, veering north-westerly later*.

I went below, leaving her to the autopilot. Paul had made his usual single corned beef sandwich, and was eating it. I waited till he had finished with the bread, and made one for myself. I said, 'We're in for a blow.'

'I heard the forecast.'

The cabin lurched as *Aldebaran's* nose slammed a wave. I levered myself across to the Decca and punched the buttons. The digital readout glowed in the dim cabin. It showed a position fifty-five miles west of Cape Finisterre, below the north-western corner of Spain. 'So what do you want to do?' I said.

'Go for shelter.'

I said, 'We won't get a landfall till night. By that time it'll be blowing force eight, nine maybe. You'll be running ahead of a gale on to a lee shore.'

He said, 'I'm not riding it out in this bloody thing.' His voice was a little too high and a little too fast.

I said, 'Think about it.'

His heavy black brows came together over his nose. 'I am sailing this fucking boat,' he said. It was cold, but there was a shine of sweat on his temples.

Don't let the bugger out of your sight, Henry had said. I said, 'We are both sailing this boat. Henry MacFarlane wants her in Marbella in one piece. You want her in Marbella in one piece. You are looking after your commission. I'm looking after the balance of the purchase price for Henry.'

He looked at me. He wanted to hit me. But he knew enough to know I was right.

'So let's shorten sail again,' I said, as soothingly as I could. 'Then we can get some kip.'

On deck, the wind hit us like a cold hammer. A gust ripped across the sea and screamed in the rigging. *Aldebaran* heeled until her shroud plates tore holes in the water. I struggled aft and put three reefs into the mizzen. The sail was so old it felt as soft as chamois leather.

'Foresail!' I yelled.

There was no question of him staying at the wheel this time. I unsheeted the outer jib, and the mizzen pulled her head-to-wind, the bowsprit drawing huge, inscrutable pictures in the sky. We groped our way along the boom to the foredeck, clung there. The tack of the outer jib was secured to an outhaul at the end of the bowsprit. I slackened the halyard. Paul shuffled forward, knees bending against the bucking of the deck. He uncleated the outhaul, and hauled.

The tack was meant to come towards him as he pulled it. It did not move.

'Jammed!' he yelled.

'I'll go,' I said.

He looked at that bowsprit. *Aldebaran* was on a crest. Below the spar, a fifteen-foot cliff of sea had opened out. As she dived into the trough, her bow chopped into the green water until the cliff was a hill rolling up and away, and the bowsprit was digging white spray out of its side. He looked at me, white-faced. I knew what he was thinking. He was thinking that back there in the cabin he had not behaved too well, and now he had to do something about it.

He clipped his harness on to the outhaul block, and began to work his way out to the snarl-up. He got there. His shoulders jerked as he wrenched at the jam. And I saw the wave.

From the base of the mast, I saw the orange timber of the bowsprit, Paul red and hooded, perched eight feet out on the spar. Beyond him was a huge grey wall that growled and muttered as it bore down. His head went up. There was a sudden lull in the wind as we came into the wave's lee. In the

96

hush, I heard him yell, saw him begin to wriggle backwards. He did not get far. As the bow lurched up the impossibly steep face of the wave, the crest curled over and began a fast, roaring slide. I flung myself forward, grabbed his lifeline, and heaved until I could grasp his hood. Then the wave hit.

It crashed aboard like a runaway bulldozer. My legs went up and my head went down, and something slammed into my face so I opened my mouth to shout, and there was only water to breathe. There was a wrenching jerk at my upper chest. Lifeline, I thought. My legs were fluttering like flags in the rush of water. Gone, I thought. Gone, we've gone.

But the water in front of my eyes was lightening. I could breathe again. The roar of the wave faded aft. My right hand was still clamped on something. Paul's hood. It was still attached to his jacket, and he was still inside the jacket. I shouted, 'Are you all right?'

He moved. He turned his head. His face was yellowish. 'Jesus,' he said. 'Oh, Jesus.'

I looked at the end of the bowsprit. The tangle had gone. So had the sail.

'Help me,' I said. 'Storm jib. Help me.'

He did not move. So I opened the sail locker hatch and wrestled out the storm jib, and wrenched its big bronze hanks on to the forestay. By the time I finished, he had gone aft.

I sheeted the storm jib to windward, scuttled aft and lashed the helm. *Aldebaran* turned her nose off the wind and lay hove-to, taking the waves under her starboard bow. That was all I could do for the moment. I went below.

Paul was asleep, wet gear and all, on the leeward settee. Shock, I thought. I put a blanket over him. I was not feeling too terrific myself. I got a Decca fix, filled the generator with petrol, and ran the pumps for a while. Then I wedged myself in a corner, and waited.

The wind rose steadily, and the seas with it. Sunset happened somewhere behind a black roof of cloud. In the twilight, the seas rolled as high as the first spreaders of the mainmast, their slopes netted with foam. I lit the cabin oil lamp. It swung violently on its gimbals, hurling shadows across the stained panelling.

At nine o'clock the night was as black as half-way up a chimney, and a lot noisier. Paul was wedged in his bunk. His face looked greenish in the lamplight, and his eyes were closed. I had stood his watch for him. Now I wanted to lie down and sleep. I checked the Decca, went over and shook him by the shoulder.

His eyes opened immediately. He had not been asleep.

'Your watch,' I said.

His pupils seemed very large. 'Wha'?' he said.

'We're hove to, fifty miles west of Vigo,' I said. 'Wind, force eight to nine.'

He lay there staring at me. It was a disconcerting stare, blank and silent. I knew what it meant. He was listening.

I had been listening, too.

Every time the boat's nose came off a wave, it banged as if someone was hitting it with a sledgehammer. Years of sailing boats made of fibreglass and aluminium made you forget the creaking and groaning and cracking a wooden hull makes as it moves. But it was not the creaking that was the worry. It was the heavy slosh of water in the bilges.

I said, 'I'm starting up the pumps again. Then I'm turning in.'

In the hold, the flashlight's beam picked up a thin sheen of water on the sides. At the downhill edge of the deck's planks, a strip of black water sluiced to and fro. Under her planks, there would be two or three feet of the stuff.

I went over to the generator and fired it up. Then I hit the switches on the pumps, which began to whine doggedly.

When I came back into the saloon, Paul was still lying on his bunk. He said, 'I'm ill. I hit my head.'

I took a bar of chocolate out of the locker and handed him half. 'Low blood sugar,' I said.

'No,' said Paul. He turned his face to the panelling.

I was too tired for theatrics. I said, 'I thought you were in charge round here.'

His head snapped back. His feet hit the deck with a thump.

'You make a very good delivery skipper,' he said. 'It's just about your mark.'

The blood whined in my ears. I said, 'You arrange to deliver a boat with no insurance to a client who won't pay you till he gets it. Then you start acting like an old woman when you get a bit of a blow. Just as well I make a good delivery skipper, because you bloody well don't.'

He smiled at me. It was an ugly smile. 'Hearts of oak,' he said. 'Heads of oak, too. You and your friend Henry and that old cow Mary. Rank bloody amateurs.'

My heart was beating slow and steady, driving the anger round my exhausted body. I said, 'So what's a big shot like you doing buying a two-bit brokerage, then?'

'I have my reasons,' he said. The smile was gaining in confidence. 'But they'd be a bit complicated for you.'

There was a heave in the back of my mind like volumes of lava, bubbling and shifting. The roar of my blood was as loud as the roar of the storm. It had been a long week, and a long watch, and I was not going to be polite any more. 'I understand, all right,' I said. 'I understand you cheated me and a lot of other guys off the Constellation Challenge. So let's try something simple for a change.' I was standing over him. 'How much did you pay for the brokerage?'

'Fifty thousand pounds.'

'I'll bet you your brokerage I sail you under the water in the Marbella Cup.'

Fifty thousand pounds was a drop in the bucket for him. For me to raise it would mean mortgaging everything I possessed. There was a silence. My stomach was a tight knot. Devereux had opened his big Irish mouth, and now he was going to have to sail his way out of it. Fifty thousand pounds was what you might call an incentive.

Paul's smile had gone now. 'Why not?' he said. His face was mean, and violent, and furious. 'And when I win you and those two pensioners can piss off and get a council flat.'

I smiled at him. 'Your watch,' I said.

'Get fucked,' he said.

Suddenly the deck rose, then fell away like a lift with the cable cut. Outside there was a roar like a train passing close by.

I ran up the companionway. The sky was dark, but between me and it there was something bigger and darker. Wave, I thought. Another bloody great wave. We were in the trough, beam-on. The wave came under. It came so fast I could feel my knees trying to bend as the deck rose. *Aldebaran* heeled far over to port. There was no wind, because we were in the shelter of the trough. But as we shot up to the crest, the wind hit with a shriek and a bang, beam-on, and smacked her over to starboard like a pendulum just as the crest came under and tripped her. She went on and on, over to starboard. The deck stopped being a deck and became a precipice. I was flung the full length of my lifeline. I hung there in the dark for what seemed like half an hour, thinking: *come up, you old bitch, come up,* calmly, as if I was talking to an uncooperative dog.

Then I heard the noise. It sounded like an avalanche, a rumbling of heavy objects falling down a slope. It was coming from the hold.

Another wave came under, but *Aldebaran* remained heeled to starboard. I scrambled back to the cockpit, crouched there with the spray and the sweat running off me. The sweat felt colder than the spray. Because I knew there was nothing to be calm about at all.

The sound had been the sound of the ballast shifting.

14

I could hear Paul shouting even over the sound of the storm. He was lying on the cabin sole, clutching his head. I stepped over him and ran into the hold.

Normally, it was a long, empty room with a wooden floor and walls. The ballast lived under the deck planking, held down by a net of cables bolted to the ribs. In the dim yellow light that was all the batteries could provide, it was a battlefield of smashed floorboards, sloping steeply down to the right. A lot of the cables must have broken, allowing the heavy ballast to punch through the rotten decking and tumble down to the starboard side.

The generator crouched silent on its bed. It was wet. But it had been heavily waterproofed. The liquid in the tank sloshed violently to port as the boat rolled, then went back to starboard. I shone the flashlight into the tank. On the starboard roll, the petrol cleared the filter on the pipe leading to the motor.

I went back into the saloon. I said, 'Put some petrol in the generator.'

Paul looked at me as if he did not understand. He started to swear, horribly. His skin was a grisly grey-blue, his eyes sunk in his head. He was so frightened he could no longer think. He had to be told what to do. I explained to him slowly. He did what he was told.

The generator started to howl, and the pumps began to whine. Then I started to clear away the broken decking.

That took half an hour. By the time I had finished, the forward end of the hold looked like a woodshed. The wind yelled on. The lake of black water down to starboard was receding, sloshing evilly through the piled lumps of old iron. I braced myself against the bucking of the sides, and began to heave the ballast uphill.

It was horrible work. The iron was mostly railway line, cut into lengths that two men could carry into the bilges, but too heavy for one man, even if that one man had not already been working his guts out for ten hours. The lengths lay hugger-mugger in the turn of the hull, like a nightmare version of the children's game where you have to move one stick without disturbing the rest of the pile. It was a tribute to *Aldebaran*'s will to live that they had not gone straight through her side.

'Paul!' I shouted.

I watched him drag himself out of the cabin and down into the black lake. He seemed to have shrunk. He was moving so slowly that I had to lift up one end of a length of iron, lay it in his hands, then pick up the other myself. Carrying it between us, we lurched up the slope of the hull and laid it on the uphill side of the keel. Then we went back for another, and another and another.

By the time we had done ten, our hands were bleeding and fiery with salt and dirt. Half a ton down, I thought. Only another nine and a half tons to go. I set my teeth and went back for the next one.

I bent, fished in the inky waters. Then I realised Paul was not with me.

He was sitting on the keelson. His head was in his hands. Blood ran down his wrists, black in the flickering light of the yellow bulb.

'Come!' I said. My voice was a croak. My throat was dry and raw.

He did not move. Outside, the waves rolled under with a hiss and a roar, and the wind shrieked in the rig. In the hold, it was

102

yellow reflections off black water, and Paul, silent, with his head buried in his hands.

I went up and grabbed him by the arm. I said, 'Do you want to live?'

He looked up at me. There were smears of black blood on his greenish-white face.

He said, 'I can't go on.'

I said, 'Yes you can. We've got a bet on.'

For a moment his eyes cleared, and I could see the hatred behind the vacant expression on his face. Then he shuffled aft to the saloon.

I thought about dragging him back. But that would have been too much effort. So I went back to the ballast, and lugged two more bits of railway on my own. I wanted to sleep. I didn't care any more if I drowned, if Paul drowned. But I had promised Henry I would get *Aldebaran* to Marbella. Marbella. The Cup. I was going to win that bet and flush him out of my life once and for all. I could not afford to drown, yet.

I bent down, groping in the water for the next length of iron. My hands met something square and smooth. I pulled it out. It was a cold-cast ballast pig, a mixture of resins and lead.

I lugged it up to the keelson, lowered it into the slot, went back. There were more of the cold-cast blocks. Someone at the yard must have taken them out of one of the wrecks, and dropped them in. I felt pathetically grateful. They did not rip at the hands like the iron ones, and they weighed a lot less. It was the first good thing that had happened for days.

At first, anyway. By the time I had made fifty trips, I was wandering in a haze of pain. I kept falling over. My ears were buzzing, and I knew that I could not go on.

I staggered aft to the saloon and ate a whole tin of corned beef, straight out of the can. Paul had made himself a meticulous bed inside his lee cloth. He was lying in it face down.

The food made me cold and sleepy. The generator thrummed drowsily from the hold. The angle of the lamp on the bulkhead was not so acute as it had been. The chronometer said 0412 hours. Six hours since the ballast went. The barometer was low, but steady.

I went on deck.

The cloud had cracked and split into flying islands that raced by in a deep gulf of stars. Overhead the three-quarter moon hung, unbearably bright after the dim yellow of the cabin. It shed an evil silver glow over the ragged edges of the clouds and licked at the great mountains of water cruising down on the port bow, turning the spray at their crests to glittering snow. It was a countryside out of hell, continuously moving, bathed in corpse-coloured light.

Shivering, I worked my way down the deck to check the jib. Spray drenched me. When I went below again the saloon seemed warm and cosy. I sat down again and lay back. It was like lying in a bunk in a runaway switchback, but it was the most comfortable place I had ever been.

I went to sleep.

When I awoke, I did the rounds as Henry had taught me, banging up and down in the Channel when I had been eighteen: check position by dead reckoning and Decca, check glass, check weather, check ship. The Decca put us fifty-one miles west of the Ria de Vigo. I marked the fix on the chart, a pencil circle with a dot in the middle. The glass had risen. Then and only then, I put the kettle on. Henry had always insisted: ship first, crew second. Paul was still huddled in his bunk. His eyes followed me balefully as I put the kettle on for coffee.

'Breakfast?' I said.

He said, 'No.' He had been drinking. His breath reeked of whisky.

I said, 'You'd better sober up. There'll be plenty to do.'

He said, 'Listen to teacher.'

I put a saucepan on the stove, tipped in baked beans and a tin of stew and a glob of chilli sauce. When it started to bubble, I scraped it into two bowls.

Paul wrinkled his nose. 'Disgusting,' he said.

I turned on the radio. A plummy London voice started talking about farming. There were five minutes to go till the forecast.

'*Shit!*' said Paul, pushing his bowl away.

'Quiet,' I said. It was time for the weather.

I scribbled down the gale warnings that rippled drearily out of the radio, read by an announcer who probably thought he was a hero for dragging himself out of bed at 5.00 a.m. and going down to a stuffy studio in Broadcasting House. I wondered what he would think if he could see this horrible saloon, full of discarded tools and sandwich crusts and wet oilskins and noise, the whole squalor of the gale.

'. . . *Finisterre westerly severe gale force nine veering north-west imminent, increasing storm force ten later,*' said the radio. I let the rest of it flow over me, thinking about breakfast with bacon and tomatoes, and how I did not want to sit in this saloon looking at Paul for another twelve hours, wet and hungry and beaten like an egg in a blender.

Paul said, 'Force ten. It's going to blow force ten. In this thing.' He got up, lurched, hung on to the grabrail above his bunk. 'Listen,' he said. 'We've got to do something.'

'Nothing we can do,' I said. 'Anyway, they're wrong. The glass is rising.'

He gazed at the barometer. His eyes were pink and glazed. *Aldebaran* took a wave, rolled far to starboard. His fingers clamped on the rail, and his tongue ran round his dry lips. 'You silly bastard,' he said. 'She could go any minute.'

I said, 'What do you suggest?'

'Mayday,' he said. 'Let's send a mayday.' His face was flushed now, enthusiastic. 'We could get a chopper out here from Spain, no bother. It makes sense, right?'

He was smiling now, a parody of his confident Old Etonian smile. He looked like a used car salesman trying to sell an insurance writeoff.

'Look,' I said. 'This boat belongs to Henry, and we are delivering it. And I am not going to sit here and watch you send maydays because you've got the bloody wind up.' I stood up. 'Go and stick your head in a bucket and sober up, and then we'll get this thing to Spain.'

For a moment our heads were close enough together for me to get the full blast of his poisonous breath. I went on deck.

It was still grey waves high as houses, and wind screaming in the rigging till your head got sore. But the clouds were higher now, the streaks of blue more frequent. I began to feel a thread of hope. Depressions had been known to change direction, and weather forecasts to be wrong. The sea was big, but the wind could not be more than force eight. Buoyed up with this thought, I moved from stern to stem, checking.

Aldebaran was in remarkably good shape, despite her twenty-degree list. The pumps were howling below, and streams of water were pouring from their hoses. I worked my way aft for another look at the glass. As I ducked down the companionway, Paul was sitting in front of the VHF, his face white and set. His fingers were clumsy on the dial. The LCD said Channel 16, emergency. He picked up the mike, thumbed the TRANSMIT button. 'Mayday, mayday, mayday,' he said. 'This is – '

It was all he had time for. Before he could finish I had dragged him out of the seat and slammed him on to the deck. The microphone clattered away on the end of its coiled lead.

He hit me in the stomach, hard. I doubled up. Out of the corner of my eye I saw his hand swing alongside my head. The Teachers bottle was in his hand. I ducked, but not far enough. Pain burst through my ear and cheekbone. The boat lurched, and my feet went from under me. I skidded down towards the radio, and my skull slammed into the lockers. Red curtains of blood hung in front of my eyes. I grabbed plastic. The microphone. I wrenched at it. The cable came away. I got up one leg, fell again, lurched into the bulkhead, shoulder and ribs. The air went out of me with a whoosh.

It must have taken me half a minute to get my breath back, gasping like a goldfish on the deck. I scrambled clumsily up the companionway. Paul was on deck aft of the cockpit, struggling one-handed with the lashings of the white canister of the liferaft.

'No!' I shouted. 'You stupid bastard!'

He turned on me the face of a man in a nightmare. 'Fuck off!' he screamed, and fumbled at his belt. When his hand came up, it held a little leaf of bright metal. A knife.

'Stay away!' he yelled. 'You're so keen on your bloody boat, you can go down with it!'

He slashed wildly at the liferaft's lashings. One of them parted.

I hesitated for a second. He was drunk and crazy. The sea was like the inside of a giant washing machine. If he went into the raft he would drown for sure.

So I jumped at him.

Aldebaran staggered as her nose hit another wave. My jump missed, but it threw him off balance. His hands went out to grab the liferaft's cradle. I saw his knife go flying to the end of its lanyard; and something else. Something that froze me in my tracks, and hung my mouth open so I could only stare.

It was the thing that had been occupying his left hand while he sawed at the lashings with his right. It was square and green, rounded off at the corners, with a brass handle in the centre of the top. I had seen it before, that object. It was a cash box. The cash box I had found in Henry's lobster pots; the cash box someone had stolen out of my Land Rover in the South Creek car park.

The cash box slid out of the crook of his arm and fell on to the steeply-listing deck. He dived after it. His fingers were closing over it when his lifeline brought him up short. It slid away down the slope of the deck, checked for a moment on the shallow bulwark, tripped and disappeared, without fuss or ceremony, over the side of the boat.

The wave thundered down.

When it had stopped rattling my head against the deck I looked up.

The liferaft was still there. The wave must have jerked the canister's release cord, because the downhill half of the deck was occupied by a big yellow doughnut with a roof like a little rubber tent. It sat on the deck as if waiting for children to come and play in it.

No children came. Instead, the next wave came cracking over the bowsprit. The world went green and white. And when it came back to its right colours, there was no liferaft.

I pulled myself up on the wheel. Something had whacked

my nose; there was blood in my mouth. Three hundred feet downwind, the yellow doughnut wheeled, slithering in the spray on the upslope of a wave. Then it flicked over the crest, and was gone.

Paul looked after it for a long time. Then he pushed his knife back into its sheath and crawled along the jackstay to the cockpit. I said, 'Where did you get that box?'

He did not answer. His face was white, and exhausted, and his eyes were terrified. I put my face close to his. 'The box,' I said. 'Who gave it to you?'

He said in a croaking whisper, 'Raistrick.'

I was too tired even to think about it. I said, 'We are going to move the rest of the ballast.'

He did not seem to hear. He kept saying, 'Oh, *Jesus*.'

I took his knife out of his belt and shoved it into my pocket. Then I led him below. The glass was up again. The 1355 shipping forecast said north-west, force three.

In the dirty grey glimmer from the skylight we moved three tons of iron ballast and cold-cast slabs from the starboard side to the centre line, and nailed planks over them to hold them down. By that time it was three in the afternoon. Paul had not said a word. He moved like a man in a trance, his face white and expressionless.

The gusts became less frequent as the evening drew on, and the waves stopped breaking. By seven o'clock it was blowing force three, and I was struggling with the brassbound spokes of the wheel as we reached eastwards over a huge green ground swell.

At midnight, I caught the loom of Panjon light whitening on the horizon. During the small hours, we moved steadily in on the rugged coast of the top left-hand corner of Spain, just north of the Portuguese border. And at six o'clock next morning, Paul picked a big mooring buoy under the castle at Bayona.

I took one look at the way we had come, where the twenty-foot ground swell was smashing itself on the Islas Cices at the entrance to the Ria de Vigo. Then I took off my oilskins for the first time in four days, and lay down in the white shambles of the mainsail in the hot Spanish sun, and went to sleep.

15

It was evening when I woke up. There was a dirty blue launch alongside, fendered with car tyres. The man aboard had a huge black moustache, and I could understand enough of his Spanish to work out that he was the harbourmaster.

An hour later we had cleared Customs and were alongside a neat stone quay. I was sitting on the deck in the scream of the gulls, sipping San Miguel out of the neck of a bottle and watching the sardine fleet coming in over a sea blue as a baby's eyes, when Paul came on deck.

He was wearing a clean shirt and a pair of white duck trousers with a sharp crease. I had been thinking about the cash box. He had not mentioned it since it had gone overboard, and he did not seem worried that I had seen it. So I had to assume that he did not know that it had been stolen. But he knew it was important, or he would not have tried to jump into a liferaft with it in a force eight gale.

Don't let the bugger out of your sight.

'Going ashore?' I said.

He nodded.

'I think I'll come with you,' I said. He shrugged and said nothing.

The noise and stink of the town was overpowering; it always is, after a week at sea.

We came out of the narrow streets and into a square. There were cafés on the pavements. In the middle there were fountains with dolphins and a Triton. Mopeds snarled round and round, for the fun of it. Beyond the far wall, the blue harbour stretched away, with *Aldebaran* lying alongside her quay.

'Let's get a drink,' I said.

'I must make a telephone call,' he said.

I said, 'You'll need a drink first.'

He hesitated. His manner had changed since the storm, as if the balloon of his self-confidence had been pricked, and he was no longer sure of his ground. I thought I knew why.

We sat at a tin table. The waiter brought two Fundadors. I said, as innocently as I could, 'Was that box important? The one that went overboard?'

He picked up his brandy, gulped at it. 'You will never know,' he said. His lips were turned in, and he was chewing at them.

'Oh,' I said. Clearly he had no idea that it had been stolen from South Creek. He was simply a courier; a courier who had made a cockup. 'Who was it for?'

Paul grinned at me. It was a very nasty grin, but it did not hide the fear in his eyes.

He looked at me, his eyes sharp slits that seemed to try and peel back my skull and see into my mind. There was a silence. Then he said, 'If you really must know, it was for Georgie Honiton.'

I sat and stared at him, and tried to imagine a set of circumstances under which His scrupulously correct Lordship of Honiton would arrange a midnight burglary, then a daylight raid, to secure somebody else's property. It was not conceivable. Unless whatever was in the box actually belonged to Honiton, and Henry had been keeping it away from him. Or unless Honiton was still an associate of my cousin James, or his Spanish partners, and they were manoeuvring him like a supermarket trolley.

'What was in it?' I said.

He shrugged. 'He asked me to bring it. That was all.' He stared at me for a moment with his haunted eyes. Then he said, 'You've got no idea, have you?' He kicked his chair back with a crash, and walked away across the square, shoulders hunched round his dark curly head.

I ordered more brandy, and watched the swallows in the blue sky and the girls in their crisp dresses. The cash box was under a lot of water, and the cash box was the only evidence. But I wanted an explanation myself, and I could not see that when we got to Marbella there would be anything to prevent me from asking for one.

Two days later, I pointed *Aldebaran*'s blunt white nose at the glittering blue wedge beyond the islands that cork the mouth of the Ria de Vigo. Paul had come back that morning, his face still as pale as when we had arrived. We had not spoken.

A fisherman looked up from the nets he was mending. '*¿Adónde vais?*' he shouted. 'Where are you going?'

'Marbella,' I shouted back.

'*¡Cuidado!*' cried the fisherman. 'Take care! Is full of thieves and drug addicts down there!' He grinned, his teeth yellow and brown in his dark face.

I waved, and knocked the throttle forward. *Aldebaran*'s hull vibrated underfoot. Drug addicts I did not know about. But I needed no convincing about the thieves.

The forecasts were good. We motored south along the dull sandy shores of Portugal, and picked up a north-easterly off Cape St Vincent. It should have been an heroic sail.

But it was not. I chafed against *Aldebaran*'s bluff nose, her flat bottom, the whine of the pumps. I came to hate the smell of paraffin and musty leather in the saloon, the creak of her ancient rigging as she barely made headway in a crisp force four. I wanted to get back into a fast boat that did what she was told, out of this marine rubbish dump.

So, apparently, did Paul. In these conditions *Aldebaran* was easy to single-hand, so we went back to six-hour watches. Paul hardly spoke; I got the feeling that he thought he had said more than he should have in Bayona.

At dawn on the sixth day, the ruby and emerald flash of Tarifa came out of the sea on the port bow. As the light grew I could see the town through glasses, its grey rocks white with bursting spray. We moved on into thickening shipping, between the jagged ranges of the Rif to the south and the long fin of Gibraltar ahead and to the north. The sky was hazed with heat, the sea ahead a white-hot dazzle in the morning sun. Slowly, diesel spewing black smoke, *Aldebaran* toiled into the Mediterranean.

It was not an abrupt transition. The clean winds and boisterous blue of the Atlantic hung on for some miles beyond the Pillars of Hercules. The sierras rose to the north, dun and hazy in the hot breeze. As the Rock went hull-down, the narrow flats between the mountains and the sea began to lose their dark fur of pines and to sprout a pox of glaring white concrete.

They started small, the pustules, an eruption here and there: little fields of apartment buildings planted by crafty farmers on the stretch of dune and badland between the coast road and the sea. I had been down this way before, taking a boat to Sardinia for the Sardinia Cup, and we had done some bar-crawling in the artificial harbours among the artificial buildings and artificial locals of places like Puerto Duquesa. After Estepona the sierras rise steeply, and at their feet the buildings jostle for space, spreading into the foothills and on to the grey beaches.

Seven hours out of Gibraltar, Marbella was coming up on the port bow. I gazed at the yellowish vapour hanging over the tangled buildings ashore. There was no wind; the sails flopped, and the braying of cars' horns drifted across the scum on the glassy blue water. Ashore, marble domes glittered in the sun. The smog stank of money-to-burn.

We had to take the sails down, facing each other across the boom as we flaked the mainsail. Paul's face was stony. He said, 'I am greatly looking forward to destroying you in the Marbella Cup. I presume the bet stands?'

I said, 'The bet stands. You'd better get in some practice.'

He shrugged and went below. I heard him talking on the radio, getting a telephone number ashore, laughing a false laugh. He came up as *Aldebaran* slid between the breakwaters into the glassy, diesel-slicked waters of Puerto José Banús.

We tied up at the *dique* by the control tower. The Customs came aboard, glum men in olive-drab uniforms. They made us take them down into the saloon and the hold, and shook their heads over the pumps and the engine, which sat there weeping black oil.

'*Sucio*. Filthy,' said one of them, with dark glasses and shining toecaps. His mate, a crumpled fellow with a big stomach trying to get out of his shirt, nodded, made drinking movements with his thumb.

'You have whisky?' he said.

I led them up to the saloon, and showed them our spirit stores, which amounted since the storm to a dozen tins of Foster's and a half-full bottle of whisky. They looked at them, and nodded. I wondered if I was supposed to offer them some.

Heavy footsteps sounded on deck. The hatchway darkened. A voice roared, 'Anyone home?'

Paul's face looked pinched and nervous. He said, 'Deke! Here!'

A man came down the companion steps. His shoulders were wide enough to blot out most of the light. He was about fifty, with a short fuzz of tightly-curled grey hair. His face was big, with the reddish-brown tan of a Northern skin that has lived for years in the sun. His cheeks were long and flat, like a boxer's, below pale-lashed blue eyes.

'This is Martin Devereux,' Paul said. 'Martin, this is Deke Kellner, *Aldebaran*'s new owner.'

'Yeah,' said Kellner. He sat down on one of the settees, hard. 'Feel that leather,' he said. 'Lovely.' His voice was hoarse South London. He took in the Customs men, and said, 'Paco. Pepe. How's it going, eh?'

The Customs men simpered. Kellner yanked two beers out of the locker and handed them one each. 'My new boat,' he said. 'Nice, eh?' The Customs men smiled weakly, and nodded. Kellner was a hard man to disagree with. 'Let's all 'ave a drink.' We all ripped the tops off beers. 'Good 'ealth,' said Kellner.

We finished the beers. Deke said, 'Let's get 'er over to the yard, then.' We stood up. I am six feet tall; he was half a head taller.

'Fanks, Paco, Pepe.' He watched the Customs men jump on to the quay. 'T'riffic blokes,' he said. 'All they want out of life's

113

a few bob for the fruit machine in Alonso's caff, and a Fanta orange once an hour. Big kids, really.'

I cast off the lines. *Aldebaran* moved across the filthy water between gleaming lines of yachts. Seventy feet long she might be, but by Puerto Banús standards she was a bath toy. Over by the Moorish tower of the harbourmaster's office a file of vast motor yachts stared sightlessly at the smaller fry from the smoked-glass domes and conservatories of their super-structures.

Deke said, 'Frightening, the amount of money you got sitting down 'ere. Put 'er in the crane dock.'

I eased *Aldebaran*'s stern into the slot in the quay. The slings were already in the water. 'You don't waste any time,' I said.

Kellner laughed, enormously, as if what I had said was really funny. 'Nah,' he said. 'Nah, we don't waste any time at all.'

We jumped on to the dock. The hoist motor whined. *Aldebaran* soared into the air, streaming water like the rose of a watering can. 'You little *beauty*,' said Deke. 'Right. Me an' Paul's got a little meeting at my house. I want to give 'im a cheque. But there's a party later. 'Bout ten. See you there?'

I said, 'See you there.'

Aldebaran settled on the concrete hard standing. Small, dark men swarmed around her with timbers and chocks.

I shouldered my bag and went through the gates in the chain link fence and into the sweltering crush of holidaymakers on the quay.

I looked back through the forest of masts towards the hard standing. *Aldebaran* was chocked now. Out of the water, her ponderous hull looked like the body of a giant dinosaur. Deke's tall, thickset figure was marching along her deck; Paul, slimmer, trailed behind.

There were taxis outside the barrier that excluded the cars of the public from the waterfront. I climbed into one, and gave the driver the name of the hotel the race organisers had booked. There was a lot to do.

16

Things have a way of looking very simple when you come ashore from a boat. They get complicated soon enough.

In the back of the taxi, I sat and poured sweat. Signs bellowed at passers-by to make a down payment on a chunk of Paradise by the sea. On the outskirts of what must once have been a pretty village, a huge sign said *Campos Elisios*, Elysian Fields. The fields were criss-crossed with sewer trenches and swept by clouds of grey dust. Beyond the dustclouds, the white tower of the Hotel El Gordo admired its reflection in the swimming pool at its base.

The walk from the taxi to the revolving door plastered the sweat with dust. The room was air-conditioned to resemble a refrigerator paved with Moorish tiles. I showered, and dried myself, listening to the clatter of drills and mixers from the Elysian Fields.

I pulled on dark blue canvas trousers and a dark blue cotton shirt, and picked up the telephone. My fingers were stiff with hauling *Aldebaran*'s ropes, so it took three tries to dial the Marbella Club.

I asked for Lord Honiton. 'Lor' Oniton is out,' said the perfect-servant voice on the other end. The voice did not know when he would be in. I hung up. It was what you had to expect, with a social lion like Honiton in a lions' den like Marbella.

I rang South Creek. Mary answered. She sounded pleased to hear my voice.

'We're here,' I said, making it sound cheerful. 'Cheque follows. Any news from Henry?'

'A postcard,' she said. 'Posted a week ago from Madrid. He said it was hot.'

'That's not much help.'

'Better than nothing. Tony's looking after things here.' She paused. 'Look out for him.'

Beyond the Elysian Fields Spain stretched away, mile after mile of beach and mountain. 'Of course,' I said, trying to fill my voice with confidence. We rang off.

I dialled the number that Charlie Agutter had given me. He answered.

'I'm here,' I said.

'Terrific,' he said. 'Come and have dinner.'

'Got to go to a party,' I said.

'Ah,' said Charlie. 'Whose?'

'Deke Kellner,' I said.

'Got a nightclub, hasn't he?' said Charlie. 'Keep your hand on your wallet, if I might make so bold as to suggest.'

'I was going to,' I said. 'Practice tomorrow, ten?'

Rather than sit under the air conditioner and freeze to death, I thought I might as well go for a walk and get a feel for the dry land. So I went downstairs and got a taxi to ferry me through the dustclouds, and climbed out a mile short of the address Deke had given me.

It was nine o'clock, and the air was cool. The road had a sinuous curve to it, with white villas peering through the dark green orange trees. After three weeks of the flat chlorine smell of the sea, it was good to sniff the woodsmoke of barbecues and the heavy scent of jasmine floating out of the gardens.

After twenty minutes the road forked sharply to the left. The right-hand fork petered out into a sandy track, leading into an area of rough grass, planted with olives. The grey-green leaves of the olives whispered in the breeze that came in from the sea. In a corner, an old man with a straw hat and a seamed brown face was cooking something over a fire of sticks. He was dressed in the shapeless blue trousers and shirt of the Andalusian farmer. I raised a hand. He waved back. Disturbed by the movement, a pair of Scops owls flew out of the gnarled trunk of one of the olive trees and settled in a eucalyptus, emitting their strange electronic cries.

Somewhere nearby, a dog started to bark. I turned regretfully away from the olive grove, and walked towards the house whose high white wall bordered it on the left.

The coloured tiles let into the white stucco of the gatepost said NUESTRA CASA, our house. There was an entry-phone above the name, a businesslike grille that did not go with the pictures of donkeys and merry peasants on the tiles. I pushed the bell and gave my name.

The voice on the other end had a background of noise and laughter. 'Come in,' it said, in fluent South London. 'Don't push the gates, they're automatic.'

I stood in front of the heavy black wrought iron. The lock buzzed and clicked, and the gates swung back with a hiss of hydraulics. They looked as if they had come off a bank vault.

The gates hissed to behind me. I was in a garden: geraniums, hibiscus, the ubiquitous orange trees. Ahead, the drive serpentined between clumps of oleanders. Above the leaves, segments of red-tiled roof and turret-like white chimneys showed. Underfoot, the turf was green and well-watered. Somebody — not Deke Kellner, I guessed — obviously put in a lot of time on the garden. But it did not look used. The air was tinged with the raw, earthy smell of woodsmoke from the fire in the olive grove next door. In contrast, the garden seemed as natural as a department store window.

As I walked into the shadow of an orange tree, a sound started inside the wall: a curious, scratchy panting. It was an oddly disgusting noise. It raised the hairs on the nape of my neck.

It was getting closer.

I began to walk quickly towards the house. The evening had turned cool, but I found I was sweating again. Calm down, I thought; you're on your way to a party.

The noise came round the corner. It came from a matched

117

pair of Doberman pinschers. They were so sure of themselves that they did not even bother to canter. They trotted, on tip toe, two barracudas on legs. They stopped fifteen feet away, and distributed themselves: one forty-five degrees to my right, the other forty-five degrees to my left, so I could not concentrate on both of them at once. Someone had taught them to do that.

My heart was beating too fast. I slid my hand to my pocket, looking for my knife. But I was off *Aldebaran*, wearing my party clothes, and I am not used to going to parties where it is a good idea to carry a knife in your trousers.

The noise had changed. It was continuous, now; a revolting hissing gurgle, from deep in their throats. Their black lips were pulled back from their white teeth. The panting was what they did instead of barking, I realised. This gurgling was what they did instead of growling. I remembered reading somewhere that dogs interpreted eye contact as a sign of aggression. So I looked at a hibiscus bush between the two of them, hard. Then I took a step backwards.

The gurgle came forward in their throats. I tried another step. By the time my foot was half-way back, the lips were curled all the way back to the pink gums, and the gurgle was a snarl like tearing steel plate. I stopped.

'Hey!' I shouted. 'Somebody!'

There was silence. The front of the house was high and white, with a streak of bougainvillaea. It had no windows, only a heavy, dark door. It did not look the kind of place where they would leave the door open. I could hear voices from the house, a woman's laugh like a tin can falling downstairs. This is ridiculous, I thought. You're going to get eaten alive sixty feet away from a cocktail party. How had the other guests survived?

We stood there, the Dobermans and me, at the three corners of an invisible triangle.

Then I heard a car's engine, and the hiss of the gate. The engine accelerated. Out of the corner of my eye I could see the car, a green Seat. I waved as hard as I dared, to attract the driver's attention. The engine slowed. Without looking around

I said, 'Open the passenger door, please.' The dogs' gurgle almost drowned the engine. A door's latch clicked at my back.

I turned and ran.

It was ten yards to the car. The first dog got me when I had run eight of them. I jerked my arm up, and felt my forearm smash into its throat at the place where the jaw joins the neck. It made a nasty coughing noise and went down on to the ground. Its friend had to swerve to avoid it, so I wrenched open the passenger door and piled in and slammed it behind me.

The window was open.

The Doberman took off ten feet away from the door. For a split second, I was looking straight into its brown eyes and all the way through to the back of its skull. Then it hit the window sill and came into the car.

If there is anything worse than being stuck outside a car with a Doberman pinscher that wants to kill you, it is being stuck inside a car with a Doberman pinscher that wants to kill you. It had gone on to the floor. I was trying to keep it there with my foot. The driver of the car said 'Hold your breath,' and leaned across me. There was a sharp hiss, like an aerosol can. The dog started making strangling noises. 'Open the door,' said the driver.

I opened it. The dog wriggled out and fell into the road and ran away, yelping. There was a disgusting smell that caught the throat and stung the eyes.

'Mace,' said the driver. 'Works rather well on humans, too.'

I stared at her; short blonde hair, nose aquiline, black eyebrows. She had had her hair cut. Last time I had seen her, she had been pale. Now, she was the colour of heather honey. Helen Gallagher. She was grinning at me, and her grey-green eyes were part of the grin.

'When you come to Deke's house, you come in a car,' she said. 'You OK?'

My shirt sleeve was in the first Doberman's digestive tract, and the second one's teeth had chipped considerable skin off my ankle. 'Fine,' I said. 'I'm glad you arrived.' I was only partly talking about her snatching me away from the dogs.

'Me, too,' she said. 'I hate to see a good man chewed.'

I sat back in my seat, and concentrated on getting my breath back. 'How come they make that horrible noise?' I said.

'Deke had them de-barked,' she said. 'Strike silent, strike sure.'

She drove through a second pair of gates, parked alongside a group of Mercedes and BMWs. It occurred to me that she knew a lot about Deke.

'One thing,' she said. 'It would be good if we didn't know each other.'

She got out of the car before I could ask her why.

I followed her into the house. She was wearing a black dress, very short, made of some stuff that clung to her breasts and her thighs. Her legs were brown, and on her feet she wore red shoes with very high heels. The effect was striking, but puzzling. There was a touch of the floozy about it that did not add up with the Helen Gallagher I remembered from England.

But I had no time to wonder about it, because she had led the way confidently past a big, flat-faced man in a dinner jacket that looked too tight for his arms, and up some stucco steps and into the roar of voices.

'Who's that?' I said, pointing at the man in the dinner jacket.

'John Elmes. They call him Jacky Damage,' she said. Then the party was upon us.

Deke Kellner walked through the throng. He was wearing an open-necked white Mexican shirt and high-waisted trousers, to show off his impressively V-shaped boxer's physique. There was a dagger tattooed on his right forearm, and two gold medallions and a shark's tooth dangled in his grizzled chest hair.

'Helen!' he said, and swept her to his chest with the tattooed arm. She looked almost frail, clasped to the shirt. She pulled away, giggling.

'Jeez, Deke,' she said. 'Trouble with saying hello to you is you get chest hairs between your teeth.' Something had happened to her voice, too; it had lost its cultured East Coast accent and acquired a Lower East Side croak that went well with the too-high heels and the too-tight skirt.

'Yeah,' said Deke, grinning and looking at me. 'Come together, did you?'

'She rescued me,' I said. I told him about the dogs. He laughed until I thought he was going to choke. 'Dear,' he said. 'Dear oh dear oh dear oh dear.'

'How about a drinkette?' said Helen.

'Yeah,' said Deke. He grabbed a bottle of champagne and two glasses from a table, and poured us some. 'So the bloody dogs 'ad a go,' he said. 'That'll teach you to go for walks in 'ot countries.' He laughed again, his eyes twinkling in their mesh of jolly wrinkles.

'I hope the dogs are all right,' I said , insincerely.

'We get them in packets of twenty,' he said.

'Ah,' I said. Helen was giggling from his elbow, gazing at me with her big grey-green eyes. Last time I had met her they had been hard and ironic, those eyes. Now they were big, dumb pools. I decided to play the naïve public schoolboy. 'Why do you need all this security, if you don't mind my asking?'

'Can't be too careful,' said Deke, with a practised grin. 'Funny place, round 'ere. Lot of riffraff. Can't count on the protection of the constabulary.' He started to laugh again. He had been drinking, I decided. 'So you and young Paulie's going to sail in this race,' he said. His eyes were watchful above the long cheeks.

'That's right.'

'I 'eard somebody say you'd lost your bottle,' he said. 'Some newspaper bloke.'

I grinned at him, because I had to do something with my face. 'You'll have to wait and see, won't you?' I said. 'Do you follow match racing?'

'Nah,' said Deke. 'But some of us put up a few quid for this Marbella Cup. Any excuse for a party.' He laughed his automatic bark of a laugh. 'I like a sail, though.'

'What are you going to do with *Aldebaran*?'

'Mend 'er up a bit,' said Deke. 'She's a nice boat. Sound boat.'

I nodded. If Deke thought *Aldebaran* was sound, he knew as much about boats as his Dobermans. Paul must have done a very good sales job on him.

I decided to change the subject. 'Have you lived here long?'

His eyes lost some of their twinkle, and became distinctly watchful. 'Long enough,' he said. 'A few years, like.'

I waved a hand at the party. 'You know a lot of people.'

He said, 'Yeah.'

'What do you do?' I said.

Helen's eyes were not dumb any more. Now, they held a suspicion of worry. 'This an' that,' he said. 'Got a club. Various business interests.' He might as well have put up a placard with NO COMMENT on it.

'Is that right?' I said. 'Well, here's to *Aldebaran*, and her new owner.'

Deke raised his glass. Helen giggled, and raised hers. I crossed my fingers in my pocket, and we drank. Deke said, 'Lissen. I got to go and see a bloke. I'll introduce you.' He swept me round the room, and rattled off half-a-dozen names in quick succession. They were mostly English, the sort of brown, smooth people you meet at expensive golf clubs, or sailing fat plastic cruising yachts round Poole Harbour. The men had unnecessarily hard handshakes and silk cravats, and the women had too much gold jewellery and the reptilian skin that comes from long exposure to sun and careful basting with expensive oils.

We spoke about the Marbella Cup. They were not much interested in the racing, but they were greatly fascinated by the size of the prizes. And all the while, they drank; not in sips, but in large draughts, mixing champagne with brandy in glasses the size of birdbaths.

As they got drunker, they talked about property. All of them seemed to be buying and selling bits of land to each other. A small Dutchman with weak brown eyes and a fawn suit took it upon himself to explain why. 'What you got here,' he said, 'is a fantastic place. The most fantastic place in the world. You go down the coast, you get wind. Not here. Just a little breeze to cool you down. And the sea.'

'Yeah,' said a brown Englishman.

'Fantastic, the sea. So the punters back home want to come here, and the A-rabs want to come here, and then you got that fantastic place over José Banús. *Plus* they're building a motorway,' he said. 'Sites changing hands for upwards of a million pound.'

Then everybody started asking me to drop round sometime. I nodded and smiled, and concentrated on not drinking as much as they were drinking. Honiton the property baron was certainly sitting where the action was.

The party roared on. Steaks appeared. The colour of the wine changed to red, and back to champagne again. Someone started playing the piano with the heavy thump of a south-east London knees-up walloper. A man with smooth olive skin, black hair greying at the temples over long, wiry sideburns, and a diamond ring on his little finger stood beside the accompanist and sang *Smoke gets in your eyes* in a voice like alcoholic treacle.

'That's Jake Schwartz,' said the dyed blonde woman beside me. 'He's singing down the club. He's got a lovely voice.'

'What club?' I said.

'The Red House,' she said.

'Ah,' I said.

'He's never heard of it,' she said, to nobody in particular. 'Isn't that amazing!' She laughed an artificial laugh that sounded like bottles clinking. 'Deke's club,' she said. ''E brought Jake out from England, and everythink.'

'Ah,' I said again.

''E was in the charts all through the early Seventies,' said the woman. 'Jake, I mean. It's a fantastic club.'

'I must drop in,' I said.

'Yeah,' she said. 'Ol' Jakie's got a lovely voice. Specially when he sings oldies.'

She lapsed into silence, a misty-eyed harpy. But I was not watching her. I was watching Helen, who was sitting with her chin on her long brown hands, watching Schwartz with adoration. There are some things I could not stomach even in a good cause, and one of them was people who sang like Schwartz. I wandered out of the big room with the piano, under the sober, incurious eyes of Jacky Damage, and into the house.

123

Under an archway off the landing outside the big room was a sort of gallery hung with pictures in department store frames. Most of them were department store pictures, except one, of an old woman. It was evidently a portrait, of the kind that is painted from a photograph. But even the crudity of the painting could not disguise the power of her face; a craggy, monstrous face, glaring out of the picture at a world from which it would take no nonsense of any kind. It was the face of a female prizefighter; the face of a female edition of Deke.

I turned to go back to the big room. Then I heard voices on the landing. One of them was Deke Kellner's. The other was Paul's. I stopped and held my breath.

Paul's voice was raised. 'It was blowing a gale,' he said. 'I couldn't help it. Honestly. I did my best – '

'But it wasn't good enough, was it?' Kellner's voice was quiet and reasonable. 'You've put me to a lot of extra trouble, Paulie. It's very upsetting.' He raised his voice. 'Jacky!' he called. The door of the big room opened. I stepped behind a brass vase of dyed papyrus plumes as Jacky Damage padded past the archway, his thick arms dangling from his shoulders, meaty hands curled at his thighs.

'Anything I can do,' said Paul. I had never heard him sound so frightened. 'Anything – '

'It's a bit late for that,' said Kellner. His voice was a low purr. I could imagine the smile on the hard red-brown face. 'Jacky. Mr Welsh was on his way downstairs.'

'I'll – '

There was an odd noise, half-way between a grunt and a moan. Then there was a dull tumbling, as of a body falling, and laughter; Deke Kellner's laugh, loud and hearty. I ran on to the landing.

Kellner was standing at the top of the flight of marble stairs, leaning against the black wrought-iron balustrading that supported the handrail. He stopped laughing as I came round the corner. His grey eyes flicked across at me, then back to what was lying at the bottom of the stairs.

What was lying at the bottom of the stairs was Paul Welsh. As I watched, he got to his hands and knees. Blood was flowing from his Greek god's nose, making a scarlet moustache on his Greek god's lip.

'Fell down the stairs,' said Deke. 'Pity.' The way he said it, it was hard to tell whether he meant it was a pity Paul had fallen down the stairs, or a pity he was not more badly hurt.

Paul pulled himself to his feet. Jacky Damage padded away. Deke said to me, 'You was probably looking for the little boys' room, am I right?'

I went down the stairs, got Paul's arm and helped him up. Deke smiled, and shook his head like a kindly uncle. 'God bless you, Martin. You're a good man.'

The lavatory was done out in brown tiles. I could feel Paul's arm shaking as I took him in. Paul splashed his face with water, and I gave him some lavatory paper for his nose. One of the cubicle doors opened, and a man came out. He was thin, with a silly grin on his face and small eyes too bright to be natural. He was tucking a rolled-up 5,000-peseta note into the breast pocket of his blue-and-white seersucker jacket. 'Evenin', all,' he said, cheerily.

I nodded to him. He stank of whisky. He banged into me with his shoulder. 'Oops,' he said. 'Sorry, sorry. No harm done.' He brushed me down with his monkey-brown hands.

'I'm fine,' I said.

'Ah,' he said. 'Sorry for being alive.' Giggling, he lurched out of the room and into the passage.

Paul's nose had stopped bleeding. I said, 'Why did he throw you downstairs?'

He opened his mouth to answer, snapped it shut again. 'What the hell are you talking about?' he said.

'They threw you downstairs,' I said. 'Kellner and his minder.'

'I slipped,' said Paul. 'Would you mind not following me around?' Holding a pad of lavatory paper to his face, he walked out of the room.

I followed him. The piano was still thumping and they were all singing along with Jakie, a dreadful baying just recognisable as *Release Me*. The voices were slurred, the faces red with sun and drink. The woman who had told me how much she loved his voice was weeping, the tears carrying streaks of black mascara down her face. Helen was standing beside the singer, her naked brown arm round his shoulders.

Suddenly I felt tired, and sober, and depressed. I had a taxi number in my wallet. I put my hand in my pocket.

The wallet had gone.

It had been in my pocket when I got into Helen's car: I remembered feeling it when I had searched for my knife. At first, I thought I had dropped it. I went round the room, looking between people's feet. It was not there. So I retraced my steps to the top of the stairs. The stairs were empty, except for a few drops of Paul's blood congealing on the marble of the bottom step. I went into the lavatory.

One of the cubicle doors was shut. There were sniffing noises coming from inside. I washed my hands. The wallet was nowhere to be seen. Bloody hell, I thought: it must be out in that horrible garden, with the dogs.

The cubicle door opened, and the man with too-bright eyes came out. He had a plastic card in his hand; he was flicking it with his thumbnail. There was a wide, fixed grin on his face. ''Ello again,' he said.

I was looking at the card. It was a Royal Yachting Association membership card. I twitched it out of his hand. It had my name on it. I remembered the pat and fumble of his monkey hands as they had dusted off my jacket.

I said, 'Give me my wallet back.'

'No,' he said. 'Not me.' His hands came up, slowly at first, then quick. I jerked my head aside. The fingers that were meant to go in my eyes gouged my forehead. My head hit the wall.

I heard the door slam, the flap of his espadrilles on the marble stairs. A car's engine started with a roar, and tyres screamed on the tarmac of the drive.

I washed the cut on my forehead and walked back to the room. Helen was by the piano, with a glass of orange juice in front of her. I said, 'Somebody's just picked my pocket.' I felt a bloody idiot. I had never had my pocket picked before.

She turned towards me. Her eyes were grey-green and bored

to tears. When she saw me, they stopped being bored. She said, 'Who did it?'

I described the man with the monkey-brown hands.

'Squeal,' she said. 'His name is Squeal. He runs the Bar Bric-à-Brac, in downtown Marbella. I guess if you ask him nicely, he might give you back whatever he took off you, unless he's sold it to buy nose candy.'

Jake Schwartz materialised alongside us in a cloud of heavy aftershave. 'Am I ever *hoarse*!' he said, in a disc-jockey's drawl, and drank deeply from Helen's glass.

'Nice singing,' I said. I found the intimacy of the shared glass upsetting.

'Well, *thank* you,' he said. He had brown spaniel's eyes, and long black lashes, and he drooped the whole set at me like a señorita on a picture postcard.

'Hey, hey!' said Deke's voice. 'Everybody 'aving a good time?'

'Sure,' said Schwartz. '*Terrific*. But I have to work, right? First set time.'

'I'll follow in my car,' said Helen.

'Can I get a ride through the pets?' I said.

Deke laughed. Schwartz said, 'Terrific. Suits me.'

I said, 'I'll go with Helen. She's saved my life once. I trust her.'

'Ooh,' said Helen, pouting her fire-engine-red lips and wriggling in her tight black dress. 'But do I trust *you*?'

That went down a storm. Deke said, 'All right, then. Ta-rar for now.' He gripped my shoulder. 'Keep your bottle, boy.'

'I'll do my best,' I said.

'Course you will,' said Deke. His eyes were cold and thoughtful and for a moment they looked straight into mine. Then he laughed, the loud, frightening laugh.

From the car park, Helen waved up at the balcony, one red spike-heel shoe raised coquettishly, bottom stuck out as she posed. I got into the passenger seat. She slammed the door.

The gates opened. As we went down the drive she said, 'You're going to have to stop following me around.'

'*What?*' I said.

'I can't move at all when every time I open a door you're waiting behind it asking idiot questions.' The East Side was out of her voice now. She sounded Ivy League, and displeased.

I said, 'I don't know what you're talking about.'

The dogs were waiting on the smooth green lawn, under the floodlights. They knew there was no future in biting cars, particularly green Seats full of people who squirted mace up your nose. The gates opened.

She said, 'You are a straight-up-and-down college boy who sails boats for a living. In that crowd you stick out like a lighthouse on a pool table. They are not dumb.'

I looked at her. She was looking straight ahead, her determined chin in profile against the big white villas by the road. And I said, 'First Southampton. Then Pulteney. Now here. What's your angle?'

'Like I told you,' she said. 'A girl's gotta eat.'

I said, 'How is hanging around with a lot of small-time hoods helping you eat?'

We had come to the main road. Her head snapped round. 'Two things,' she said. 'Don't ever make the mistake of thinking that Deke Kellner is small time. And don't ever tell me what I should do.' She paused. 'But if you want to get hurt, just keep right on asking the questions.'

Her hair was brassy gold in the light of the passing cars, and the moon shone silver in the whites of her eyes.

Suddenly she leaned over towards me, and I felt the faintly sticky touch of her lips on my cheek. 'Don't get hurt,' she said. 'You have lipstick on your face. Now get out of here.'

And the next thing I knew I was standing in the hot night under the hazy stars, and her tail lights were howling under the palm trees down the wide road towards Marbella.

17

It would have been a long walk home, if I had not had a 1,000-peseta note in my trouser pocket. As it was, I got a taxi to where the tarmac stopped and walked through the Elysian Fields, barren and lunar in the grey starlight, towards the floodlit finger of the Hotel El Gordo.

The crew meeting next morning was at the Club Deportivo marina in Marbella. I caught the nine o'clock bus. It was already hot enough to stick my shirt to my back as I walked down the white road between the dusty building sites to Calle de las Rosas, home of Squeal.

The sign said BAR BRIC-A-BRAC – BEER – INTERNATIONAL ATMOSPHERE. The plate glass window needed a clean, and the blind inside was spotted with fly-dirt. It was closed. It looked like the kind of bar that did not open till much, much later. As I walked back along the promenade, the Mediterranean rustled among concrete groynes on my right. Thick-necked blond tourists were already drinking beer in the beach bars. I found a quiet bar, and sat at the zinc counter in the cool inside and drank coffee. While I drank it, I wondered why Helen had kissed me last night under the palms by the side of the big road, and what she was doing with Jake the singer. It was a small cup of coffee, so I did not wonder for long. When I had finished, I shoved twenty-five pesetas into the telephone and dialled the race office. They told me Honiton was away, but he would be returning in the evening, if I wished to make an appointment. I made an appointment, paid, and left.

At ten to ten I was on the Dique de Levante breakwater that flings an arm round the marina. The sea breeze was just getting up. There was hardly enough of it to tickle your face, but it blew away the race office and the sunburned early beer-drinkers and set my heart thumping with pleasurable anticipation as I walked towards the eight tall, slim masts at the end of the quay.

They were already working on the boat when I got to the end of the breakwater. It was the usual routine: seizing anything that could come unscrewed, taping anything that could chafe, sticking woollen tell-tales to the sails. When you are racing against some of the best skippers in the world, you do not leave anything to chance.

Charlie looked tired, as usual. Scotto and Noddy and Dike looked large and brown and hot.

We cast off the lines, and I backed the boat out of its berth, and motored past the white ends of the breakwater and into the dazzling blue Mediterranean, frosted with little patches of breeze.

The sails went up. I turned off the engine and pulled the nose off the wind. In the new quiet, the cockpit sole came suddenly alive underfoot, and the chuckle of the wake became a tiny roar at the tail of the long, sloping transom.

'Trouble with sailing in Marbella,' said Charlie, squinting up at the long, smooth curve of the slot between the mainsail and the genoa. 'Not enough wind.'

I nodded, not really listening, getting used to the boat in the way you learn if you do a lot of match racing. My senses had run to its extremities; I could feel the tiny vortices at the tip of rudder and keel, the kiss of the wind flattening the tell-tales on the aerofoil curve of the mainsail, the slide of the boat's flat sections over the little ripples the breeze was kicking out of the Mediterranean. After the wallowings of *Aldebaran*, it was pure pleasure.

'Boat doesn't mind,' I said.

'She's not too bad,' said Charlie, pulling the long peak of his cap down over his eyes. He was a man acutely afflicted by modesty.

There was so little wind that a lot of cruiser-racers would have been dead in the water. But the Bayliss 34 flew wings of brilliant nylon, and caught the zephyrs, and the little roar at her transom never slackened, while the trimmers moved softly at their winches so as not to knock her out of the groove.

'Good boat speed,' said Charlie.

Under the boom, the white palaces of Marbella sprawled in the trees behind their dirty grey beaches. There were other sails on the water, little white triangles twisting and turning on the glittering blue, practising.

Scotto said, 'There's Fournier. And Paul Welsh.'

Fournier was a Frenchman, a charmer off the water and a Great White Shark on it. He was going to be a problem.

'Paul,' I said. I saw again the crumpled figure at the bottom of the marble stairs. And I thought of fifty thousand pounds and the Senator's Cup. The white palaces were suddenly sinister. Honiton was in there somewhere, fretting over a tin box that had never arrived. And Henry, up to nobody knew what. 'We'll murder the bastard,' I said.

'Yeah,' said Scotto, and grinned.

By twelve o'clock we were settling down into a nice, easy rhythm. The sun was directly overhead; even in a hat, it was like balancing red-hot iron bars on your skull. We were dried and salted like peanuts.

Charlie said, 'Let's get some lunch.'

I was so absorbed in what we were doing that I nearly agreed. Then I remembered Squeal. We headed for the shimmering line of the shore, and I banged the boat alongside. I walked straight from the marina up into the sweat and dust of the town. The pavement cafés were filling up. I tried to keep in the little wedges of shade in the angles of the buildings, but I was not thin enough. By the time I got to the Bar Bric-à-Brac, my shirt was sticking to my chest, and my shoes felt as if they were half full of sweat.

This time the blind on the dirty plate glass window was up,

and when I pushed the door it swung inwards. On the left-hand side was a long mahogany bar with nobody behind it. Above the bar was a wrought-iron rack from which hung a line of pewter tankards. On the walls were dozens of narrow shelves, full of cuckoo clocks, jam jars, old bottles, candlesticks, presents from holiday resorts in England, and a lot of other stuff that looked as if it had come out of an antique dealer's dustbin. The place stank. It stank of spilt beer, and cigarettes, and dirt, and failure. Maybe that was the International Atmosphere.

A blonde girl came out of a door at the back. She looked as if I had woken her up. When she had given me a San Miguel, I said, 'Where's Squeal?'

She clicked her tongue. She had puffy brown skin and sour black eyes. 'In bed,' she said. 'He 'ad a late night.' Her accent was somewhere between Madrid and Stepney.

I knew about his late night. 'Where?' I said.

She frowned. 'Who are you?'

'Friend,' I said.

'Oh.' She did not seem impressed. ''E usually pops round to get his heart started about now.'

I looked at the greasy smears on the glass she had given me, and decided to drink out of the bottle. The beer spread freezing tentacles through my dehydrated body. 'Have you worked here long?' I said.

'Long enough.' She picked some knitting out of the corner by the icebox and went to sit as far away from me as she could. I sipped at the beer. Neil Diamond moaned away about the difficulties of being a man and misunderstood.

The door opened and Squeal came in.

He was wearing a dirty beige linen suit, and he did not look at all well. His face was coppery, as if there was no colour under the tan. He hoisted himself on to a stool and said, 'Give us a vodka, dear,' in a voice like dead leaves rustling on Hackney Marshes. He did not even look at me.

The bottle blonde brought him a tumbler of vodka mixed with a little tomato juice, and a big dollop of Tabasco. He lifted it to his lips with both hands, and took a couple of gulps. She gave him a napkin to dry his streaming eyes, and said, 'You got a visitor.'

He turned round to look at me. His eyes had lost their unnatural glitter. They were very close together, his nose long and reddish at the end, drooping futilely over a small, ineffectual chin. Last night, with the glitter of cocaine in his eyes, he had had a sort of presence. Today, he looked like a rodent with a very bad hangover. There was no recognition in his face. But he smiled, an ingratiating smile that showed chipped yellow teeth. 'And what can we do you for?' he said.

'You can give me my wallet back,' I said, and stepped off my stool so that I was between him and the door.

'What wallet?' he said.

'The wallet you took out of my pocket at Deke Kellner's party,' I said.

The hangover round his eyes turned to something much worse. A muscle twitched in his cheek. 'I don't know what you're talking about,' he said, and picked up his drink, and gulped it down.

'Have another,' I said. I made my voice nice and casual. 'All I want is the wallet back.' His eyes swivelled left and right. I thought about Deke, the solid presence of the man, and decided to take a little gamble. 'Otherwise I'll ask Deke to get it back for me.'

It worked. The eyes shifted away and ran around the stains on the top of the bar as if they were looking for a map marking the emergency exit. Deke was someone to be frightened of, if you were Squeal.

The girl had given him a new glass. This time I distinctly heard it rattle against his teeth. He worried a Ducado out of its blue-and-white paper packet and lit it slowly, to give himself time to think.

'Ask him, then,' he said, finally. The yellowish eyes glanced across at me to gauge my reaction.

'Think about it,' I said. 'Old Deke might be a little upset about your thieving off his guests.'

He looked at the dirty tiles under the legs of his stool, then at the girl. Neither of them seemed to be much help. Then he gulped the last of his drink, and dived his nicotine-stained left hand into the pocket of his jacket. 'I never nicked no wallet,' he said. 'I found one on the ground, though. I meant to 'and it in to Deke, but . . . well, you know 'ow it goes. I forgot. Is that yours?' He held it out towards me. It was mine. I took it.

'I do believe it is,' I said. 'What a bit of luck.'

'Yeah,' he said. '*Well* lucky.'

'Pity about the money,' I said. Twenty thousand pesetas in cash was missing from the inside compartment.

'Money?' he said. 'I never saw no money in it.'

'Of course you didn't,' I said. He was looking at his empty glass. I tucked the wallet away. 'Well, you've done me a big favour. Have another drink?'

He pretended to wonder whether he should or not, and finally gave in gracefully. His hand had stopped shaking now, but he must have drunk the best part of a quarter of a bottle of vodka, and his movements were becoming vague and clumsy. We drank to each other.

'Nice bar you've got here,' I said.

He looked round as if he had never been there before. 'Yes,' he said. 'Nice little place. Nice little business. Course, season hasn't started yet. Bit slow, this year.' He paused, contemplating the filthy junk on the shelves, and the fact that nobody ever came in. 'Funnily enough I was just thinking of putting it on the market. Save me the trouble, make me an offer.'

I tried to look depressed, and said I could not afford it. He shook his head, and had another vodka. 'Pity,' he said. 'Pity.'

'Are you going back to England, then?' I said. 'Selling the bar, and all?'

He shook his head at his glass. 'Nah,' he said. 'Few problems up there, know what I mean.'

I thought I did. 'Trouble with the officers?'

He nodded, looking at me sideways across his long nose. 'Thass it.' He had drunk enough to unbutton. 'Bit of a misunderstanding. I used to sell life insurance door to door, and, well, the company didn't always get the premiums, know what I mean?' He said it as if he was Robin Hood, ripping off the Sheriff of Nottingham. 'So I done a runner. And here I am. Sun, sea and señoritas.' He waved a hand to encompass the filthy bar and the puffy woman knitting on the icebox.

'And old Deke is in the same boat,' I said.

I knew as soon as I had said it that I had gone over the top. Squeal had spent too much time in too many interview rooms not to recognise a leading question when he saw one.

His eyes became suddenly wary. 'Deke,' he said, 'is a very 'ard man. And he would not like me to discuss what I may or may not know about him with a bloke who is trying to get me pissed dinner-time in my own bar.' He stood up, suddenly, his face twisted with anger. 'So piss off,' he said. 'Go on, 'op it!'

I stood up. He stood up, too. But he had underestimated the effect of the vodka on his legs. He took a step backwards, tripped over the stool, and crashed into the narrow shelves on the wall behind him. They collapsed in a cloud of dust, sending a shower of bric-à-brac on to the tiles. I pushed it aside with my feet, heading for the door.

Then, half-way to the door, I stopped.

One of the objects off the shelf had slid a little further than the others. It was a slim box made of patinated grey metal, curved so it would fit comfortably into a pocket. I stooped, and picked it up, and looked at the inscription on the lid. My mouth was dry, and everything had suddenly become quiet and still.

Because I knew that box. The inscription on the lid said *To H.M., from the crew of HMS* Rutland, *1942.* The box was a gunmetal cigarette case, and the last time I had seen it, six weeks ago, it had been the property of Henry MacFarlane.

18

I held the box in my hand, turning it over and over. It was a smooth, sympathetic shape. I had admired it, as a child; later, I had thought it part of Henry's stubborn eccentricity that he should use a cigarette case at all, let alone one made of gunmetal.

Behind me, Squeal said, 'Go on! Piss off, before I call the cops!'

I turned round and walked towards him. His mouth fell open, and his skinny body shrank as if someone had let the air out of him. My hand went out without my wanting it to, and grabbed the front of his suit. I walked him backwards across the bar until one of the benches along the wall caught him behind the knees, and he went down with a crash.

I held the gunmetal cigarette case in front of his little yellow eyeballs. 'Tell me,' I said, through lips that felt clumsy with shock. 'Where, *exactly*, did you come across this?'

His eyes closed. There was sweat on his forehead, and he smelt of booze and cigarettes and fear. 'Can't remember,' he said.

I picked him up and shoved him against the wall. His skull made an ugly knocking sound on the stucco. 'That case belongs to a good friend of mine,' I said. 'A very good friend of mine. I am going to keep banging you against the wall until you tell me where you found it.' I banged him again. More bric-à-brac clattered on to the tiles. 'And then I will tell Deke who swiped my wallet,' I said.

'Police,' gasped Squeal. 'Mona, police.'

I looked over my shoulder. Mona was still knitting. 'She knows what you ought to do,' I said. 'So do it.'

'Let me go, and I'll tell you,' he said.

I dropped him. It was a pleasure not to be close enough to him to smell him.

'I was doing a little job,' he said.

'Who for?'

'Company,' he said. 'Property company.'

'Name of the property company?'

'Morris Holdings.' He simpered. 'It's this geezer I know, he does a little private detective work, process serving, anything.'

'Where is he?'

'Out of the country,' said Squeal.

'Where did you find that cigarette case?'

'I 'ad to go and deliver some stuff to a geezer. Some papers. I seen that little box lying on a table. I thought it looked like it would, you know, fit the decor. So I nicked it.'

'Very nice,' I said. 'Who was this geezer?'

'Bloke called Neville,' he said. 'Major Neville.'

'Where does he live?'

Squeal's yellow incisors showed under his sharp upper lip. 'He *did* live down Guadalmina,' he said. 'But he probably don't live there no more, because of the papers I served him. They was something to do with him getting out of the house.'

'How long ago was this?' I asked.

'Three weeks.'

Three weeks ago, *Aldebaran* had been sailing away from the loom of Oar Head.

'Write down the address,' I said. He wrote it down. I paid for the drinks and left a small tip for Mona. She did not thank me.

I went to the bank, then hired a car and headed for Guadalmina. Someone had built a lot of villas down there. But the road eventually became a track, and the neat gardens of oleander and orange petered out into a patch where there had been a fire. Pine trunks stuck like rotten teeth through a carpet of black ash. Among the ashes were billboards. 25 BEAUTIFUL VILLAS, they said in English; LUXURY APARTMENTS. Eventually even they stopped, and the road came to an end in a pool of sand. To the left, an iron gate under a big almond tree led through a wall. There was a long, low house in there, walls painted white, green shutters, red-tiled roof. There had been a garden, once. Now, the lawn was scorched with lack of water, and geraniums hung brown and lifeless from the stone pots on the terrace.

A lizard skittered from under my feet as I opened the gate. Over the wall of the sandy paddock in front of the house, the Mediterranean shifted against a narrow grey beach. It was a wonderfully quiet place, and the sound of the waves and the cicadas only deepened the silence.

I walked to the front door and banged the knocker. The sound echoed in the house with the peculiar ring of tiled floors. There were no footsteps, no voices. I knocked again, walked round. Doors and shutters were locked tight. The Nevilles had gone.

A voice behind me said, '¡Hola!' When I turned, an old man was standing there. His scrawny brown shoulders stuck out of a filthy singlet, and on his feet were sandals made of old car tyres. On his head was a straw hat, pulled down hard over eyes like wet grapes.

I asked him where I could find Señor y Señora Neville. He launched into a torrent of Andalusian Spanish. He seemed to be saying that they had left three weeks previously, and that he looked after the garden for them. I asked when they would be coming back, and he tut-tutted. 'No,' he said. 'Casa vendida. The house is sold.'

I asked him where the Nevilles were now.

'Banús,' he said, gesturing to the east. 'Banús.' Then he pulled at my arm. 'Perro,' he said. 'Perro.'

Perro is Spanish for 'dog'. He tugged at my arm again, pulling me towards a clump of bushes in a corner of the garden. He made frantic signs with his hands and his brown, wizened face. I allowed myself to be led.

He led me towards a tree. I could hear the flies buzzing long before we got there. He nodded and grinned and held his nose. It was true: the smell was terrible.

There was a small slab of stone under the tree. It looked new. On it were engraved the words: WINSTON, R.I.P. By the side of the stone was a hole with a mound of earth beside it. The mound looked as if it had been excavated by dogs. Beside the hole, a buzzing swarm of flies crawled over something on the ground. Something that had once been a dog. But now, the dog had no head, and it had not been improved by having been buried for a while. For, say, three weeks.

'*Han cortado la cabeza*,' said the man in the straw hat. They had cut its head off. I watched the maggots wriggling in the matted black pelt. It was reasonable to suppose that Henry had come to Spain on business connected with whatever had been in the cash box. According to Paul, the cash box had been destined for Honiton, who had made a lot of money in property. And here was a house Henry had visited, which had recently been sold.

It was not difficult to connect Squeal with headless dogs. Honiton, the Pall Mall stickler, was another matter.

I told him to bury it again, with big stones over it, and gave him two hundred pesetas. Then I went off to Puerto Banús, into the harbourmaster's office in the Moorish tower at the south-western corner of the basin, and asked for the Nevilles.

The man in the office looked bored, and said, 'Motor cruiser, *Shearwater*. Down the far end,' and waved a limp hand beyond the floating palaces, across the alleys of grimy water to the far jetties where the boats were smaller and scruffier, and the sightseers did not bother to walk.

Shearwater was a twenty-eight foot wooden motor boat of the kind that English brokers try to make more attractive by claiming that they sailed with the Little Ships that brought the British Expeditionary Force back from Dunkirk. She was kept well; the gangplank that came over her stern shone as if it had been dipped in syrup, and the green awning over the cockpit looked as spruce as if it had been ironed.

I knocked on the rail, and called, 'Anyone home?'

A woman's head came out of the companionway. The hair was grey, the face that of an elderly and aristocratic parrot. 'Good morning,' she said, without visible enthusiasm.

'Mrs Neville?' I said. 'Have you got a minute for a chat?'

She cocked her head at me like a bird. 'What about?' she said.

'About Henry MacFarlane.'

She frowned. Her sharp eyes ran me up and down, checking: Admiral's Cup T-shirt, navy-blue shorts, Henri Lloyd deck shoes, untidy blond hair, peeling nose. It was a combination scruffy enough to add up to respectability. She said, 'You'd better come aboard.'

It was very hot on the boat; there is seldom a breeze at Puerto Banus. The cabin was panelled with mahogany. A man was sitting at the table. He had a thin brown face and a clipped white moustache, and the backs of his hands were covered with liver spots.

The woman said, 'This young man thinks we know someone called Henry MacFarlane.'

The man's eyes were old, and watery, and suspicious. 'Does he?' he said. He had on a cream shirt, and a silk cravat, and under the table his knobby brown feet stuck out of a pair of espadrilles. He did not look like the kind of man who was naturally rude to strangers.

I said, 'I understand a man called Squeal served some papers on you, three weeks ago. While he was in your house he stole a cigarette case that belonged to Henry MacFarlane.'

'Are you some sort of policeman?' he said.

'No,' I said. 'Henry MacFarlane is by way of being my stepfather.'

Mrs Neville said, 'Philip, I think you should.'

'Should what?' said the Major, irritably.

She did not answer. The Major frowned at his old fingers on the table. Finally, he said, 'What's your name?'

I told him.

'Sailor?' he said. 'Read about you in the papers.'

'Yes. Henry and I are partners in a boatyard. He brought me up there.'

'Ah,' said the Major. 'Yes.' The pouches under the eyes deepened as he looked at me. 'That adds up.'

'What do you mean?'

'I think we ought to tell you,' he said. 'He came to see us. Said he was chasing a company that was trying to diddle him out of some property somewhere. Someone had told him we were dealing with the same company.'

'Sea Horse Land,' I said.

'That's right.'

'Those terrible people,' said Mrs Neville.

'He asked us not to tell anyone he'd come to see us. He said it would be dangerous.'

'And we believed him,' said Mrs Neville. 'After what happened.'

I took a deep breath. Henry, you old brute, I thought. Off to Marbella to play detective. But how did you know where to come, and where the hell are you now?

'Looked like a chap who could take care of himself, though,' said the Major.

'How long ago was this?'

'Three weeks. Two and a half. Three days after we got notice to quit.'

'Have you seen him since?'

'Said he was off to Madrid,' said the Major. 'Actually, we've been a bit busy, since.'

'You sold your house,' I said. 'I went there, looking for you.' Outside, the air filled with thunder as a powerboat cowboy tested his engines. The roar of tourists' voices came from the quays, and the water slopped against the side like oil. 'It must have been a wrench to leave it.'

Mrs Neville laughed. It was not a pleasant sound. The Major said, 'Worst mistake we ever made.'

'But we couldn't *help* it,' said the woman.

The man raised his hands, let them fall again. The suspicion had all leaked out of him. What remained was despair. 'Oh, well,' he said. 'That's all gone, now. We must look to the future.'

I said, 'It's very rude of me to be so inquisitive. But would you mind telling me what happened?'

They looked at me as if they had forgotten I was in the room. Then Major Neville said, 'Sit down. Sit down. Have we got any tea, Hilda? Or would you prefer a drink?'

I said tea would be fine.

'La Residencia,' he said. 'Bought it years ago. Just after the war. Then forgot about it. Came back to live here ten years ago. Well, I mean, whole place'd changed, but luckily I'd bought the farm when it was nothing but goats, pretty thin goats too. So we thought, useful place to retire, really. And we upped sticks, sold a couple of acres inland, near the golf course, and there we stayed. Jolly nice place.'

'A lovely place,' said his wife, passing bone china teacups forward from the galley. 'Terribly peaceful.'

There were two engines under test now, and a helicopter was landing someone on one of the floating palaces by the Torre de Control.

'Anyway,' said the Major, raising his voice to make himself heard above the racket. 'About four months ago, chap came to the door and said he wanted to buy the house. Well, there've been dozens of them over the years. I suppose it must have got pretty valuable.' I thought of Deke's bronzed guests, discussing million-pound building sites. 'Never occurred to me to check. This chap was a bit persistent. Spaniard, he was. Oily. Grinned a lot, handshake like a wet rag. I told him to go away. He went, easy enough. That night, the woods caught fire.'

'The woods?'

'Pine trees. Scrub. That sort of thing. Nice place. Good for snakes and so on, you know. Well, there it was, burned to a cinder. Lucky it didn't get the house. And then who should pop up but Menendez. That was his name, Menendez. Said he was sorry about the woods, accidents would happen, couldn't be easy to patrol the land, at our age. Said we really should consider going somewhere . . . nicer.' He snorted. 'Nicer! Little brute. Well, I told him where to stick it pretty sharpish, I can tell you. And off he went.'

'And then it all started to happen,' said his wife. She had sat down, and her face was pink and animated. 'The orange trees died. Somebody put battery acid on the roots. There were graffiti all over everything. There were always people on the beach, drinking, and one of them hit Alec when he asked him to leave. Someone put a dead pig in the well. We had our own water, you know. And then − ' She screwed up her face, as if she did not even want to think about what happened next.

'We had a dog,' said the Major. 'A black labrador. Winston. We never had any children. I suppose you get silly about dogs. Anyway, we came down to breakfast one morning, and there was poor old Winston.'

'Poor old Winston,' said his wife.

'In the middle of the dining room table. Somebody had cut his head off. Actually we never found the head. So we went out and buried him in the garden. We were getting pretty stubborn by then. So they changed tactics. There's a land register in Madrid. When we bought the house, nobody ever paid any attention to it. So we never registered. Didn't know it existed, actually. This lot went to the descendants of the chap I bought it off, got a *factura* off him − '

I said, 'What's a *factura*?'

'Bill of sale,' said the Major. 'Sworn in front of a lawyer. They bribed the chap, got a crooked lawyer, took it to Madrid, got the register changed. And that was us gone.' There was a silence. 'Actually it wasn't as much of a wrench as we'd thought. We'd come to hate the place, you see. Everything was going to hell. I suppose they'll build houses all over it, or turn it into a night-club.'

His eyes were far away. 'We've decided to give up. Go back to UK. I expect we'll get by.'

The wife said, 'Yes.' She turned her face to me. For a moment she looked less like a parrot than an eagle. She said, 'But we're not giving up. I've got a lawyer. We've served writs on them. Today.'

'Courts here, we'll be dead before anything happens. We're

143

old, and they know it,' said the Major. 'Anyway, they can't be bothered with foreigners. Still, it's plug, plug, plug.'

'We liked Henry MacFarlane,' said Mrs Neville. 'I hope you find him.'

I finished my tea, and left them in the wreckage of their lives.

19

The Marbella Club was a village of white stucco cottages peering through heavy swags of jasmine and geraniums. I negotiated the glare of the evening sun off half-a-dozen Rolls Royces, and made my way carefully, so as not to break any of the cottages, to the fake Andalusian door of the Honiton residence.

Honiton was sitting under a white umbrella on the terrace. There was a glass of what looked like gin and tonic on the table, and he was contemplating the end of a cigarette in a short black-and-gold holder. He was wearing a blue blazer, Pall Mall Yacht Club tie yanked up tight, and white trousers. When he looked up, his crafty amber eyes were narrow and hostile, but he smiled. *Noblesse oblige*, that was Georgie Honiton.

'Well?' he said. 'What can I do for you?'

He did not offer me a chair. I pulled one up anyway. His glass rattled as I put my elbows on the table. I said, 'You have made a lot of money out of property.'

He frowned. 'I was under the impression you wished to see me on race business.'

I said, 'There are some things we should discuss first.'

He fitted a new cigarette into his holder. The narrow eyes were watching me very carefully.

'An object was stolen from the South Creek Boatyard,' I said. 'That object turned up again in the possession of Paul Welsh.

When I asked him what he was doing with it in his possession, he said he was delivering it to you. What I want to know is, what is someone like you doing receiving stolen goods?'

There was a long silence. A man's voice was speaking Arabic somewhere in the compound, and swallows chirruped as they flew to the red roof-tiles. Finally, Honiton lit his cigarette. He put the lighter on top of the packet, straightened it, and said, 'This is an extraordinary allegation.'

I felt like a bull in a china shop. But I charged on anyway. 'You are a business associate of James de Groot,' I said. 'You collaborated on Las Brisas. I've seen the photographs. And through James you are linked to a company called Sea Horse Land, which has been operating a sabotage campaign against a business in which I am a partner – '

'Stop,' said Honiton. All right, I thought. Let's hear it. 'You say that Paul Welsh told you this?'

His voice was perfectly calm; too calm. My stomach was suddenly cold. He should have had everything to lose, but he was talking like a man who had nothing to fear.

I nodded.

He sipped his drink, and blew smoke out of his nostrils and down his immaculate lapels. He said, 'I fear you have been misled. I have no connection with Sea Horse Land.'

I grinned at him. I was back on solid ground. 'In the library of my cousin James's house, there is a photograph of you with the Mayor of somewhere or other, at the opening of Las Brisas, a Sea Horse Land development.'

He nodded gravely. 'A year ago,' he said. 'Eleven months ago, I resigned my directorship.'

The sinking feeling returned. 'Why?' I said.

'I did not like some of the . . . business methods . . . of the other directors,' he said.

'Such as?'

He smiled primly. 'I do not propose to lay myself open to an action for slander.'

I shrugged. I knew about the business methods of Sea Horse Land. I said, 'So why would Paul Welsh say he was acting on your behalf?'

He swirled his glass, jingling the ice-cubes. 'That,' he said, 'is the most puzzling aspect of the affair. I can only assume that he was telling you an . . . untruth because he wished to divert suspicion from someone else.'

'Friendly of him,' I said.

Honiton's eyelids were heavy with the cynical wisdom of his class. 'There are certain pressures none of us can resist,' he said. 'Paul is a very promising young man. I don't propose to hold this slip against him.'

I nodded. 'So what was the pressure?' I said.

He got up and walked into the house with his straight-backed, stiff-legged gait. When he returned, there was a piece of paper in his hand. He passed it to me. 'I am giving you this for Paul's sake,' he said. 'Not because I give a damn what happens to you.'

I looked at the paper. It was a letter. It said:

Dear Honiton,

It is most distressing that you feel compelled to resign as a director of Sea Horse Land. I should like to thank you for all you have done for the company, and I know that in saying this I speak not only for myself, but for Deke Kellner as well.

Yours sincerely,
James de Groot.

'Deke Kellner,' I said. Suddenly I could see the photograph in James's library, the man who might have been trying to hide his face from the camera.

And I knew by the hair and the set of the shoulders that it had been Deke Kellner.

Honiton said, 'I expect you will be wanting to get along. I shall watch you race with interest.'

I stood up. I was thinking of Paul, in Bayona, terrified because he had lost the box. And last night, his nose pouring blood at the bottom of the marble staircase. He had lied to me in Bayona because he had been scared out of his wits. And James had been scared out of his wits, in England. Both of them had

147

been scared by the idea of admitting they had dealings with this Kellner.

'Thank you,' I said. 'That is very interesting.'

Then I went back to the hotel, and rang Mary.

She sounded glad to hear me. Her pleasure was as good as a tonic. 'Any news?' she said.

'He's been around,' I said, sounding as confident as I could. 'He's here somewhere. Near Marbella. I've met some people who have seen him.'

She said, 'You are telling me the truth, aren't you?'

'Of course,' I said, trying not to let my voice sound hollow. Mary knew me well enough to see straight through any white lies. I said, 'I must go. Look after yourself.' Then I rang off.

Mary would not be content with the call, but it was the best I could do. Henry was seventy-one years old. If he was out gunning for a hard nut like Deke Kellner, there was plenty to worry about.

I had dinner at the hotel, and wondered what I should be doing, besides going to bed early and thinking about winning match races. The answer was not hard to come by. I should be getting out and about, and keeping a careful eye on Deke Kellner, not to mention Helen Gallagher.

I went and had a couple of drinks in a bar. Then I drove to the long, low building under the palms by the coast road that was the Red House.

It was coming up to midnight. As I went up the steps and under the thatched portico, my legs told me that I had been on the move since early in the morning, and that they would like eight hours' sleep at my earliest convenience. I told them to shut up, and went into the club.

It was like most nightclubs: a dance floor, with tiers of tables alongside and a stage at the far end. I went and got a beer from the operative behind the thatched bar. There was enough light for the customers to be able to stare at each other. I recognised a tennis hero, a couple of footballers, and a millionaire songwriter, each neatly placed under a spot. But I was not particularly interested in celebrities. I saw a mop of blonde hair at a table in the half-dark near the stage, the flash of a red light glinting off the bluebottle-coloured dress she was wearing. Helen. There were two men with her at the table; one of them, by his hulking shoulders and frizzy grey hair, was Deke. The other was Paul Welsh.

The house lights went down. A spotlight caught a man in a glittering dinner jacket as he trotted across the dance floor and on to the stage. It was Jake. His teeth were shiny between his long black sideboards. The band started to play, and he started to sing *It's not unusual*, jerking his sequinned groin at the audience.

I strolled across the floor through the frenzied gibber of the music, climbed up the steps to their table and sat down. I greeted Deke first; he was the sort of person who would expect that. Then I nodded to Paul, and turned to Helen.

She was watching me vacantly, head on one side. 'Terrible singer,' I said, and grinned at her.

'I think he's terrific,' said Paul. I could see in the gloom the whites of his eyes flicking towards Deke, to see if Deke approved.

''E is fucking terrible,' said Deke, and laughed, so loud that the singing faltered. He banged me on the knee, and I could see his teeth smiling in the big, dusky oval of his face. 'You're a good boy, Martin,' he said. ''Ave a drink, eh?'

I had a beer. The singing stopped, eventually, and the discotheque started to bang. Jake came and sat down with us. There was sweat running out of the black curls of his sideboards. Helen snuggled up to him. I kept my eyes off her.

Deke said, 'You was fantastic, Jake. Wasn't he, Martin?' He winked at me, so Jake could see. Jake pouted sullenly.

I was not in the mood for sitting around bitching at nightclub singers. I said, 'Shall we have a dance?'

She shrugged. Her shoulders were bare, except for the bootlace shoulder-straps of her dress. The skirt was very short and very tight. '*Can* you dance?' she said. She patted Jake on the shoulder and kissed his cheek, then led the way on to the floor, with the exaggerated swing of the hips that went with her Lower East Side voice.

They were playing a Tammy Wynette song. She hung on to me, and we danced close together. She said, 'OK, you can dance.' She was still using her Lower East Side voice, but now it was soft, and for fun.

We rocked side to side for a few bars. Her body was firm and pliant.

I said, 'What the hell are you doing here?'

She said, 'Merging with the landscape.'

'Have you seen an old guy called MacFarlane?'

'Who?'

'Grey-haired man. English. Sunburned. Smokes.'

'Not that I know of,' she said. 'Easy with the questions.'

'There are things I wish to know,' I said.

I felt her crisp blonde hair brush my cheek. 'Like I told you,' she said. 'You want to be very careful what you do, because people will be watching you.'

We danced a moment in silence. 'Like who?' I said.

'Like our genial host,' she said. 'He watches people very, very hard. He watches me, which is why I am making out I am deeply in love with that faggot Jake, who is deeply in love with him. And of course Deke is after my body. You want to give him something to watch.'

We had pivoted. Deke's hair was a red aureole under the spot. His eyes were on us.

'You have a bet with that creep Paul,' she said. 'Deke loves a bet. Give him that to watch.'

'What are you doing here?' I said again.

'If I tell you, you will get us both hurt,' she said. 'So I won't tell you.' She reached up her hand, and I felt the light pressure of her nails at the nape of my neck. 'Like I said last night,' she said. 'Don't get hurt.'

'Nor you,' I said. Our hands clasped, briefly.

'*Ow!*' she shrieked. 'Jesus! My foot!' She started to hobble off the floor. When I tried to take her arm, she batted me away. I could feel the blood rising to my face. Deke's laugh rang down from the table.

I sat and grinned like an idiot while Helen explained that I had feet bigger than a New York cop, and that her toes were jelly. Deke listened with half an ear, watching the dancers from under the fleshy hoods above his upper lids. After a while, she leaned over and whispered in his ear, her eyes narrow and mischievous, flicking between me and Paul.

Deke laughed, for a long time. Then he said, 'I've got a little bar down Banús. Come and 'ave a drink. Percy's.'

'I'm off,' said Paul.

'Suit yourself,' said Deke. He was obviously the kind of team leader who did not like his players to go to bed before him.

It was 3.00 a.m., but bedtime was not a concept with which the inhabitants of the Costa del Sol appeared to be familiar. The walkways along the quays were jammed with people.

Percy's was half-way down the quay, and it was everything the Bar Bric-à-Brac would have liked to be but was not. There was English motorway café food, cane chairs with peppermint-green cushions, a waitress in a T-shirt that was big as T-shirts go but small as dresses go, and a white baby grand with a black pianist playing *The Entertainer*. In a corner, Jacky Damage was sitting at a table by himself, nursing an untouched light ale in his crane-hook of a hand.

Deke looked after the conversation. He ordered steak, egg, chips and peas. Then he and Helen and Jake started an argument about the rules of tennis. I sat and sipped coffee, and concentrated on being part of the landscape. The pianist's meanderings trickled over my mind like warm glue. I knew I would have to get home soon. There were seven races tomorrow, and sleeping in a cane chair is not a good preparation for seven races. I pushed my chair back, ready to get up.

Outside, there was a big, flat *boom*. The windows rattled. The voices of the passers-by hushed for a moment. A woman screamed, then another. I had heard big, flat explosions like that before. I went through the door with twenty years of boatyard-bred reflexes driving my legs.

The promenaders were looking into the basin. The water was calm and black, except where the crests of its smooth ripples were touched with dingy orange reflections. Beyond the reflections, a yellow wraith of flame wriggled up from the press of hulls moored on the pontoons.

Gas explosion.

The flames were not rising from the floating palaces. They were coming from the far jetties, where the boats were smaller and scruffier, and the sightseers did not bother to walk.

I barged through the crowd and began to run, fast, towards the column of fire. It was a good two hundred yards, but I must have covered it in well under half a minute, tired legs or no tired legs.

But half a minute was a long while too long. The sweat was pouring down under my coat, partly because it was hot, but partly because I knew what came next.

It came. There was a heavy roar that rattled across the slimy harbour and round the windows of the apartment buildings. Something big leapt flaming into the air and fell into the water, towing a comet's tail of blazing debris.

Fuel tank, I thought.

By the time I got there the fire was roaring like a small volcano, flinging sparks at the stars gazing out of the dead black sky. It was too hot to get near. I stood and looked at it for five seconds. There was no awning any more, and the cockpit was a crater of fire. But the name was still on the transom.

Shearwater.

I shouted, 'Major Neville! Mrs Neville!' My voice was submerged by the roar of the flames.

I pulled the hose off the reel on the jetty and spun the stopcock. It kicked in my hands as I trained it on the flames. I felt the heat sear the sunburn on my face, and watched the honey-coloured varnish on the gangplank blister and blacken. A crowd was beginning to gather, held back by the heat of the flames.

Someone was asking if there was anyone on board. I did not answer. Sirens were sounding now, down at the entrance to the marina. There was a lot of shouting.

The water from the hose was making a difference. The stern was steaming and blackened. Most of the coachroof had gone when the fuel tank blew. I was shooting water down into the pit of flame that had once been the saloon. As the fan from the hose swept across that pit, the flames abated for a moment, and

I saw what had been the two bunks that ran down either side of the cabin. The Nevilles had slept on those bunks. The Nevilles were still there, what was left of them.

I pushed the hose into the hands of a fat man who was craning his neck to get a better view. Then I shoved my way back to the other side of the jetty, and was very sick indeed.

They towed the hulk away, still burning, and left it on the breakwater in case it set fire to the other yachts. People with fire extinguishers ran round *Shearwater*'s neighbours, putting out the little bonfires of blazing debris on the decks. An ambulance trundled along the breakwater, siren screaming. The crowd muttered and eddied like greasy brown water.

A policeman came and asked me what I had seen; I had been very quick, he said.

'Gaz,' I said.

He nodded, his face dark against the sky. In the Channel it is collision; in the Mediterranean it is always gas, because gas is heavier than air, and if someone comes home drunk and forgets to turn off the stove when he has made his midnight coffee, a pool of the stuff forms in the bilges of the boat. Then a thermostat trips, or someone starts the engine, or lights a cigarette; any little spark will do. And the gas goes *bang*, and the top of the boat blows off, and if it is a wooden boat, with cushions and nice little blue curtains, the whole works goes up in a sheet of flame, and takes the people in the boat with it.

'*Problema, gaz*,' said the policeman. I gave him my name and hotel. Gas explosions may kill people, but they are too common to be any big deal in the marinas of Europe.

This is why a lot of sensible yachtsmen have a gas alarm on their boats, a machine that sniffs the air for hydrocarbons and sounds a buzzer if it finds any.

As I sat there with my forehead resting against the cool concrete of a bollard, I put my mind back into *Shearwater*'s cabin, Major Neville glancing at the clock, with the gas alarm next to it. When a gas alarm goes off, it makes enough noise to wake the dead.

Which left various possibilities. One, that the sniffer was not working. Two, that they had slept through the buzzer. Or three, that someone had disconnected the buzzer, turned on the gas tap, and waited for the bang.

I got up. My hands were sore when I put them in my pockets, and my forehead felt tight with heat. Sea Horse Land had killed Dick to get what it wanted. Had it killed the Nevilles?

The night air felt suddenly cold. I saw in my mind Jacky Damage, waiting in the piano bar as we came in, nursing his untouched light ale. He moved quietly, Jacky, and he did what he was told. The gas must have been hissing from the Nevilles' stove while he sat in front of his glass.

He watches people very, very hard. Helen had said that. Deke could have watched the Nevilles go to their lawyers. He could have decided that the Nevilles were making trouble for him, and they needed shutting up.

But if the Nevilles needed shutting up, so did a lot of other people.

Including Henry.

20

I got up and walked shakily down the jetty. Deke and his party were on the way out of Percy's.

'There 'e is!' cried Deke. 'The fire brigade!'

They laughed. But the laugh went quickly from Helen's face, and under the heavy makeup she looked tired. She said, 'Deke's having a party.' The skin around her right eye trembled in the beginning of a wink.

'Yeah,' said Deke. 'All you boating people. Celebrate that Marbella Cup. Tomorrow night. Bring your crew. Paul'll bring 'is, and we'll try and get a few more of 'em organised. Get stuck into the ol' rum drinks. Ta-ra for now.'

I watched them disappear into the crowd, laughing. It was late, and I was burned and exhausted. I wondered if I had imagined talking to the Nevilles earlier in the day.

But tired as I was, I knew my imagination was not that vivid.

Deke's laugh rang out above the murmur of the crowd. I shivered and went back into Percy's lavatory and tried to wash some of the sting out of my face with cold water.

The waitress was leaning on the bar as I came out. She looked bored, but she cheered up when she saw me. She was dark and pretty, and she was not wearing very much under her T-shirt.

I said, 'That bloke who looks like a boxer. Was he in here long before us?'

'Jacky? He came in at nine, when we opened.' She had a faint Swedish accent. 'He stayed there. One beer, no tip.' She made a face.

'Does he come in a lot?'

She shrugged, and her T-shirt fell off her shoulder. She made a little performance of hoisting it up again. 'Enough,' she said. 'He's a pig. Can't keep his dirty hands to himself, you know what I mean.'

I nodded. If he had been in all evening, he could not have turned on the Nevilles' gas.

'But tonight he was ill,' she said.

'Ill?'

'The runs. He spent a long time in the lavatory.' She laughed.

I did not laugh back. I went into the lavatory.

The window led into a narrow alley. It was easily big enough, even for Jacky. On the sill the paint was scuffed, and splinters of new wood showed through.

'Hey,' said the waitress when I went back to the bar. 'We're closing. You want to go for a drink somewhere?'

She had a nice smile. But I was wobbling with exhaustion, so I said some other time, and headed for the car.

That night I dreamed of flames. Next morning I felt as if I had slept in a microwave oven. I crawled out of bed, wrapped up against the air conditioning, and looked at myself in the bathroom mirror. Same old face, redder than usual; some of the yellowish hair scorched off at the front, dark circles under the eyes. I had a quick breakfast of coffee, hard bread and butter, climbed back into the car and headed back for Marbella harbour.

Someone had hung a banner between two of the palms in front of the Club Deportivo. It said ¡HOY MARBELLA CUP! There was a TV van there, and a few photographers. Flashguns went off in my face as I walked up the steps and into the big, crowded room on the ground floor. There were three men on the platform at the end. Two of them I did not recognise. The third was His Lordship of Honiton.

156

He flicked his amber eyes at me, and the corners of his thin mouth turned down. 'Now we're all here, I shall explain the rules,' he said in his cold, dry voice. 'For the benefit of the press as much as the skippers.'

He explained. It was the same set-up as the Iceberg Cup. Two marks, a mile apart, one directly upwind of the other. The start half-way up the windward leg; a gun eight minutes before the start gun. The course was twice round the circuit, except in the semi-finals and finals, which would be decided on the best of three single-circuit races. The umpires were in powerboats astern. In the event of a protest, they would decide on the spot who had been in the wrong, and instruct him via the radio of the appropriate penalty, which for minor infringements would be a 270 degree pirouette. There were to be heats during the first day, all against all. The top four point scorers would move on to the semi-final, and the winners of the best-of-three semi-finals would sail the finals.

I saw Paul near the front of the crowd. He was frowning at his clipboard. His Adam's apple moved as he swallowed; too often, I thought. He was nervous. It was good to see him and Honiton in the same room. It produced a healthy burn of anger in the pit of my belly, a clarity of vision. Winning was a job that had to be done, and barring accidents we were going to do it.

After the briefing I pushed through the crowds and up towards the taped-off area at the end of the quay. Charlie and the crew were waiting. 'Blimey,' said Charlie. 'What have you been doing?'

'Night life,' I said, and jumped into the cockpit.

'Who have we got first?' he said.

'Gilchrist.'

Gilchrist was an Australian offshore racer. He was a good helmsman, but he was new to the one-on-one aggression of match racing. We sailed out into the blue morning in line abreast a little ahead of him.

'Hold her back,' I said quietly.

Charlie gave the mainsheet winch a couple of turns, so the boat stuck its white plastic side down into the water, dissipating forward motive power as she heeled. We slowed.

Half a mile away on the port bow, an inflatable plastic champagne bottle jutted from the glittering water. A couple of hundred yards to its east was another. The start line buoys. I could feel the adrenalin beginning to dry my mouth. Over in the other boat, Gilchrist looked across at me. His eyes were narrow. He was a nice enough guy. But today, he was just someone to beat.

The gun banged. The manoeuvres began.

His crew were good, but Scotto and Noddy and Slicer were better. Two minutes before the start gun, he was tooling along on the starboard tack, pinching our wind.

I said, quietly, 'Stop.'

Noddy and Dike jumped on to the coachroof, planted their Docksiders on the non-slip, and shoved the boom out at ninety degrees to the boat's centreline. The wind slammed into the wrong side of it. The boat stopped dead.

'*Go!*' I roared.

Things began to happen with the smooth, deadly rhythm which comes when you are sailing really well. Scotto wound in the genoa so it backed. We spun away on port. The winches howled as we tacked all the way round; and I felt a surge of pure triumph as I saw Gilchrist, his boat dead in the water, gazing at us slack-jawed as our bow bore down on him at seven knots, close hauled. On the foredeck, Noddy was shouting '*Starboard!*' Sweat gleamed on Gilchrist's face as he spun the wheel. But he had no steerage way, and nothing happened. I jinked off the wind and ducked under his tail. Our weather rail passed two inches from their transom.

'PROTEST!' we roared, and broke the red flag out on the backstay as we came up to windward, stealing their air. The radio crackled as the jury boat upheld the protest. We waltzed across the line a hundred yards ahead of them, and led them in procession all the way round.

The rhythm stayed with us. The next start was against Gulbransson, a Swede. We went into the middle of the starting area and sat on his wind while he tried to sail backwards out of our shadow. Next one along, we edged Richie Barrett over the line ten seconds before the gun, compelling him to go back and recross, which put us a minute in the lead.

We had lunch on the water, and sailed four races that afternoon. We won all of them.

When I stepped on to the quay, I felt eight feet tall. A journalist came up to me and said, 'Congratulations.' He was young, with brown wavy hair. 'I've never seen anyone sail like that before.'

I grinned at him. 'How's Paul Welsh doing?'

He shrugged. 'OK, I guess. He won his. But not like you did.'

I said, 'Keep watching,' and went down the quay to my car.

I pulled up the road past the pavement cafés on the seafront, and into the dust of the building sites. The Bar Bric-à-Brac was open, but there seemed to be no customers. The sight of it depressed me. It reminded me of the Nevilles, and Henry's cigarette case.

Then I jabbed my foot on the brake pedal, and the car squealed to a halt.

Major Neville had said Henry had visited them a couple of days after Squeal had served the papers on them. So how could Squeal have found Henry's cigarette case at the Nevilles? Someone was telling lies, and I was ready to bet that it was not Major Neville.

I dragged the car round in its tracks, and drove back to the Bric-à-Brac.

The blonde woman was behind the bar, knitting. Her puffy black eyes were suspicious.

I said, 'Where's Squeal?'

'Out,' she said.

'Where does he live?'

She shrugged. 'Dunno,' she said.

I pulled a 5,000-peseta note out of my shorts, and put it on the bar. 'Address,' I said.

Her hand came out. I covered the note. She said, 'Edificio Granada. 6038.' When my hand came off the money she whipped it away and shoved it down the front of her dirty pink crochet sweater. 'But he's not there.' She smirked, as if she was being very clever.

I said, 'Where is he?'

She gave me a tight-lipped smile.

'No more money,' I said. 'Just police.'

She thought for a moment, and decided that she did not want police. ''E's gone to a party,' she said. Her voice became querulous. 'And 'e wouldn't take me, would he?'

'Where?' I said.

'Mr Kellner's,' she said, with a sort of reverence.

Back at the hotel, there were twenty telephone messages. Everyone liked the way we had sailed that day. I dialled London. The voice on the other end said 'Guardian.'

'Newsroom,' I said. 'Harry Chase.'

When they put me through, I said 'Have you heard of a Deke Kellner?'

'Kellner,' he said. His voice was heavy with Carlsberg Special Brew and Tom Thumb cigars. 'Nah. Why?'

I told him I was in Spain, and described Deke.

'Costa del Crime, eh? Won't be his right name, then. I'll ask around.'

I thanked him, and hung up.

I changed into black trousers, clean deck shoes, navy-blue shirt and seersucker jacket. I put a knife and a little flashlight into my trousers pocket; if I got a chance to look round at Nuestra Casa, I wanted to be equipped. Then I headed for the Shark Club at Puerto Banús, where I had arranged to meet the crew.

Charlie was sitting at a table with Scotto. I ordered a beer.

Scotto said, 'Some poor bastard got burnt last night.'

I said, 'I saw it.'

There was a silence. We looked at Shearwater's burnt-out hull, hauled up on the breakwater. The hole where the coach-roof had been gaped like the socket of a tooth.

'Gas?' said Charlie.

'That's right.' I did not want to talk about it.

Charlie said, 'What time are we supposed to be at this party?'

'We've got an hour.'

'Let's have a look at that ketch you brought over.'

We paid the bill and walked along the waterfront, past

Percy's Bar and the shops selling snakeskin bikini bottoms. *Aldebaran* was chocked in the far corner of the yard, towards the sea.

'Jeez,' said Scotto. 'What a heap.'

For all his eagerness when we first arrived, Deke did not seem to have touched her since. Her hull was a peeling barrel against the sky. There was a ladder propped against her on the seaward side. I went up it and across her gaping deck seams. Charlie and Scotto dived into her bowels. Her main hatch was open.

I was wrong; someone had been at her. The deck in the hold had been torn up, and some of the ballast had been removed. Charlie came through into the hold from the saloon, craned his neck up at me. 'You're lucky to be alive,' he said.

'*¡Oiga!*'

I looked over the side. A small man in blue overalls was coming towards me. He was wearing a badge and shaking his head. I told him I had sailed the boat to Marbella, and he too told me I was lucky to be alive. Then he escorted us to the yard gate.

'You're telling me this Deke bought that thing off a photograph?' said Charlie.

I nodded.

'And it passed a survey?' We walked on. 'Strikes me,' said Charlie, 'that your friend Paul Welsh maybe had a word with the surveyor.'

'I reckon he bribed the bastard,' said Scotto. 'If I was this Deke bloke I'd kick his arse all over Spain.'

'Maybe he is,' said Charlie. 'Paul was very timid today, I hear.' I did not say anything. I had my own views on why Paul was being timid.

'He's still a problem,' said Scotto. 'Timid or not.'

Night was falling. The lights came on suddenly. The horrible burnt-out thing dragged up the breakwater faded into deep shadows. We had another drink. After half an hour, we set out for Deke's party.

'Bloody hell,' said Scotto. 'Someone's been spending a few bob.'

From the gate, I could see cars parked in front of the heavy front door. The dogs must be locked up for the evening.

I stopped the car. 'Take her in,' I said. 'I'm going for a walk.'

The air was warm. I went out of the gate. I wanted to see the lie of the land outside the walls.

A little breeze ruffled the trees in the olive grove. I liked the olive grove. It and the Nevilles' house were the only two places I had seen on this filthy coast that had any trace of wildness. The evening's last birds were singing in the thick of the trees. Deke's garden wall was like a blank dam, keeping out a world that did not care about important things like money and property. The olive grove was land, not real estate. At its end, the wall curved round the top of a low, scrubby cliff above a beach. I scrambled down on to the beach. The sea murmured; the wall ran on to the left, with a door in its centre. Steps led to the door. I tried the handle. It was locked.

Beyond the door, the wall met the neighbour's fence. It was reinforced with prickly pears, and I did not fancy climbing through it. I went back the way I had come, following the wall through the olive grove.

It was rough underfoot, hard to negotiate in the growing dusk. I kept my eyes on my feet. Half-way along, something pale caught my eye at the base of the wall. I stopped, picked it up, shone my flashlight on it.

And I stood very still, not even breathing.

It was a little brown plastic bottle. There was a label on the bottle. It said: *One three times a day or as required. Commander H. MacFarlane.* The bottle was empty.

I slipped it into my pocket with a hand that shook. Above me, a red-tiled roof ran down to the top of the wall. Garden sheds. Deke's garden sheds.

Slowly, I walked out of the orchard, and through the heavy iron gates.

21

The floodlights were on in the garden. The orange trees threw no shadows, and the front of the house was a windowless sheet of white stucco. There were no hiding places.

The heavy oak door swung open. Beside it stood Jacky Damage, like a lethal butler.

There was a roar of voices from the marble stairs. I walked past the paintings and the dyed papyrus plumes, and on to the balcony. Charlie and Scotto were by the bar. Deke came towards us, wearing his usual white shirt and high-waisted trousers, carrying a bottle of champagne.

I introduced him to Charlie and Scotto. I could feel the bulge of the pill bottle in my pocket. Charlie said, 'So that's your ketch in the yard?'

'Yeah,' said Deke, grinning. His eyes were cold as camera lenses. 'What d'you reckon?'

'Needs a bit of work,' said Charlie.

'That's right,' said Deke, nodding. 'That's right.'

'Are you going to do it here?' said Scotto.

'Haven't decided,' said Deke, with a big, thin-lipped smile. 'Somewhere or other.' His eyes roamed the crowd. 'You seen Paulie?'

I shook my head.

He winked. 'No,' he said. 'No. Probably reckons he needs his beauty sleep, after the way you sailed today.' He laughed, and punched me on the arm, and moved his big shoulders off into the crowd.

Charlie watched him go. 'You ever tried to get a boat rebuilt in southern Spain?' he said.

'Must be insane,' said Scotto.

'He'll never do it. Why the hell did he make you bring it all the way out here when he could have had it mended in England for half the money?'

The first time I had heard *Aldebaran* had been sold, I had jumped to the conclusion that the purchaser was either an enthusiast, or very rich and very stupid. Deke was neither of these things, and it was hardly credible that he should have used the boat merely as a vehicle for Paul and his tin box. 'Very hard to say,' I said. I was going to say that I was planning to find out. But at that moment, I caught a glimpse of a tan shoulder and a head of greasy, thinning hair on the other side of the balcony. I went after it.

The greasy head went through the balcony door. Heading for an interview with his little packet of face powder, I thought. I caught up with him at the head of the stairs. I said, 'Squeal.'

His face was yellowish and sallow. It went paler when he saw me. His eyes were snapping; he had been at the white goods already. 'What do you want?' he said.

'Where did you find that cigarette case?'

He said, 'Keep quiet,' in a terrified hiss.

'Not till you tell me where,' I said.

'I told you. Nevilles.'

'Try again.'

'Jesus,' he said. 'Here. It was here.'

'Over the wall,' I said. 'In the olive grove.'

He said, 'How did you know?' His face was white as paper.

This time, I knew he was not lying.

I said, 'Where is the man those things belong to?'

He was not listening any more. He was looking over my shoulder, and his face was a terrible colour. Then he turned, and ran down the stairs. The front door slammed, tyres screamed, and he was gone.

I turned to go back to the balcony. Jacky Damage was

164

standing behind me. My stomach turned over, once. He smiled, a wide smile that stretched the stony skin of his face like rubber. ''Scuse me,' he said, and went down the stairs at a horribly agile run.

I went back to the balcony, right to the edge, to get some good, deep breaths of the clean night air. Henry had been in the olive grove. He had dropped his cigarette case and an empty pill bottle. What had he been doing there?

I looked across the garden. Over against the wall there was a long white shed. There was a barred area in the middle, the kennels. At the far end there was something that might have been a garage. This end, there was a door, and a shuttered window.

Of course, I thought. It was not necessary for Henry to have dropped his cigarette case and pill bottle in the orchard. He could have thrown them over the wall, from inside.

My mouth was suddenly dry. I had to look those sheds over. I was inside the walls. The dogs were locked up.

Tonight was the night.

'Cor,' said Scotto. He was leaning over the railing. There was a swimming pool down there, a blue porthole in the lawn. The trees and shrubs around it were heavily floodlit, draped with fairy lights. But Scotto, leaning over the railing nearby, was not admiring the fairy lights. What he was admiring were the three girls in the swimming pool. They were very pretty girls, and they did not have any clothes on.

'Makes you shudder just looking at 'em,' said Scotto, taking a deep draught of his beer.

A woman's voice behind me said, 'Darling.' I turned. It was Camilla. Her tan was like milky coffee and her wide turquoise eyes were shining with goodwill. She was wearing a very small but very expensive looking black dress. 'You were *fantastic* today.'

I should have been pleased to see her. But tonight she was a distraction.

'I came with Georgie Honiton,' she said. Her long fingers twined in mine. 'And I hear you're quarrelling with Paulie.'

Over her silky brown shoulder I could see Helen Gallagher. She was wearing red stilettos, a pair of satin see-up boxer's shorts, and a singlet that said JOE BUGNER TRAINING CAMP. There was a gold slave bracelet on her left ankle.

I said, 'I'm terribly sorry, but I must go,' and walked down the steps to the pool. A small voice in my head said: *that is Camilla, and you are walking away from her.*

I scarcely listened to it. My mind was on the open grey spaces of the lawn, and whatever was in the shed beyond.

The girls were still swimming. I watched them for a couple of minutes, fixing a pebble-beached grin to my face. Nobody seemed to be taking any interest in me. So I started to fumble with my fly, and stumbled into the bushes. Stumbling was good camouflage, by this time of the evening.

Once in the bushes, I pulled off my pale-blue jacket and hung it in the branches. My heart was beating too fast. The bushes thickened towards the little hut at the end of the pool. I took a deep breath and tried not to think about Jacky Damage. Then I crept away from the noise and the floodlights, and pulled myself over the wooden fence of the pool enclosure.

The cicadas yelled in the bushes, and the party roared on the balcony and round the pool. But the garden was horribly silent. I could hear my own breathing, and the thump of my feet on the Bermuda grass.

I got into the dead ground at the back of the pool hut. At the end of the garden, the floodlights were a little less bright. There was the high, white wall, with the door to the beach. There was bougainvillaea growing on the white stucco, and a frieze of some sort of plants in a bed at the bottom. The wall curved round to the right, towards the huddle of sheds and the garage. Anyone walking round there would stand out against it like a lump of coal on a wedding dress.

I took a deep breath, bent double to keep as much of me as possible against the black shadow of the herbage, and made for the sheds.

It was a horrible feeling. I walked slowly, expecting at any moment to hear the yells that would stop me in my tracks. But there were no yells, only the roar of the party, and the rustle of the sea beyond the wall, and from the olive grove next door the electronic beep of the Scops owls.

I was against the end gable of the sheds where it stuck out at right angles from the garden wall. There was a little prism of dark shadow in the angle. I crouched in its shelter, waiting for my heart to slow and the sweat to stop running over my body inside my shirt. The house was a sculpture of white sugar with red tiles, clad in a green-and-grey nimbus of floodlights. Water flew up from the pool, and laughter crashed off its stucco surfaces. As my breathing quieted, my confidence came back.

There were three sheds, joined end-to-end. I ran up to the far end, past the kennels. The dogs stirred in their sleeping quarters, gurgling. The end shed was a garage, as I had suspected. There was a silver Mercedes in there, and no door in the end wall. I sheltered in its darkness a moment. If Henry was here, he was in the shed at the other end.

So I moved very cautiously back the way I had come, and slipped into the prism of black shadow by the door.

The door had a padlock on it. I pulled the screwdriver off my knife, moved sideways into the glare of the lights, and took out the three screws that held the hasp. Then I turned the handle.

In the middle shed, a breathy rasping started. The dogs were barking. I opened the door and slid inside.

It smelt like a garden shed. The palm-sized yellow disc from my flashlight travelled over lawnmowers, rakes, a shelf of weedkiller bottles. A gecko scuttled down the wall. It was all pure and innocent as mother's milk.

There was a connecting door on the inside far wall of the shed. I said, 'Henry.' There was no reply. I pushed it open, stepped over a pile of old flowerpots and in. The yellow disc ran over hanks of string, packets of seeds, an old wheelbarrow. I stood there feeling weak with disappointment.

In the corner was a pile of what might have been potting compost. Everything in the shed looked grey and dusty. But the compost was warm, chocolatey brown, as if it had just been emptied there.

I picked up a bamboo cane that was leaning against the wall, and dug it into the brown pile. An inch under the surface, it met a solid obstruction.

Bending, I brushed away the brown dust. There was a silver-grey surface underneath, metallic yet not metallic. I got hold of a corner, and pulled. I had to use both hands; it must have weighed fifty pounds. I held the flashlight in my mouth, and looked at it: a silver-grey slab the shape of a big dictionary. And Henry went right out of my mind.

I had seen this slab before, or plenty of slabs exactly like it. Last time had been in the hold of *Aldebaran* in the gale. It was cold-cast ballast, a mixture of resins and lead that you mix up and cast to whatever shape you require. And I remembered looking down through *Aldebaran*'s main hatch earlier this evening, seeing the planking torn up from the decking of her hold, the dark shadows where the ballast pigs should have been.

There were more in the pile. I covered them up quickly, picked up the one I had found first, and went back into the first shed.

Very cautiously, I put my head round the door.

There was the sharp-edged prism of shadow, and the flat grey lawn. The noise of the party had intensified. Someone was playing a trumpet. The rasping still came from the kennels. But in the wedge of my vision, nothing moved.

I switched off the torch, pocketed it. Then I picked up the silver slab, tucked it under my chin like a medicine ball, and flung it at the top of the wall. It was heavy. It hit the stucco a foot below the top, bounced back, and landed with a dull thump on the lawn. The rasping from the kennels grew stronger. Waterfalls of sweat ran out of my hair.

I picked it up again, threw again, as hard as I could. This time it hit the wall six inches from the top.

My arm was aching fiercely where I had broken it. I knew I was not going to be able to throw the slab over without help. I went back into the shed. There was an old table in the corner, stacked high with flowerpots. I pulled them off, laid them in stacks on the ground, struggled outside with the table, and pushed it against the wall. My breath was coming in ragged gasps. I climbed up on to the table. The line of shadow from the shed fell diagonally across the white surface of the wall. My head and shoulders would be showing above it, making a perfect silhouette for anyone who was watching. I heaved the slab, up and out, heard the *thump* as it hit the ground on the far side, and waited for the shout from the house.

There was no shout. The voices from the balcony roared on.

But underneath the voices, I heard another sound. Somewhere in the house, deep in the part of the house where the guests did not reach, a bell was ringing, on and on.

I got down from the table, heaved it into the shed.

I shoved the screws back into the hasp, crouched low, and started to creep back round the swimming pool. Then the sound came from behind me.

There was the kind of buzz an entry-phone makes when someone opens the door by remote control, and a gurgling.

The dogs were out.

22

They trotted on to the grass, their black-and-tan bodies monochrome phantoms among the black pudding shapes of the floodlit trees. I caught one glimpse of them out of the corner of my eye. Then I began to run for the palisade.

This time, I did not care who saw me. I wanted to get far away from those teeth, and that was the end of it.

I hit the palisade like a train running into the buffers, pulled myself up and got a foot hooked over the edge. The first dog ran up the wall as if it was flat ground. Its teeth clashed by my right shoulder. I felt the rip of cloth. It fell back. I got a foot hooked up. My body rolled over the fence, and went down the other side with a bang that knocked the breath out of me.

There was shouting now. Through the bushes, the water of the swimming pool shone sapphire blue. I could hear bodies brushing through the shrubbery. I grovelled my way across the dead leaves under the bushes away from the palisade. My clothes, I thought. They're filthy, they'll give me away.

Beyond the bushes, there was laughter and the sound of splashing. And I knew what I had to do.

I ran through the last of the bushes and dived into the cool waters of the pool.

When I came up, people were shrieking, ''E's got 'is clothes on!'

The crashing in the bushes had stopped. Deke came out and

strutted up to the edge of the pool. His thumbs were hooked into the cummerbund of his high-waisted trousers. The light made a bright aureole of his grey, curly hair. I could not see his face. 'You tore your shirt,' he said.

I looked down. 'So I have,' I said.

'You want to be more carefuller,' said Deke. He spun on his heel and walked away.

I stood in the middle of the pool while the swimmers splashed and giggled around me. A girl said, 'You look cold.'

I grinned at her with a face that felt like marble. She was right, I was cold. But that was not why I was shivering.

I collected Charlie and Scotto. We got into the car. Both sets of gates were shut now, and the Dobermans trotted from bush to bush, heads pointed.

Outside the outer gate, I cut the lights and turned into the olive grove. The car bounced across the rutted ground until we were opposite the rise of the shed roofs. The ballast slab gleamed dull grey in the dry grass where I had found the pill bottle. I heaved it into the boot, turned the car round and drove back on to the road.

Charlie said, 'What is this?'

I said, 'Ballast from *Aldebaran*.'

He said, 'What do you mean?'

I said, 'I think I have just discovered why he bought the boat.'

Charlie said, 'Why?'

I said, 'Tell you in the morning.' I dropped them at their apartment, and drove into the town.

Squeal's little yellow eyes had watched a lot of what went on at Deke's house. I wanted to find out exactly how much.

The lights were on at the Bar Bric-à-Brac. They were dim, so from outside the window the dirt did not show up too badly. But they were bright enough to show that there were five people sitting up at the bar. I moved closer. They would not be able to see out of the windows because of the reflections. The people at the bar were tourists. Mona was in her corner by the icebox, her rubbery brown fingers moving over her knitting. No Squeal.

I started the car and headed uptown. Away from the front and the Old Town, the only signs of life were a blond man in Union Jack shorts being sick into a drain, and a couple of taxis. One of the taxi drivers directed me to the Edificio Granada. I left the car a block away and walked. It was a tall white block of a building. Washing hung on the dark, empty walkways. The sound of snoring filtered from open windows. Far away a radio was playing flamenco, and a dog was barking.

I went up to the sixth floor. There was a light on in thirty-seven. Thirty-eight was dark. The front door was closed. My heart sank.

I pushed. My hand caught ragged wood. I peered at it. In the dim light from next door I saw that someone had dug away the rebate with a chisel, so they could get at the lock. The lock was a Yale. Its tongue was exposed.

Pulling out my knife, I dug the point of the blade into the brass tongue and pulled it back.

The door swung quietly open.

The stink was revolting; old grease, stale tobacco, dirty clothes. I was in a kitchen, breathing through my mouth so I did not have to smell it, listening. Silence. Not the silence you get from a place that is inhabited; the silence that you get when there is nobody in.

My hand went to the light switch by the door, flicked it down. Nothing happened. Bulb gone, I thought. There were some matches in the filthy litter on the kitchen table, *cerillas*, little sticks of wax that burn with a big, clear flame. The first one cast huge shadows over the ceiling, glinted dully in the grease on the walls. I went through a door and into another room; a living room.

It was empty, except for the smell, two chairs and a coffee table. There were white specks on a mirror on the table. I flicked the light switch. That one did not work either. Fuse, I thought, and lit another match. The bedroom was empty. The smell was worse in there. The bathroom door was ajar. I pushed it open, and went in. Then I took one big breath, quickly, and my heart started banging as if it was trying to hammer its way out between my ribs.

Squeal was in the bath, watching me. His eyes were wide open. His face was twisted into a horrible caricature of a grin. But the eyes were not seeing me. They would never see anything again. Because the cable from the shaver socket, the Spanish shaver socket, no fuse, ran to the big radio that sat on Squeal's scrawny belly in the bath, with the water half-way up it. And I knew why the lights would not turn on.

The match burned my fingers. I lit another, put my finger on Squeal's shoulder. It was cool, but not cold.

Turning, I ran out of the apartment, slammed the door behind me, and pounded the streets to my car. The yell of the tyres shook the blank-eyed frontages as I roared away into the night.

A gas explosion, a radio in the bath. Accidents.

When I got back to the hotel I double locked the door of my room, kicked my clothes on to the floor. Then I went to the window and looked out.

The Elysian Fields were grey under the stars, and beyond them the moon was making a silver road over the ebony sea. Jacky Damage, I thought. He went after Squeal, and Squeal told him what we had said. And Jacky had made an accident happen. And the next on the accident list would be Martin Devereux.

The smell of Squeal's flat stank in my nostrils. I went into the bathroom and turned on the shower.

Someone knocked on the door.

I stopped dead, with my hand on the shower tap. Squeal would have arrived home, panting, got out his mirror and his joy powder for a bit of consolation. Then the knock on the door. He had not answered. After that, the smash and rip of the chisel . . . I found my hand shaking so badly I had to grip the shower tap to stop it.

'It's Helen Gallagher,' said a voice.

I wrapped a towel around my waist and started for the door. Then I stopped. Was she alone?

'Please,' said the voice. It sounded tired; it had no Lower East Side in it.

I thought, Devereux, you are a bloody fool. Then I opened the door.

She was alone. She had taken her shoes off, and was carrying them in her hand. She looked small, and brown, and defenceless, and very pretty. 'Come in,' I said.

She came in. Her grey-green eyes travelled from my feet to my head. She said, 'Do you have a drink?'

I gave her some whisky in a tooth mug.

She sat down in an armchair and threw her shoes across the room. 'Oh, that feels good,' she said. 'Listen, I have to hurry.' I poured myself some whisky and sat down on the bed.

The room shrank. I was in a survival capsule, just me and Helen, while outside in the grey moonlight, men with the minds of wild animals prowled the dusty flats of the Elysian Fields.

She said, 'I didn't want to disturb you.'

I watched her through the whisky, and said, 'I'm not disturbed.'

She made an impatient movement of her hand. 'I found this,' she said, and passed me a piece of paper.

It was crumpled, as if it had come out of a waste paper basket. There was a lot of typing on it, in legal Spanish. It looked like a bill of sale, referring to a piece of land. The piece of land bore a number, no doubt referring to a large-scale map.

But it was not the text that caught my attention. It was the area below the typewriting. There was the signature of a lawyer, and of a purchaser, all neat and correct. On the left-hand side was the signature of the vendor, above a typed name. Except that the vendor had not signed. Instead, he had written in black ink NO SALE.

I knew the writing. It was loose and straggling; but it was unmistakably a version of the firm hand that had appeared on the weekly envelopes that had arrived on the oak mail-table at school, and later at the bottom of the correspondence of the South Creek Boatyard.

The name typed under the scrawl was Henry MacFarlane.

I looked at the date. It was dated this morning.

I said, 'My God.'

She said, 'I found it in the waste basket in Deke's room. That was the guy you were looking for, right?'

I stared at her. 'Today,' I said. 'He was with Deke today.'

'I guess so,' she said, and looked at her watch. 'I pulled it out of the waste basket this evening.'

'So where is he?' I said.

'Who knows?' Her face suddenly looked thin and worried. 'But don't ask. Don't do anything at all, right now. Martin, you're in trouble.'

I did not want to think about me being in trouble. I wanted to be able to ring Mary, and tell her that I had found Henry, and he was fine.

She said, 'Deke's angry.'

I began remembering things it was healthy to remember. Squeal's disgusting face leered at me out of the bath. I said, 'Someone killed Squeal tonight.'

Her face was very still. She said, 'Jesus.' There was a silence. The room was not warm and safe any more. It was full of the smell of wild animals. 'He saw you,' she said.

'Who?'

'Deke. He saw you running across the grass at his house with the dogs after you. I was watching.' She paused. 'He was laughing. He said, "Better luck next time." '

I said, 'I can look after myself.'

She said, 'If you knew Deke as well as I do, you wouldn't be saying goddamn stupid things like that. So far he's been playing with you. Now he'll kill you.'

I said, 'I'm going to get him first.'

She said, 'What are you trying to do?'

I told her about Henry MacFarlane, and Mary, and South Creek. Not just the police report outlines, but what it all meant, the background. When I had finished she sat and said nothing. I thought, you bloody fool, you've got no evidence that she hasn't been sent here to find out what you know, warn you off. You don't know anything about her that she hasn't told you herself. The bill of sale could be bait.

I said, 'What are you?'

She said, 'I'm an actress.' She sat there in her page three girl's

175

clothes, knees together, hands between her brown knees, and she started to cry. I forgot about bait, and being warned off. I went over to her and put my arm round her shoulders. She said, 'It had to happen like this.'

'Like what?'

'I come half-way round the world to do a job. And in the middle of it all I meet this guy who's tearing round like a bull in a china shop, trying to get himself killed. And he's after the same thing as I am.'

'Which is?'

She got up. 'Listen. Stay in crowds. Don't go to the cops, because you never know who he is paying off. And when you have finished your races, you get the hell out of here. And tomorrow, I will shift about and see what I can find out about your friend Henry MacFarlane. Come to the Red House car park at two tomorrow morning, and follow me home. Now I have to go.'

I said, 'What were you doing in Deke's waste paper basket?'

She said, 'It's a hobby of mine. I'll tell you tomorrow.'

She came close to me. Her bare arms went round my neck. She kissed me hard on the lips. I kissed her back.

I said, 'Stay.'

She shook her head. 'I have to see Jake,' she said. 'Take my place in the household. That way, they don't notice I'm there.' She took a deep breath, and wriggled her toes into her red high-heeled shoes. 'See you tomorrow,' she said.

The door closed, and the clack of her heels faded down the marble corridor.

When she had gone, I looked at my watch. It said 1.00 a.m. She had to catch Jake's second set at the Red House. I poured myself more whisky, and sat in the armchair, and tried to work out why Henry would be refusing to sign bills of sale, and to stop my thoughts latching on to Squeal, in the bath with the radio on his belly.

Helen's lipstick was faintly scented on my mouth. The whisky drowned it. The first time I had seen her in Spain, she had tried to warn me off. The second time, she had taken me into her confidence. And now she was dangling carrots inscribed by Henry MacFarlane, and asking me to follow her God knows where, at an hour of the night when fatal accidents were easy to arrange. She practically lived in Deke's pocket. If you wanted a perfect set-up, she was it.

I finished the whisky and climbed into bed. When I closed my eyes, my mind said *Squeal*. But I thought of Helen, and Squeal went away. And I knew that I was going to be waiting in the Red House car park tomorrow at 2.00 a.m.

23

First thing next morning, I rang Mary. As I dialled, I tried not to let myself think that if Helen was right about Deke, this could be the last time I would be speaking to her.

She sounded cheerful. 'Read the paper,' she said. '*The Times* says you are inspired.'

'I've got some news about Henry.'

'What?' Her voice was suddenly tense and anxious.

Keep it light, I told myself. 'Nothing much,' I said. 'Just someone who's seen him around, yesterday.'

'Oh.' Her voice held a mixture of disappointment and relief: disappointment that it was so vague, relief that he was alive. 'Is he all right?'

'By the sound of it,' I said. I did not like the scrawling quality of his usually precise handwriting. But the 'NO SALE' was authentically Henry. 'Did he ever talk about property in Spain?'

'No,' she said. 'Never. At least . . .'

'Yes?'

'He used to go there bird watching. D'you remember? Until about five years ago, with his friend Sam Ethridge. Every spring, when he should have been painting boats. Then Sam died, and he didn't go any more.' I had a vague memory of Henry packing a Panama hat and field glasses, and heading for destinations unknown accompanied by a grey-haired man with a large moustache. But Henry had always been off somewhere, so it made no specific impression. 'Why do you ask?'

'I've got an idea he's selling some land.'

'Oh,' she said. 'I hope he's not making deals.'

'No,' I said. 'I don't think he is.' Or he would not have been writing NO SALE on carefully-prepared legal documents.

'So he can't do too much damage.'

I made a soothing noise. It would not be reassuring to tell her what I suspected about Mr Kellner's business methods. She said goodbye, and wished me luck in the semi-finals. And I went out into the heat and glare of the morning.

I walked out to the car park on the fringe of a knot of tourists, talked to one of them, making sure I was part of the crowd, too noticeable to become an accident victim. At a hardware store in San Pedro de Alcantara, I bought a lump hammer and a chisel, and went round to Charlie's apartment. I took the ballast slab up in a sack. I laid it on the kichen floor, put the chisel on it, and split it in half.

'I suppose it beats ripping up telephone books,' said Charlie.

'Wait,' I said, and banged the two halves into quarters.

'Do you have to?' said Scotto, who was making faces at his first cup of coffee.

Charlie said, 'Now he is going to break the quarters in − '

He never finished. Because I had put the chisel on the first quarter and banged it, and the quarter had fallen in half. In the middle of the flat surface of the break was a rumpled, resin-stiff polythene bag. I cut away the plastic film with my knife. 'Look what our Deke keeps in his potting shed,' I said.

On the palm of my hand, the morning sun was shining on two little stones. They seemed to drink in its rays through the facets cut into their sides, and then pour them out again, dyed the colour of blood, so the white ceiling of the room swam with little motes of light.

'Strewth,' said Scotto.

'Quite,' said Charlie

We chopped the slabs up into dust, then. There were five more rubies. And a lot more slabs in Deke's potting shed.

Charlie sat there for a moment, with the specks of red light chasing each other in and out of the hollows of his face. Then he got up and pulled a bottle of Famous Grouse from a cupboard, and splashed a good measure into three glasses. I do not drink in the morning, but this morning was an exception.

'Ballast,' said Charlie. 'Strike me pink.'

I said, 'You were asking why Deke didn't have that ketch done up in England.'

Charlie nodded. 'Hardly worthwhile,' he said. 'A one-trip wonder.'

Scotto said, 'Who loaded them up?'

'He had his own special surveryor,' I said. 'Paul looked after the repairs. He hired his own men.'

'So let's ask,' said Scotto.

'It'll wait,' I said.

'Go to the cops,' said Scotto. 'Now.'

I said, 'Not yet.'

Helen had said that Deke had friends in the police. I wanted to wait until after two o'clock in the Red House car park before I made any moves against him. All the same, I was aware that trusting Helen Gallagher was not the act of a sensible person. So I felt I had to make an excuse.

'This bloke's into everything,' I said. 'Jewels, extortion, you name it. If the police move in, things are going to get confused. He'll go to ground. And nothing will stick. *Aldebaran*'s not the only boat in Spain with cold-cast ballast.'

Charlie was still looking at the jewels. 'Enterprising chap, your friend Deke,' he said. 'Wonder where he got them from.'

I picked up the telephone, dialled the *Guardian* and got Harry Chase.

'Oh, there you are,' said Harry. 'Your friend Deke Kellner sounds a bit unsuitable.'

'In what way?'

'Also known as David Blackah,' said Harry. 'Family man, south-east London style. Cousins everywhere. Armed robber, wanted for questioning in connection with the Walstein's robbery.'

I had never heard of the Walstein's robbery. I told him so.

'Blimey,' he said. 'Don't you read the papers? It was five years ago. He had some mate who worked there who knew when the shipments came in. So one day, Mr Walstein is looking through a box of sparklers at his office in Hatton Garden, and Deke comes in with a couple of family friends. They all had sawn-off shot-guns. They got Mr Walstein out of his chair. And to stop him getting to the alarms, they made him put his hands in a filing cabinet drawer, and then they slammed the drawer and locked the filing cabinet.'

'Jesus,' I said.

'Yes,' said Harry. I heard the flick of his lighter as he lit a Tom Thumb. 'Mr Walstein will never play the Warsaw Concerto again. Deke scooped up the jewels, about three million quids' worth, and left. He was laughing, my friend said. Out loud.'

'He's got a wonderful sense of humour,' I said.

'And then he turned up in Spain,' said Harry. 'Nobody knew how he got there. He just popped up one day, passport stamped, resident's permit, the lot. No luggage, though.'

'No,' I said. 'We brought that for him.'

'What?' said Harry.

'Nothing,' I said.

'So why the interest?' said Harry.

I said, 'Why would anyone want to bring jewels to Spain?'

'Córdoba,' said Harry. 'Jewellery capital of the Mediterranean. Sell your gold, launder your stones, recut the bloody Crown Jewels if you want them to. Listen, cock, have we got something in the way of a story, here?'

I said, 'You will be the first to know.'

I hung up.

We put the jewels in a safe deposit. Then we spent the afternoon practising.

When we came ashore that evening, Paul had sailed seven, won six. We had sailed seven, won seven. The draw for the semi-finals was in the Club Deportivo. Honiton's lips compressed in a thin smile as he unfolded the slips of paper. 'Welsh against Gibson,' he said. 'Devereux against Fournier.'

Fournier was good. But he had a disadvantage. He was trying

to win the Marbella Cup, and I was trying to beat Paul Welsh. There was no comparison.

I stayed with the crew all evening. We went to a brightly-lit restaurant, and drank beer in a brightly-lit bar, places with no dark corners where an accident could happen.

At 1.45 I left the bright places and went to my car, and drove on to the dark roads that led to the shadows under the royal palms in the car park of the Red House.

Fairy lights looped in the branches of the trees, and made an avenue to the entrance. The distant howl of a guitar solo came even through the wound-up window of the car:

> *There's a Red House over yonder*
> *that's where my baby lay . . .*

People straggled down the steps. The guitar solo ended. There was applause. A clot of people spilled out on to the grit, laughing and leaning on each other. Cars began to move away. Then two people came down the steps: a man, long-legged, in glittering trousers, and a slim woman with a short skirt and blonde hair. Jake and Helen. She reached out an arm and touched him on the shoulder; he blew her a kiss with a camp flick of the wrist. They walked to their respective cars. It was all mild, and innocent, and safe as milk.

The sweat was running off me. I set my teeth and followed her out of the car park and left on to the main Marbella road. There were hundreds of headlights. Any one of them could mask the cold eyes of Deke or Jacky Damage.

She turned through a pair of floodlit wrought-iron gates that said EL GENERALIFE in iron letters. Inside were villas set well back from the road, separated by stretches of scrub and umbrella pine. There was a pair of headlights in the rearview mirror.

The headlights in the mirror turned off to the left. I found I was breathing too fast. She turned off down a track. A small white house gleamed in the headlights, set among trees. Her car stopped. I parked alongside and got out, slowly. The feet would come out in hard, deadly thumps, running. I stood with my back to the car, waiting for it to happen. But there were only the cicadas in the warm night, and the howl of a distant motorbike.

'Come in,' she said.

Suddenly everything was warm and ordinary. There was sand underfoot, and pine needles. No manicured garden, no floodlights. Inside was the echo of an empty house, white walls with pictures of bulls, and red terracotta floors. I began to relax.

She opened the door of a big room and said, 'I'll be right down. There's beer on the shelf.'

I sat and watched a column of ants walking across the terracotta tiles, and half-waited for Jacky Damage to come in at the door with a sawn-off shot-gun. He did not come. Instead, Helen came, wearing a black towelling dressing gown that looked very good against her short blonde hair. She had scrubbed off the heavy make-up. She went across to the alcove by the fireplace, poured a couple of fingers of whisky into a heavy tumbler, and sat back on the sofa. She said, 'I was thinking about what you told me last night. I guess you and I are after the same thing.' She looked up at me, and her face was tired and distant.

She said, 'I was at the house all day. I didn't see or hear your friend Henry MacFarlane. I'm sorry.'

'That's fine,' I said, to cover my intense disappointment.

'I'm sorry,' she said again.

I said, 'Do you know who Deke Kellner is?'

She laughed, without humour. 'If you know a guy's waste-basket, you know the guy.'

I said, 'So you know about the Walstein robbery?'

She stared at me. 'Uh-uh,' she said. 'No.'

So I told her about the shot-guns, and the little man scream-ing with his fingers slammed in the filing cabinet. And she chewed her lips from the inside, and nodded.

When I had finished she got up, went to a cupboard and pulled out a big red scrapbook. She tossed it in my lap. I opened it.

The first page held a glossy brochure. QUAGUE LANDING, it said. EXCLUSIVE SPACE FOR YOU – AND YOUR DREAMS. There was the usual picture of boats, an artificial harbour, houses with steep-pitched roofs. On the next page, the newspaper stories began. TWO DIE IN BARN FIRE, said the first one. The rest were variations on the same theme, clipped from papers ranging from the Boston *Globe* to the Quague *Examiner*. The story said that Jack Walton, a retired Harvard professor, and his wife Una had died in the blazing ruins of their hay barn during haymaking. The theory was that the grass had been too wet when stacked, and that the bales had spontaneously combusted. Jack and his wife had been shifting the bales at the time of the fire, and had been unable to escape. The Quague *Examiner* had plenty to say about the Waltons, who had been greatly loved in the local community, not least because they owned the mouth of the Quague River, on which was a landing used by all and sundry during the summer months. The Walton farm, landing included, had been sold to a property company.

I did not have to read the company's name to know that the company was called Sea Horse Land.

'Who were the Waltons?' I said.

'My parents,' said Helen. 'Jack never made hay out of wet grass. They burned them alive in the barn, that was what happened. First they found the landing. Then they made rumours that Jack and Una were having money problems. Then they drew up a bill of sale, and forged Jack's signature. Then they killed them before they could get their lawyers on to it. But nobody believed that, except me. I've heard them talking about it.'

'I believe it,' I said. I was thinking of the things that had happened at South Creek, and of what that lifting of the curtain of flame had revealed on *Shearwater*'s bunks in Puerto Banús. 'But how did you get this far?'

'I took a look at Sea Horse,' she said. 'It's registered in the Isle of Man. They wouldn't talk to me there. So I hung about and waited and made good friends with a guy in the office.' She looked at me with her steady grey-green eyes. 'And he gave me

James de Groot's address, and, well, I got to meet James. People like to meet me.'

'I am not at all surprised,' I said.

'So I got to be just good friends with James, who is an asshole, as I guess you will have found out by now. He is a director of Sea Horse Land, did you know that? He does not enjoy violence, or anyway knowing about violence. But Deke thinks he has class, so he is useful. James lines up the deals. He doesn't ask too many questions about the way Deke . . . negotiates. And nobody has ever told him that Sea Horse is a laundry for the money Deke makes out of selling second-hand jewels, because he has never asked.

'Sea Horse is making a lot of money. Buy some property by the water, the kind of stuff that never comes on the market because you can only get hold of it by killing people. Develop it, sell it off.' She shrugged. 'Big profits.'

'What about Paul Welsh?'

'Paul Welsh is a gofer,' she said. 'He thinks it is cute to hang out with bad guys. I guess Deke has him around because he likes to see him wriggle.' She paused. 'You know, I think he kind of likes you, because you make Paul wriggle, too. Not that that will stop him killing you.'

I said, 'How do you know about this?'

She said, 'I work in the front office. He thinks I'm too dumb to be a problem. So I get leads, and I follow them. And when something lands in the wastebasket, I copy it.' She patted the second red file at her side. 'It's not evidence. But a lawyer who did not have to put in time acting dumb and wiggling her ass could make it evidence, no problem.'

'So you'll take it to the police?'

'He has plenty of friends in the police. He'll be hard to catch, in Spain.'

'But they won't extradite him anywhere else?'

'No,' she said. 'He'll go of his own accord.'

I stared at her. 'What do you mean?' I said.

'He moves around,' she said, matter-of-factly. 'England, Germany, all over. He trades passports, takes the return half of a charter flight, you name it. It's no problem. He has a lot of

185

good friends. So next time he's out of the country, I find out where he's going, and I tell the police, and they take him.'

I said, 'How long can you keep this up?'

She smiled. It was a fierce smile. 'Won't be long. He's going to England any day now.'

'How do you know?'

'Your friend Paul Welsh is helping him out.'

'Paul?'

'They were talking about it in the club. Thought I didn't understand. He is kind of arrogant about women, our Deke. His mother's ill.'

'His mother?'

'Terrible old woman.'

I said, 'How's he going, and when?'

'You'd have to ask Paul,' she said. 'His mother lives in a place called Sheerness. She won't leave the country. She's very sick. They're a close family, the Kellners.'

'The Blackahs. How do you know?'

'He told me.' She shrugged. 'He has her portrait in the house.'

I remembered the dreadful old lady under the archway at Nuestra Casa. 'I've see it,' I said.

'He puts flowers in front of it. She's dying.'

She was looking tired, all of a sudden. I said, 'How long have you been . . . collecting evidence?'

'Three months,' she said. 'Three . . . goddamn . . . months.' She took a sip of whisky, and made a face. It was meant to hide the tears that ran down the side of her nose. It did not.

I went to sit beside her. I put my arm around her. I said, 'Don't worry. Not tonight, anyway.'

She put her head against my chest. Her body was stiff in my arms. The tears were soaking through my shirt. Then she relaxed, and pulled her head away, and said, 'OK. No worrying.' She sat up and dried her eyes. Then she said, 'Would you come to bed with me? I would like someone to be with.'

'Anyone?'

She smiled at me. 'You,' she said. 'Irishman. That's what Paul calls you. Mad Irish bastard.'

So we went upstairs. And on her big white bed, with the warm breeze sighing in the umbrella pines, we made love. It was simple, and straightforward, and tender; an extension of the close world we shared, away from the animals snarling in the ruins. After it was over she lay in my arms, and I watched the glints the pale oblong of the window made on the curved lines of her body.

She said, 'That was the first natural thing I have done in months.' She rolled over and took my face in her hands and kissed me. The line of her back was like satin. 'Would you mind if we did it again?'

'Twist my arm,' I said, and saw the white shine of her teeth in the friendly shadows.

The telephone rang.

'Leave it,' I said. 'It's four in the morning.'

'Uh-uh.' I saw the light on her hair as she shook her head. 'It'll be Jake. He needs his hand held.' She picked up the receiver. 'Yeah,' she said. 'Jake.' The Lower East Side was back. 'Poor honey. Poor Jake.' The receiver jabbered in her ear. I stroked the little golden hairs on the back of her neck. Then she said, '*What?*'

The voice on the other end was high and agitated. She said, 'Poor honey. Relax, baby. It's over, now. You go back to the apartment and take one of your little pills.'

The voice jabbered again.

'We will have lunch,' she said. 'Lots of yummy cakes at Pepe's, the way you like them. Trust mamma.'

The jabbering faded. She put the telephone down. I said, 'Mamma?'

'Jake's a big baby,' she said. 'The dogs got out at Deke's.' She sat up, her arms clasping her knees. Her voice sounded strained. 'There was some guy in the garden. An old British guy. Jake said he shouted a lot.'

I sat up fast. 'Did the dogs get him?'

'They pulled him down. Jake said he couldn't watch.' Her

voice was level, monotonous, telling me because she had to, not because she wanted to.

I was already into my trousers, pulling on my shoes. 'Where did they put him?'

'Jake said they put him in with the dogs.'

'No,' I said. 'They can't have. They'll kill him.'

She shrugged. Her face was glossy with tears. I stood there, frozen with horror. Why would they want Henry eaten alive?

Then I knew.

Once again, I could see the label on the pill-bottle gleaming in the dry grass of the olive grove. And I knew.

You bloody fool, I said to myself. He's been there all along. You bloody fool.

She was standing in the moonlight, her brown body gleaming. 'They'll kill you,' she said. 'You'll never get him out.' She wrapped her arms around my neck. I could taste the tears.

I said, 'I'll be back.'

She stood in the door as I started the car. The light from inside shone through her hair in a golden halo. The tyres screamed as I braked under the wrought-iron sign, pulled on to the main road, and headed east.

Down at the Club Deportivo, a pair of green-clad policemen were leaning on their bikes and watching the young element falling down the steps of the discotheque. I ran down the quay to the jetty, fumbling in my pocket for the key. The bolt-cutters were in the starboard locker. On the way back down the quay, someone tried to sell me some cocaine. I went straight on past him, climbed into the car and drove back towards the road, looking for building sites.

There was no shortage. I found a gate down a side street, cut the padlock with the bolt-cutters, and dived in. The town was quiet now, with only the distant thud of a bass guitar. The polythene awnings of the site crackled like sails in the breeze.

It did not take long to find the site hut. I unlocked it with the bolt-cutters, pulled out a short ladder and a pile of old sacks. I jammed the ladder into the back window of the car, tossed the sacks into the driver's seat and got in after them.

There were no lights in the long road down to Deke's house. I drove the car all the way into the olive grove. When I turned off the engine, the only sounds were the cicadas and the rattle of leaves and the plunge of the sea on the beach. I pulled the ladder out of the window.

The leaves were rustling in the wind from the sea. In the eastern sky there was a faint lightening. I leaned the ladder against the wall where the shed roofs stopped, and started to climb.

24

The floodlit lawns spread like a pool of poisonous water below. I laid two sacks over the broken glass set into the top of the wall, climbed up, and let the ladder down the other side. To my left, the disgusting rasp of the dogs began. I swallowed, dry-mouthed. Then I went down the ladder.

I landed by the door at the end of the sheds, where I had climbed on to the table to throw the ballast pig over the wall. I left the ladder where it was, and moved slowly round the end. The kennels had a sort of barred porch. Inside the bars, the dark forms of the Dobermans moved quickly to and fro, like sharks in a tank. As I came closer they began their gurgling, flinging themselves against the bars. Their teeth shone in the flood-lights. The house was dark.

The palms of my hands were slippery with sweat. I knew where I had to go. Through the bars I caught the hot, yeasty smell of the breath rasping from their throats.

Good dogs, I said quietly. *Good dogs*.

They hurled themselves against the bars, mad for blood.

The porch gate was in the centre. It closed with a simple spring latch. The bars were vertical, with a horizontal brace half-way up. I breathed deeply, once. Then I threw the bolt-cutters through the bars, and opened the door.

The dogs came out like torpedoes, so fast that I could hear their paws skidding on the grass as they turned back to tear me into little pieces. But by now I had my foot on the bar, pushing up and round, over the top of the door. The dogs bounced up, snapping at my legs. I went over the top in a sort of clumsy gate-vault, landing on the concrete with a thump, my hand on the bars, pulling the gate as hard as I could as I fell back.

One of them was half-way through. I heard a *crunch*, the resistance of a body. I pushed the gate outwards, hard in the face of the other one, kicked the body out of the cage, and slammed the door with a metallic crash that seemed loud enough to wake the dead.

Then I stumbled back and leaned against the wall to get my breath.

Across the grey lawn, the big white house was dark and quiet. The remaining Doberman raved throatily by the body of its companion. I turned my back on it, picked up the tools, and examined the wall.

There was a door in it, bolted. When opened, it led to a little room that smelt of dog. I closed the door, and turned on my flashlight. The beam played over bare cement walls, and another door. This one also had a bolt. The bolt was padlocked. The bolt-cutter went through the padlock like cheese. I pulled back the bolt, and the door swung open.

It was a room that might have been a toolshed, except there were no tools in it. It had cement walls, and a concrete floor. On the floor stood a galvanised bucket, and a hard chair. There was something in the corner that might have been a pile of rags. I went down on my knees beside it.

The pile of rags moved. It said, 'Piss off.'

The voice was blurred and indistinct. But it was unquestionably the voice of Henry MacFarlane.

I said, 'Henry. It's Martin.'

'Balls,' said Henry. 'Go away.'

I said, 'Look,' and shone the torch in my face.

There was a groan, and the sound of stirring. Then he said, 'By God. It's you.'

The beam had temporarily dazzled me. I said, 'Come on. Let's get you out of here.'

'Not easy,' he said.

The dog was flinging itself at the bars outside. The sound was coming through two doors. Soon, someone in the house would hear.

The flashlight beam caught his face.

When I had last seen him, it had been square and solid as a rock. Now it was the colour of lead, a mass of pouches and hollows. His breathing was loud and hoarse.

'Hands,' he said.

I shone the flashlight. The fingers were thick and blackened, because someone had trussed his wrists together with wire, and looped a chain round the wire, and padlocked the chain to a ringbolt in the wall.

'Got out,' he said. 'They came with my grub. Put the dogs on me.'

I could not speak. The bolt-cutters sliced through the chain, and I cut the wire from his hands as gently as I could.

He struggled. 'Help me up,' he said.

I helped him sit up. The effort made his breath thick and stertorous.

'Can you walk?'

'Just.'

He was in no state to run away from dogs. I shone the flashlight beam round the walls. There were no windows.

We were stuck.

Then I remembered. 'The pill bottle,' I said. 'How did you get it out?'

He was bent over his hands. The returning blood must have made them agonisingly painful. 'Roof,' he said.

The beam of the flashlight flicked up. It shone on pole rafters supporting heavy, curved tiles.

'Stood on chair,' said Henry. 'Shoved 'em with bottom of bucket.'

I pulled the chair up against the end wall, stood on it. I was taller than Henry, but I still could not reach the rafters. I came down and picked up the bucket and threw its contents into the far corner. Then I put its open end down on the seat, stood on its bottom, and reached up.

My fingertips touched the rafters. Taking a deep breath, I bent my knees and jumped.

My left hand caught one of the battens supporting the tiles. My right slipped off a rafter. The bucket clattered on the floor with a noise like a car crash. I groped with my right hand, ramming the fingers between tile and rafter. The fingers found a purchase, tightened. I walked my feet up the wall until I was hanging from the rafters like a sloth, found a lodging for my left foot, hung a moment to catch my breath. Then I got my right one in among the tiles, and kicked.

They gave, then fell back into place.

I kicked again. Again they gave, and fell back. But this time I heard a grating as they moved.

My fingers were cramping, and the tendons of my forearms felt like red-hot wires. I kicked again.

There was a long scraping slither, and a crash. The night air flowed in through a hole the size of three tiles. I kicked the battens away, shoved a leg through, and wriggled my body out on to the roof. The night air smelt delicious.

'Getting a ladder,' I said, into the dark hole. He was coughing, a hideous bubbling cough.

I went along the roof to the wall and pulled up the ladder. A couple of tiles skidded underfoot, bursting like bombs on the stony soil of the olive grove. The dog set up a harsh, breathy roaring on the lawn. I fed the ladder through the dark hole and went down.

Henry was still sitting on the floor. I said, 'Come on.'

He looked up at me, and grinned. 'Ticker,' he said. 'Can't.'

'Yes, you bloody well can,' I said. I was angry now. Angry at Deke, and Damage, and the other bastards who had locked Henry in this stinking hole. 'Get up.'

I grabbed his wrists, and pulled. His skin felt loose and flaccid, the skin of an invalid.

'Now get on to the ladder,' I said.

He half fell against it. I held him upright. The torch clattered to the floor, and went out. I left it.

'Climb,' I said.

There was a silence. 'Can't move,' he said.

I bent down, and put my head between his legs, as if I was giving a child a lift on my shoulders. 'Hang on with your hands if you can,' I said. Then I took his weight, and started to climb.

He was surprisingly light. As he came out of the hole in the roof I felt him flop sideways. His legs unwound from my neck. I pushed through, into the grey half-light of the dawn. The sound of his breathing almost blotted out the sound of the dog.

A yellow oblong showed through the trees. Someone had switched a light on in the house.

I said, 'Sorry about this.' I hung on to the rafter with one hand. Then I grasped his left wrist and pushed his body off the wall. He groaned as the weight came on his arm. I dropped him the last three feet. Then I jumped after him.

He was not moving, but I could hear him breathing. I dragged him to the car, bundled him into the passenger seat. Someone was shouting on the other side of the wall. I heard a starter motor cough in the garage as I twisted the key. My own engine started first time. The back wheels spun in a cloud of dust. We bounced towards the gate.

The wing of a car came past the gatepost. A Mercedes. I floored the accelerator, aiming for the shrinking gap between the wing and the gatepost. It flew towards us. We hit with a huge, metallic *bang*. The Mercedes slewed away, and the black serpent of the road wound clear into the half-light. I looked quickly round. Water was spewing into the Mercedes' head-lights. It must be coming from the radiator. They stayed immobile in the gateway, reflecting in the puddle of water. My own car was wobbling strangely, but did not seem to be vitally injured. The needle came round to 140 kph, and I kept it there. There were no lights in the rearview mirror as we turned on to the main road. Henry stirred. His face was a bad, ashy white. 'We'll get you to a hospital,' I said. Not in Marbella, though. Accidents could happen in Marbella. 'In Malaga. Can you last out?'

He struggled in his seat, fighting for breath. We were entering the outskirts of the town. I pulled over into the bus station, helped him upright, fastened his seat belt and got back on the road.

His colour improved a little. He said, 'There's no parking in the olive grove.'

'Quiet,' I said. 'Save your breath.' I might as well have been talking to myself.

'No parking in the olive grove,' he said. 'You know why?'

I shook my head.

''S my olive grove.'

'What olive grove?'

'Next door to bloody Kellner.' He was breathing hard.

'The olive grove next to his house belongs to you?' He's raving, I thought.

'Bought it in 1947,' said Henry. 'Like old Neville. Except I registered mine, in Madrid. Used to go birdwatching there. Migrants.'

I looked round. He was watching me with his ravaged face. The eyes glittered with the old Henry spark: *I am a sly old dog who knows more than anyone*, they said.

'Kellner tried to get it,' he said. 'I went to see the bastard. Last five beachfront acres for miles. Worth millions. Don't need millions. Like the trees. Like the birds.' The words came out slowly and painfully, with many pauses for breath. 'Came to negotiate. Didn't want it built on. Argued. Went away for a few days. He asked me back. Next thing I knew, bastard locked me up. Tried to get me to sign it away. I wouldn't sign. So he tried to persuade me. All that stuff at South Creek. That was to persuade me.'

'You rang up,' I said. 'After Dick died.'

He nodded. The effort seemed to tire him. 'They told me about that,' he said. 'It was Paul Welsh that kept 'em in touch. They said he knew where that box was.'

The road was empty except for a couple of beer trucks heading for Torremolinos.

'But he didn't,' said Henry. 'My bloody fault he got it. Should have left it in the pots. But I panicked. Told you to take it to the bank. Bloody fool.'

'What was in it?'

'*Factura*. Bill of sale. Once he had that, he could burn it, put his lawyers on to it, make a new one, change the register, nobody the wiser. Dropped it overboard, I hear.'

'Yes.'

'So then he said he'd kill me. Killed the Nevilles. Had me locked up by then. When I saw that, I knew he meant it. He had a new *factura* drawn up. Put it in front of me. All legal. I wouldn't sign.'

'I saw it,' I said. 'No sale.'

He laughed, a slow wheezing laugh.

The sun was up. Ahead and to the left, an airliner was roaring into the morning air over the Malaga Coca-Cola plant.

'Beautiful place, that olive grove,' said Henry. 'Lovely birds.' He lapsed into silence. Then he said, 'Late night. You racing today?'

'Semi-finals,' I said. 'If I get through, I could be racing Paul.'

'Beat the bastard,' said Henry. 'Hammer the little swine.'

He lay back, panting. I said, 'Henry. I want you to rest and get better. Then we will get together, and what you know will put Deke Kellner in prison for twenty-five years.'

'Fine,' he said. 'Fine.'

We turned into the gates of the hospital. I jumped out, ran in and explained to the receptionist. They brought a stretcher. As Henry went through the doors, he said, 'Race. And look after yourself.'

I hesitated. My eyes stung with tears. It was typical of Henry to use up precious breath on my welfare.

Then I got back into the car, and headed for Marbella.

25

It was seven o'clock when I got back; too late for nightclubs, too early for work. The town was clean and silent, except for the whisper of the jacaranda leaves in the square. I parked outside Charlie's apartment and rang the bell. There was nobody in the street, but it was a nasty, naked feeling as I waited for him to answer.

When he let me in, I told him what had happened. Then I lay down on the sofa and went to sleep suddenly, as if I had been hit on the head. When I woke at one o'clock I felt refreshed, with a good prickling of adrenalin in the stomach. We had coffee and omelettes in a cafeteria. Then we went down to the Puerto Deportivo.

As we motored out of the marina, the wind that had been blowing the leaves in the olive grove last night was still coming in off the sea. It was a solid, heavy breeze. The forecast said it was going to stay that way, due south veering south-westerly later.

'Right-hand side,' said Charlie.

'We'll try,' I said. If there was going to be a windshift, we would want to be able to protect the right-hand side of the course, to stop the enemy taking advantage of the fair wind, and stay between him and the buoy. Fournier was already on the water. He was a fair-haired man, with a blond beard. He waved when he saw us.

Up in the starting area, Paul Welsh and Joe Gibson were weaving around each other, dogfighting, each trying to get on the other's tail. There were a dozen or so spectator boats.

'There's Deke,' said Charlie, pointing at a big Sunseeker, yellow with black tiger stripes.

I did not look. All my attention was on the white triangle of Fournier's sails, rocking-horsing over the indigo waves a hundred yards to windward.

'Three minutes to first gun,' said Charlie, stabbing the buttons on the Brooks and Gatehouse with his thumb. 'Plan?'

'We'll take it very slow,' I said.

The committee boat was getting bigger. Attack, I thought. Attack.

'Strewth,' said Scotto, watching the boats in the area. I could see his Adam's apple move in his huge neck as he swallowed.

I grinned, a grin that used all the muscles in my face, to clear the tension.

'One minute,' said Charlie.

'There they go,' I said.

The boats in the starting area had split apart, and were hammering one for the left-hand, one for the right-hand end of the line. The left-hand one was Paul. He seemed to be doing marginally better.

'Here we go,' said Charlie. The gun thumped.

'Tacking,' I said, and moved the tiller over.

The boom clacked across, and the lee rail pulled a long, roaring gurgle out of the sea.

'He's tacked,' said Charlie.

'Tacking,' I said. The boom slammed over, the winch sang, and we were back on starboard. Fournier was only twenty yards away now, on port. We were coming into the area. 'Bit of hailing.'

Up on the weather rail, Noddy and Slicer began to yell. Not that there was anything to yell about; but if Fournier's nerves were jumpy, it was worth a try.

It probably had nothing to do with the shouting, but he tacked again. It was an unnecessary tack; it put him dead level with us, and downwind. We were in the area now.

'Luffing,' I said. Scotto let go a couple of turns of mainsheet. Great ripples of air shook the sails as the wind got behind them. The boat hung pitching in the low, short swell from the south.

Fournier had stopped too, down to leeward. He was perhaps twenty feet away. The rattle and boom of his sails came across the water nearly as loud as our own.

I turned to look at him. He was looking at me. I caught his eye, and grinned.

He grinned back, but he let his eyes drop first.

We stayed there. We sat in the water on the starboard tack, with right of way, and did absolutely nothing. And there was just about nothing Fournier could do, except sit there with us. Out of the corner of my eye, I could see the sweat shining on his forehead. I took off my white peaked cap, and rearranged it. I was sweating too, but not the way he was. There is a kind of radar you have to have, in match racing. It tells you how the other guy feels about his boat, his breakfast, about you. Today, it told me that Fournier was on the defensive.

Which suited me fine.

The digital timer on the coachroof above the companion flicked down. On the other boat, the crew were muttering in French. I let the numbers tick past 1.15. At 1.10 Fournier's men were fingering the sheets. At 1.05 I said, quietly, 'Now.'

Our sheets came in with a bang, and the sails made a hard, dry *snap* as they filled. Fournier's crew were too ready. Their nerves put them maybe half a second behind, and during that half-second we had the nose in front, and our sails were taking the edge off their wind, and they were stuck. The gun went when we were well behind the line. But the opposition was more important than the gun.

'The more we are together,' said Charlie, sighting across at Fournier's bow, level with our mast, 'the happier we shall be.'

'Tack now,' I said, on the line.

And we were away on the right-hand side of the course, waiting for Fournier where we had to be to catch the windshift.

'Murdered him,' said Noddy.

'Too easy,' I said. 'He was nervous. He won't be so easy next time.'

And we sailed up on the right-hand side of the course, for the windward mark.

Fournier's nerves stayed bad. The start seemed to have rattled him, and he never recovered. Charlie and the boys worked well. The spinnaker popped out like a huge orange at the windward mark, and we flew round. The windshift did not materialise, but that was no problem; morale is everything, and Fournier's had taken a hammering at the start. So we came over the line a full thirty seconds ahead of him.

But there was no back-slapping. There were two more races to sail.

Fournier's grin was not so convincing at the start of the second race. We sailed him out of the water, and crossed the line ten boat lengths ahead. And that was that.

'You're in the final,' said Charlie. 'Nice work.'

The radio crackled below. Scotto put his head out of the companion hatch. 'Paul Welsh won his,' he said.

Beat the bastard, Henry had said.

I grinned at Scotto. I was truly and honestly delighted.

In the clubhouse I sipped a beer and grinned at journalists. After twenty minutes I and my crew trooped outside on to the steps, and flashbulbs popped. Then we went into the car park, to collect our cars and head for the showers. I peeled off the bunch for the twenty-yard walk to my car.

There are trees outside the Club Deportivo. Dusk was coming on, and their leaves were black against the sky. The motorcycle policemen had not yet taken up their stations in the forecourt. A green Seat was parked under the trees at the far side of the little roundabout beyond which I had parked my car. As I took the keys out of my pocket, a voice said, 'Martin.' The window of the Seat was down. Helen Gallagher leaned out of the window. She said, 'They – '

I did not hear the rest of what she said, because at that moment something collided with the base of my skull. A jagged star of pain exploded in my head, and my knees turned to rubber bands. I pitched forward. A car had drawn up behind me. Someone opened the back door. It drew me in like a whirlpool, that open door; and as I fell into the dark inside, something hit me again, same place, just as hard as before, so I wanted to scream that it hurt, stop it. But nothing came out, and my face was on cushions and none of me worked. And I thought, with a deep misery, Helen, you bitch, you were stringing me along. Then there was a sound, a trace of a sound; a laugh, long and loud. Deke's laugh. But the laugh was being squeezed between two big black shutters, moving further and further away. The shutters shut with a clang, and it all went black.

It was cold: so cold that I was shivering like one of the leaves in Henry's olive grove. The pain arrived in the back of my neck and behind my eyes. It spread into my stomach. I rolled onto my side. My brain slopped in my skull like cold porridge. I was sick over the edge of something.

Being sick did not make it any better. There was a noise of some kind. Sluggishly, I worked out what it was. Water, slamming against a hull. The sound of a boat under way. An engine. But the boat seemed to be tilting. Heeling, you called it. So it was a sailing boat. What was I doing on a sailing boat?

My mind scrabbled at the question, got a grip. The nausea came back. I was sick again. There were footsteps. 'Ugh!' said a voice. ''E's 'ad a puke.'

'Filfy bastard,' said another voice. There was a noise behind the voice; the growl and bubble of a big engine. Not the noise of a yacht's auxiliary. 'Let's do it here.'

I still did not understand what was going on. But down in my scrambled brains, some part of me knew. I found I was shuddering like a stunned fish.

Feet rattled on the cabin sole. I tried to get my legs under me to kick. They would not co-operate. Hands gripped my arm.

'Christ,' said the voice. ''E's bloody 'eavy.'

'Lucky fish,' said the first voice.

I said, 'What is this?' All that came out was a thick, gluey croak.

''E's awake,' said the first voice.

'Not for long,' said the second. I knew that voice. It belonged to Jacky Damage. They both laughed, a desperate giggle, like

201

schoolboys planning a midnight feast. But they were stronger than schoolboys. I felt myself being dragged towards the companionway, legs trailing. My head did not like being upright. It spun and throbbed evilly.

There was a light breeze blowing across the cockpit. I could see lifelines, a tiller, white fibreglass under the moonlight. We were aboard a cruising boat. The sails were up. We were sailing on a broad reach, kept there by the autopilot nudging at the tiller.

The breeze felt cool on my hot forehead. It became easier to think. Out there in the night, motoring parallel to the boat, was a big motor yacht. Sailing yacht and motor yacht carving parallel wakes on the black sea under the moon; a getaway cliché.

'Go on, then,' said Jacky Damage. 'Get up on the edge.' Like a dentist. *Open wide.* My knees were against the seat in the cockpit. I could hear the ticking of the autopilot, the thump of my heart above the long bubble of the wake. All of a sudden, my head was clear. The knowledge brought the strength back into my legs. Bracing one foot against the seat, I shoved violently backwards.

The man on my left arm grunted. I saw his hand go up. Something banged into my skull where it met my neck. If it had hit clean, it would have taken my head off. But it glanced off sideways. Agony exploded in my head, and I tried to shout. No sound came out. Things were happening out there beyond the red haze of pain. Somebody pushed me from behind. Something hit the front of my legs just above the knees, and tripped me. I went forward, hands out to brace myself against the fall.

The hands did not work, because I was not falling on to anything hard. Arms outstretched, I went smash into deep, black, salty water.

26

I went in with my mouth open. Water poured in, and I choked. I could feel myself rolling, and for a moment I did not know which way up I was. But the Mediterranean is salty, and it floats you easily. My head broke water, and I got rid of the bitter mouthful. *Get organised*, I told myself. The pain in the head was very nasty indeed; the water was cool, but it did not seem to be helping. *Get organised*.

I heard the sudden thunder of engines in the night. A disc of light appeared, a little sun throwing off dazzling white rays. Searchlight, I thought, in between the hammerings of the head. Down, down. They'll run you down. So I struggled down again, into the cold black. The surface glared suddenly white as the searchlight beam passed over the top; I could hear the rapid ticking of the Sunseeker's propellors in the water. Holding my breath made my head worse. I did not want to be seen on top of the water, but I could not stay down any longer. I let myself come up, gasped air.

The searchlight went out. The engines faded. The moon gleamed palely in the sky.

The sea was black, and huge. It heaved with a long, slow lift of swell. To my left I could see red and green sidelights, a white stern light, the pale loom of a sail in the moonlight. In my fuddlement, I lifted my hand and opened my mouth to shout.

Then I knew what it was. It was the cruiser from which I had been thrown overboard, sailing away on autopilot towards the coast of Africa. Must have slipped, they would say when the boat came ashore. Promising chap. Sad, very sad.

Suddenly the sea was cold, and the cold penetrated my shirt and trousers and my skin, and struck in, towards the heart and stomach.

Far away to my right, a frieze of orange and white lights was strung along the horizon, dipping behind the gleaming backs of the swell when I went down into a trough. They would be the lights of the coast. But they were too widely-spaced and jagged to be the lights of Marbella. My numb brain gnawed at the problem. Where was I?

A wave bigger than the rest rolled under me. From its crest, I saw that along the base of the lights, the individual points coalesced into a glowing mass. The chill deepened. The lights over there were scattered among the mountains above Marbella; that glowing mass visible from the big wave would have been the town itself.

That would put me more than ten miles offshore. Ten miles is a long, long way to swim in the middle of the night, even if you are fit.

I blinked at the lights, and tried to tell myself that the jagged lump of pain in my head would go away, and that I could swim ashore easily, if I took my time. Then I saw Deke's high boxer's cheeks and his flat, calculating eyes. He would have done his homework. I would no more be able to swim to Marbella than cross the Atlantic on roller skates.

I trod water, and spat out salt, and concentrated very hard on keeping my breathing slow. Panic would be no good. But I thought of the tiredness: the aching limbs, the slow sink into the water. And the fierce struggle against choking, far away, where no one would hear.

Water slopped into my mouth, and I choked. Suddenly I could feel the hundred yards of black water below me; I saw myself as an insect, kicking in the surface film of this vast black trap. Water came into my mouth again, and I started to sink. Somewhere at the back of my mind, a tiny voice said: Why string it out? It's better this way. Let go; close your eyes, float down into the dark, away from the agony in your head, the fear —

My head broke the surface. I shouted, '*No!*' The sound was flat and pathetic in the dark heave of the water. I kicked off my trousers, and pulled my shirt over my head. Then, turning my face to the lights, I began to swim.

It was easy swimming at first. The day's heat had faded from the mountains inland, cooling the air, which flowed down the slopes and out over the sea in a light offshore breeze. The lights of the town came and went, came and went with the big roll of the sea, so it was not difficult to stay on course. There were four blotches of light high on the mountains, roughly arranged as the corners of a diamond. I used them as my main mark. Soon my shoulders started to hurt, and the pain spread up into the bruised patch at the base of my skull and over into my eyes. My legs were stiff, too. The diamond of lights floated in the blackness. It was not a diamond, but a cross. And I was on that cross, nailed up. The agony in my neck and shoulders was because I had been seen hanging there by my arms all afternoon, in the sun. But the wind on my body was cold and wet —

Cold water ran into my mouth. I rolled on to my back and rested, looking up at the sky. It was deep black, set with billions of heavy yellow stars that looked down at me and did not give a damn. For some reason, that cheered me up. Sod you, I thought, I'll show you. And I rolled on to my stomach again, and began to kick for the lights.

Visitors began to arrive. Helen came and told me that everything was all right. That was annoying, because any fool could see that everything was exactly the opposite. But I could not argue, because by this time Paul was sitting on my shoulders, driving my face into the water and telling me about his plans to fill in South Creek and open a supermarket. He was heavy. I began to sink. Breathing was painful and difficult, and the salt had burnt the inside of my mouth into a dry, bitter cavern. But worse than that was that when I put my face down, I could see Squeal down there. He looked unhappy, even for Squeal, and I knew that if I went down to join him I would never come back again, and the prospect of spending eternity with Squeal was very undesirable indeed.

I breathed water again, choked, and managed to roll over on to my back. This time, it must have taken ten minutes to get my strength back. I was very tired. Out of the corner of my eye, I could see the thick slab of light that was Marbella, in full view now, spread along the edge of the sea. It was perfectly obvious that it was too far away, and I knew I was going to die. I was angry. Angry that I would not be out in the races tomorrow, with a chance to put Paul through the mincing machine, and win the bet. Thinking of Paul set me thinking about Deke. Thinking about Deke made me angrier. And the anger gave me the push to roll on to my front once again, and start propelling my throbbing skull across the black swell towards the shimmer of the lights.

Cold water does not encourage anger. It faded quickly, and the weariness came back. I felt my arms becoming slower and slower, rested again. It was getting harder to float, so I rolled back. Soon the arms would stop, and that would be that. Squinting at the dazzle of lights on the horizon, I struggled on.

One of the lights moved.

Car, I thought. Late night driver. Going home, bed, wake up in the morning. Lucky bastard.

The light moved again, out of the bright patch that had hidden it, and across a less brilliant patch. I felt my heart speed up, breathed a faceful of spray. There were three lights. The lowest was red; a ship showing her port side. Above it, floating against the dazzle of the city, was a white light, with directly above it another red. They came and went, those lights, losing themselves against the background. But I knew what they meant as well as if I had the almanac open in the water in front of me. *In addition to sidelights, two all-round lights, red over white. A vessel fishing, other than trawling.*

It could not be more than half a mile away, that vessel fishing other than trawling. Clenching my teeth, I began to plod heavily towards it.

I wanted to live now. The visions had gone. Now there was only pain. The lights had stopped moving. I could see the

206

spidery black lines of a mast and rigging, hear the clank of an elderly diesel. *Stay there*, I yelled in my mind. *Stay there*.

My arms were numb; they moved like the paddles of an old, old steamer. The boat was only two hundred yards away now. I could see its side like a black wall, the figures of men moving in the working lights on her main deck, hear the clank of some kind of windlass. I stopped in the water, raised a hand, shouted. But there is a lot of noise on the deck of a fishing boat, and my voice sank into the racket like a stone into deep mud. I swam on. *Stay there. Stay there.*

I was a mere hundred yards away now. A man was standing looking up at a machine on deck. He had his back to me. I yelled, thrashed the water. He did not turn. I'll get close, I said to myself, planning. Then I'll yell again. My shoulders were on fire, my legs like iron bars. I was twenty yards off the side, now. The man's back was silhouetted against the deck lights. He was so close I could see the sleeves of his T-shirt fluttering in the breeze. The clatter of the diesels was very loud. I opened my mouth to shout.

The engine noise fell lower. White water churned under the counter. Slowly at first, then gathering speed, the fishing boat began to move ahead.

I was too late.

I went mad, or as mad as you can go when your arms are dropping off your shoulders and your legs no longer function. I moved the last twenty yards to the ship's side, felt the kick of the propellor's wash spin me over. Then I was watching the tall black stern moving into the darkness; ten yards away, then fifteen, and the lights of Marbella were winking once more, eight miles away over the black swell.

I trod water, and watched salvation fade into the dark.

Something bashed my arm. I jumped away from it, thinking, shark, dolphin, creature of blackness. It brushed me again. My heart hammered furiously, full of a sort of mad fear of anything that came in the dark. I put my hand out to put it away, and felt a smooth, round object.

A net float.

My hand tightened, and closed on rope. The rope was moving. It tried to pull my arms out of their sockets. I hung on, buried in water, my legs tangled in the meshes, as the net went through the sea and walloped me against the lovely steel plating of the fishing boat's side. I was shouting as I went up the side. Someone heard the shouting as I came over the rail, and stopped the big steel roller that was winding in the net. I saw brilliant lights, and three stocky men who had not shaved, staring with their mouths open in the black stubble. One of them had just taken a small swordfish out of the net.

'*Bueñas noches*,' I said.

Then everything went hazy. I have a vague memory of being led to a bunk that smelt of rotten fish and wine and black tobacco, and looking at my fingers, which were as wrinkled as a washerwoman's. Then I must have passed out.

The next thing I knew, someone was shaking me by the shoulder, which hurt a lot. It was one of the fishermen, grinning out of his unshaven monkey face and shoving a cup of coffee at me.

When I swung my feet off the bed, my head hurt, and the muscles in my shoulders felt as if they were all mixed up with broken glass, and I could not be sure I was not going to be sick. But I managed to grin and choke down some of the coffee, which was heavily laced with brandy. The brandy burned down into my stomach with the gentle warmth of a red-hot blowtorch. The fishermen gave me a pair of overalls, much too small. I went on deck.

The Puerto Pesquero of Marbella was burning white-hot under the morning sun.

'*Bien dormido*,' said the fisherman. 'You slept well?'

'*¿Qué hora es?*' I said.

He showed me his watch, an elaborate Japanese object. It said five past ten. I nodded and grinned. The sun was hammering down on the harbour and the smell of the city was hot and acrid in my nostrils. It was so far from the cold, wet terror of last night that for a moment it blew all the rest of it away.

But only for a moment.

I went and shook hands with the whole crew. They looked mystified, but seemed pleased I was alive. Then I hobbled down the gangplank and collared a black-and-green Mercedes taxi to the marina. I was bulging out of the overalls, but since it was Marbella nobody looked twice, and I had more important things on my mind than clothes. Helen, I thought. Helen needs talking to.

But Helen had set me up. What was more important than Helen was the race.

Down at the end of the breakwater, the sails were already up. The taxi driver followed me out there through the crowds. Charlie looked up from the cockpit and said, 'Where the hell have you been?' His face was drawn, with black crescents under the eyes.

I climbed stiffly down. Charlie paid the driver, and Scotto lent me a pair of shorts. 'Sorry,' I said. 'Got held up.'

'You're not supposed to be alive,' said Charlie. 'They found a boat sixty miles off of here at six this morning, head to wind, autopilot alarm going fit to bust, nobody on board. Someone said you'd been seen going out to her, drunk, earlier.'

I said, 'Who said that?'

Charlie shrugged. 'Rumour.'

Somebody else had heard the rumour. Down the dock, Paul Welsh was putting elastic bands on his spinnaker. Or had been; because now he was staring across at me, like a Greek god who has seen a ghost.

I called, 'Morning, Paul. You ready?'

He grinned, a weak, watery grin that hardly stretched his face.

Charlie said, 'What's wrong with him?'

I said, 'His friend Deke Kellner took me out on your missing boat. They banged me on the head and threw me overboard, out there.' I pointed at the blue sheet of the sea, molten under the sun.

Charlie looked at the sea, then at me. 'Overboard?' He frowned at me. 'Out there?'

I told him. He said, 'Are you sure you're fit to sail?'

27

The spectator boats came out with us, black against the glitter of the sun; Honiton and Archer, and the men with the note-books and lenses. Their engines buzzed like flies gathering before a dogfight, drooling for wounds. Best of three races, one circuit per race, winner takes all.

'Gun,' said Charlie.

Eight minutes to the start. I went into the area fast, stayed in the middle, luffing on the starboard tack. Paul squeezed up to leeward, trying to grab the advantage, knock me on to the other tack. The dogfight began, the looping and weaving and shouting. Suddenly there was a direct line from the brain through the hand on the tiller and into the boat. I could feel the certainty radiating out of me like light. Get ready, you bastard, I thought. Get ready, because we are going to feed you to the flies.

'One minute,' said Charlie.

Paul was sitting on our starboard rail as we went down for the left-hand buoy. I could hear the wakes roaring between the plastic hulls, see from the corner of my eye the white slope of his cockpit, his face under the boom, expressionless, staring straight in front of him. The buoy was dead ahead, in the slice of blue between the forestay and the shroud. Any more to port, and I would be outside it, forced to go round again. Any more to starboard, and the umpire would make me do a 270 degree turn for sailing above my proper course. We were spot-on, our noses dead level, racing down for the line with perhaps a foot between us. I wiped sweat off my forehead with my sleeve, said, 'Sheet.' I saw Charlie lick his lips as Scotto eased the mainsheet. He was counting: fifteen, fourteen, thirteen. He looked worried. We were going down at a horrible pace.

Then what I had known would happen happened. Easing the sheet had slowed us, and Paul's bow had inched ahead. We got a little blast of dirty wind, turbulent from his sails. He seemed to shoot out in front as we slowed, bounding forward as the buoy came up ten yards ahead.

'Nine, eight, seven,' said Charlie. '*The bastard's over early.*'

Paul's bow had crossed the line a good six seconds before the gun. I could hear him screaming at his mainsheet man.

'Protest!' we roared.

He was so close that I could hear his VHF crackle as the umpires told him to do his turn. We crossed the line bang on the gun. Next time I looked, he had got round, and tacked out for the right-hand side. When we crossed tacks he was a long way back. We held him all the way up the windward mark: nobody knew more than Charlie about getting boatspeed from a Bayliss 34. Our spinnaker popped out nice and easy, and we headed down for the buoy with the wind on the backs of our necks. Paul got round two hundred yards behind. Noddy and Slicer, right aft to get the weight right, made insulting remarks as he tried to aim his wind shadow at us. But he was too far astern to do any good. We were a minute and a half ahead at the gun.

We sat and let it all flap and drank orange juice while we waited for the next race. The other semi-finalists went by. I should have been watching them. But I was drenched in sweat, sitting on the cockpit bench because I was not sure my knees would support me.

'You look terrible,' said Scotto.

'You should see the other guy,' I said.

He nodded and grinned and loped away on to the foredeck at his fast gorilla shuffle to see to the spinnaker. Charlie said, 'Couple of minutes to the next gun.'

'Let's get it over with,' I said. Best of three. The elation of the first start was fading. One more race would be enough.

The trimmers sheeted home. The breeze snapped the sails into their tight, gleaming curves, and I pointed the nose at the left-hand end of the line. Over to starboard, beyond the umpire's inflatable boat, I could see the taut white triangle of Paul's sails as he headed for his end of the line. They were a long way ahead – much too far for a voice to have any chance of carrying. I said, 'We'll go ballroom dancing.'

They nodded. They knew what I meant. That was the point of practice.

We were outside the buoy now, at the left-hand end.

'Minute to gun,' said Charlie.

'Let it all go,' I said.

The sails, unsheeted, roared as the wind caught them both sides and made them flutter like flags. Ahead, the two bottle-shaped buoys of the start line sat one on top of the other, like the sights of a rifle. On the far side of the sights, Paul's boat was heeling gently, spilling wind, a little white moustache in the ink-coloured water under her bow.

'Thirty seconds,' said Charlie.

'Go,' I said.

The winches roared. The sails became hard white wings, and the wake hissed like a snake where the rudder cut the water. The buoy flashed past to port. Paul was coming straight for us, on starboard tack, with right of way. His foredeck men were shouting. I paid no attention, eased the tiller to port. Our nose dipped to starboard. The spray of his bow-wave sluiced up between our bows, and his side whizzed by a foot to port as I dipped to give him right of way.

'Ready about!' I shouted, and shoved the tiller away.

The conventional move would be to tack, to get on to his stern. Paul's head snapped round. His eyebrows were a heavy bar over his eyes as he watched my boat's nose seek the wind. The thoughts were as easy to read as a cartoon strip: *got to get on his tail*. Winches jingled as he bore away, ready to jibe, the standard countermeasure to our attack.

'Go!' I shouted. And instead of carrying on up into the wind, bringing it across the nose, I pulled the tiller towards me, hearing the wake roar as I sailed into a long, freeing curve, accelerating till the boat banged over the wavelets instead of ploughing through them. At the bottom of the curve the boom smacked over as we jibed, losing no speed as the wind passed round our stern. And we were on starboard tack, with right of way, and from where I stood the forestay was right on Paul's bow, and we were closing at a combined speed of close to twenty knots.

'Hail,' I said.

'*Starboard!*' roared Noddy and Slicer.

The razor-edge of Paul's bow wavered and fell off as he gave way. I heard him swearing as I luffed hard, the trimmers trimming smoothly and fast. The rudder spewed foam as she carved her turn. And there we were, on starboard, sitting between Paul and the line, in control. I looked down at him. He looked back, his face furious, and spat over the side.

'Temper!' said Scotto, loud enough for him to hear.

We started three-quarters of a boat's length ahead on the port tack. Three-quarters of a boat's length is not far, but it is far enough, because on the first windward leg it meant that we were not only between Paul and the buoy, but polluting the wind in his sails with our dirty air.

It did not last, of course. The dirty wind slowed him down, and he began to fall back. I saw his forestay drop past me, the water throwing ripple-patterns of light up the sail. Then I could not see it any more. But I knew what was going to happen next.

When I turned my head I saw Paul, across the coachroof, standing so he masked the tiller with his body. His left shoulder dipped. I smiled at him, saw the sick uncertainty spread on his face. But it was too late for him to change his mind.

'He's going,' said Charlie, between his teeth.

I heard the slide of the genoa across the mast, the bang of the boom as he went about. But by that time, I had my tiller over, and my boom banged a second after his.

And there he was, his mainsail rippling uneasily in the vortices that poured back from the curve of our main.

'Watch him,' said Charlie, between his teeth.

I was watching. When you are behind, sailing to windward in a two-boat race, your only chance is to break away from the leader's cover, and go off on your own. The only way the leader can lose the race is to relax his cover, or make a cock-up.

We did not relax our cover.

The sweat was pouring down my face as the inflatable bottle of the windward mark grew in the haze beyond the shrouds. My shoulder muscles felt as if they had been tied in knots, and my head was throbbing in the molten glow of the sun off the water.

'He's keeping up well,' said Charlie.

He was. He was one and a half lengths behind, now. If he had had our boat speed, I would have expected him to come on through. The certainty I had felt at the start had slipped. I could feel the headache, and the pain in my shoulders.

The grotesque bottle grew; you could hear the waves slapping against it over the rattle and hiss of our progress and the bubble of the umpire's launch. 'Snappy with that kite,' I said.

Noddy and Slicer, foredeckman and mastman, nodded. There had been no need to speak. Being snappy with spinnakers was how they earned their living. Gently, I began to bear away for the buoy in a long, smooth acceleration curve. There was the dark frost of a gust on the water ahead. Sun and sea swam in my eyes. The nose came round. The kite went up, Noddy's arms moving with the urgency of a boxer on the punchbag. I was sailing too fast. The puff hit as we were halfway round, before Dike could clip the pole on to the sail. It swung to starboard. The buoy rushed up, three feet away. And as we passed, the big yellow bulge of nylon swung sideways and brushed against the top.

'*Jesus!*' said Scotto.

We held our breath. We did not have to hold it long.

'PROTEST!' roared the voices astern.

The VHF began to crackle. I did not wait to be told that we had touched the buoy and were therefore liable to re-round it. I slammed the tiller over. Noddy let the kite fly. We were round again in twenty seconds. But a boat sailing at eight knots can go a fair distance in twenty seconds. As we came off the buoy and the spinnaker sheet came in, Paul's boat was eighty yards down the track, kite up and drawing, and we were nowhere.

Charlie said, evenly, 'He's got a long way to go.'

I steadied my breathing. He was right. Gradually, the fat half-moon of his transom grew. I was squinting up at the masthead, watching the tell-tales, laying our wind shadow off a little ahead of him, like a man shooting pheasants. As we drew near the leeward mark, I could see that it was working. But it was very late; we had a terrible lot of catching up to do.

He came round the buoy and hauled in his sheets just as we came down on it. I saw his face under the boom. The sun was shining on the sweat, emphasising the hard knots of muscle at the corners of his jaw. When he saw me looking, he grinned. It was a nasty grin, and he raised a hand from his tiller and put up the middle finger and jabbed it in the air towards us.

'Very sporting,' I said. Then I hauled the tiller towards me and in came the spinnaker in a billow of sun-coloured nylon, and the winches roared as we dug the lee rail in and galloped up on his tail.

But he had us covered, and there was nothing we could do. I split away for the far end of the line, but he got the gun ten seconds ahead of us.

And we were level: one race all.

We sat there and did not say anything for a while. I wanted to put my head down on the seat, and go to sleep for a couple of weeks. But that would not have been good for morale. So I started to think about Paul instead.

He knew I was better than him. Rather than lose, he would sail foul. He had done it in Australia, and unless we watched him like hawks, he would do it again. So I sipped orange juice, and squinted across to where he and his crew were sitting in their cockpit, heads close together. One race; twenty minutes, fifty thousand quid, the Senator's Cup.

'Watch him,' I said. 'He'll get nasty now.'

They all nodded; Charlie, dark and thin, Scotto, large and blond, and Noddy and Slicer, bullet heads on necks that ran straight into their shoulders. They knew what was at stake. They could get nasty, too.

'Three minutes,' said Charlie.

We moved along to the end of the line. Overhead, two helicopters clattered. Television boats hovered outside the start area, closing in tight as we began our run down. The breeze was hot, pouring over the sea from the south. Mixed with the chlorine of the sea was a hint of dust: Africa. The cameras whirred. The binoculars flashed. There was another smell on the wind.

Blood.

28

We were at the right-hand end of the line this time, coming in on starboard tack. A puff of smoke floated off the committee boat, followed by the little *thud* of the gun. The breeze was freshening. It laid us over on our port side, and we stuck our nose into a wave that shattered and flew aft and slammed into my face. Ahead, Paul was bearing down on wings of spray. He was coming fast. I held my course. I could see his face now, his eyes slitted as he tried to decide which way I was going. I had right of way. There was twenty yards between us when I eased the tiller towards me. As our nose bore away, I saw the white side of Paul's boat a couple of inches off our nose. He luffed violently, jamming his nose into the wind to avoid the collision that would have disqualified him. I heard him bellowing over the roar of unsheeted sails, and permitted myself a very small grin. Confident men did not bellow.

Our boat had picked up now, rattling across the waves on a reach as I bore away, then came up and crashed through the wind, Scotto on the genoa sheet pumping frantically as we came on to Paul's tail.

Beyond the right-hand buoy, puffs of wind were playing on the water. They were coming not from dead ahead, but further down to the west. That was the side to go. We would be sailing with the wind at an angle to our course for the next mark

218

instead of directly from it. On the port tack, we would be lifted towards the mark. I could cover Paul tight on port, and keep a loose cover on starboard.

All this went through my mind in the half-second it took to shoot up to starboard of Paul, let go the sheets, and sit there, luffing on the starboard tack, on his bow. As long as we did not fall off the wind and collide with him, we were safe.

I looked across. He was ten feet away. His face was dark and twisted with anger.

'You're coming down on me!' he yelled.

'Bullshit,' roared Scotto.

'So protest,' I said.

He did not protest. He went for the tiller, to bear away. I made to follow him. He brought his nose up again. I brought mine up, shy of touching him.

He grinned nastily. 'Chicken,' he said.

A gust was rolling its shadow across the water on our starboard bow. It smacked into the genoas. We both pointed up, the tall silver wands of our masts leaning away as the wind wailed in the shrouds. I saw the man on Paul's genoa move his hand, stealthily.

Scotto had seen it too. His hand moved like a snake, knocked the genoa sheet out of the self-tailer. Our genoa spilt wind, and the mast bounced upright. So did Paul's, scything through the air like a great silver sword against the heat-washed blue of the sky. It whizzed through the place where ours had been a second before.

'Tack!' I yelled.

'Forty-five seconds,' said Charlie.

We came on to port and moved away to the right. Sweat was pouring down my body. If our masts had touched, it would have been deemed that I had rammed Paul, the right-of-way boat. At best, it would have been a 270 degree turn. At worst, it would have been disqualification.

Charlie said, 'Seven . . . six . . . five . . .'

Scotto was up on the top rail now, his great weight flattening the boat in the water as I bore away, picking up speed as the buoy came closer.

'Zero,' said Charlie.

The buoy hissed past two seconds later. Looking down the line, I saw the other buoy still obscured by Paul's white hull. We were ahead, by maybe a second. All right, you bastard, I thought. Stand by to get yours.

'Tack now,' I said.

And over we went on to starboard, with right of way, heading back into the middle of the course.

I was concentrating on breathing, and keeping my heart beating, and judging where that white pyramid of sails coming towards us on port was going to arrive when we crossed tacks. It was the crucial moment in the race, that crossing of tacks. Whoever was ahead then stood an excellent chance of staying there.

As he came closer, I could feel the grin beginning.

We passed a length and a half forward of his nose, and tacked to cover. They were all shouting at each other now.

He tacked again, to escape our wind shadow. We tacked again, to stay between him and the mark. The game of cat-and-mouse began.

The next five minutes was an edgy clatter of tack and counter-tack. By the time we were up on the buoy, we had increased our lead to three lengths, and even Charlie Agutter was sweating.

The buoy came up on the starboard bow. This time, we were far enough ahead to save hoisting the spinnaker until we were well round.

'Go,' I croaked.

Noddy began to haul. The yellow nylon soared aloft. It stopped half-way.

'Go!' I croaked again.

Noddy gave two jerks at the halyard. 'Stuck,' he said. My stomach turned over. Scotto was already on his feet, pounding along the coachroof to the mast. He squinted up against the glare. My head banged pain at me as I glanced over my shoulder. Ten yards away, a big yellow bubble of nylon was bearing down above the sharp white bow.

'Got it!' shouted Scotto. The spinnaker went all the way up, wobbled and filled. The wake started to bubble at the transom, a long, hilarious chuckle of delight.

But none of us was laughing. For while we had been wrestling with the halyard, Paul Welsh had gone through, and now he was a good two boat lengths clear.

I took a deep breath, and let it out. My head was pounding like a big drum. On the masthead, the wind direction indicator pointed dead ahead. I moved the tiller, aiming the shadow of the spinnaker at the black curly hair on the back of Paul's neck. Ripples of uncertainty ran up his mainsail. We began to gain ground. 'You're holding him,' said Charlie.

Paul jibed, drew away. I concentrated on trying to creep over to port, where the puffs were coming from. My head was buzzing like a beehive. My tiller arm felt like wet string. *Last night I swam this course.*

Charlie was looking at me. We had strayed over to port. Paul had pulled away. There was no extra wind. There was only the sun, pouring floods of white-hot light into the crucible of the sea.

Concentrate, I yelled silently. *Concentrate, Devereux, you bastard.* I leaned on the tiller. Inch by inch, we began to move up again. I saw his main flutter in my dirty wind before he jibed. We jibed. He jibed again. All that existed was heat, and the men on his foredeck, and the crash of the boom. Three hundred yards, I thought. Three hundred yards, three hundred jibes, we'll catch you.

But we did not have three hundred yards. The buoy was twenty yards on his starboard bow, and there was a length of clear water between him and us.

'Make it good,' Scotto was saying, to nobody in particular. 'Make it good.'

We went round the buoy on starboard, hardening up as we rounded. And there he was, sitting on our wind, our nose level with his stern.

'Here we go,' I said.

They all looked at me. Their eyes were sceptical. 'We're racing,' I said. 'We're still racing.'

They nodded.

'Tacking,' I said.

We whistled away from under the stern, heading up for the right, where we had looked for wind on the downwind leg, and found none. I watched Paul. He looked at us, then at the line, three hundred yards away. Then he tacked.

As he tacked, I felt the lift of a little puff of breeze. It was just enough to lay us over and shove us forward. He was going through the wind as it came, his sails empty, so he did not get the benefit of it.

The crew made a noise. It was a low groan, but it had nothing to do with pain. Because the genoa hitched on the mast on its way over, and as he came round, and he stopped. And when he settled on port, we were dead level, sailing under him.

We went through the water six inches apart, hard on the wind, heeled at precisely the same angle, the wakes sloshing and quarrelling between our hulls. He'll tack away, I thought. And I knew I did not have the strength to make another tack. The noises sounded enormous. Everything was turning red at the edges, and I wanted to be sick. It had to end, now.

I looked at Scotto, and I said, 'Sheet.'

Then I shoved the tiller away from me.

Scotto eased the genoa. The boat came suddenly on to an even keel. There was a harsh clatter of metal in the sky. Paul's mast, heeled over our decks, had collided with ours.

'*Water!*' I yelled. It came out as a croak. But the rest of the crew got the idea, and the yelling bounced in my head like red-hot tennis balls.

Paul turned away. It had been my right of way. Thank you for the idea, I thought. He went through a penalty pirouette. We left him for dead, sailed over the line sedate as a flotilla cruiser. The gun banged.

I sat down on the cockpit seat, and let my head fall into my hands.

'You did it!' roared Charlie. 'You did it!'

I nodded. My head was too heavy. If I had let go of it, it would have fallen on the ground. I beat the bastard, I thought. I beat the bastard.

29

Honiton was on the quay, standing to attention in his blazer, his Pall Mall Yacht Club tie flapping in the breeze. He walked up to me. His smile was as thin as a razor-slash.

'Congratulations,' he said. 'I shall be recommending that you be invited to compete in the Senator's Cup.' The words sounded strained, as if he was forcing them out with great difficulty.

'I beat the bastard,' I said, and walked past him, pushing my way through the crowds on the quay. Helen, I was thinking. Now Helen can explain.

My car was under the trees, where I had left it twenty-four hours ago. I climbed in and screamed between the glaring white hotels, out on to the main road. Horns blared at me as I roared across the east-bound lane. I turned off under the wrought-iron lettering that said EL GENERALIFE. There was a wind, a blast-furnace wind, stinking of dust. It made the umbrella pines by the road writhe and twist. Sand was blowing as I stumbled out of the car and up to the front door of Helen's house.

The front door was open, flapping on its hinges in the wind. I walked straight in, and into the living room.

There were books all over the floor. Someone had pulled the pictures of the bulls off the wall. One of them had been smashed over a standard lamp. The telephone receiver was dangling at the end of its cord. I opened the cupboard under the drinks tray, where she had kept the scrapbooks. The scrapbooks were gone.

The wind was hot, but I was suddenly cold. I ran through the rooms shouting her name. There was smashed china, broken pictures. In the kitchen, ants were crawling over a floor gritty with spilt sugar.

Upstairs, it looked as if wild animals had been fighting. The bathroom was a shambles. The cabinet above the washbasin was closed. It was the only closed door in the house. I opened it.

The door was covered in red smears. For a moment I thought it was blood. But it was not blood. It was lipstick, fire engine red. The smears were writing. *Mart Gone Eng Dekes mom ask Paul*.

I remembered her face the last time I had seen it, in her car under the trees. She had not been trying to set me up. She had been trying to warn me.

I went through the rest of the house like a hurricane, found nothing but wreckage. Deke's mother was dying in Sheerness. But if Deke went to England, Deke would get arrested. So he would not be climbing on to a scheduled flight with Helen on his arm.

I put the telephone back on the hook, got a dialling tone, dialled Deke's house. A woman answered. She had a heavy Spanish accent. She said, 'Señor Kellner no here. They have gone for holiday.'

Deke had been through her house and found her dossier. Now she was insurance for him against people like me.

I drove back to the hotel, and rang Paul's number. He had already left. I would have to catch him in England. I got myself the first seat out, on an Iberia flight in four hours' time. Then I drove to Malaga, and went to the hospital.

Henry looked very old, and very thin. There was a drip in his arm and oxygen cylinders by his bedside. He said, 'Mary's coming out. She's taking me home.'

I would have liked to see her myself, drink in her massive calm. But there was a long way to go before I could be calm. I said that was good, and patted his hand. Mary was safety, and someone to look after him. That was what he needed now. The difference between this Henry and the Henry who had left South Creek six weeks ago was appalling. I sat with him a while in the antiseptic hush, soaking up the distant hiss of doors, the birdsong of women's laughter. As I got up to leave, he said, 'You beat Welsh?'

'Yes.' I hesitated. 'We had a side bet,' I said. 'My share of the yard against his. He doesn't own the brokerage any more.'

Henry stared at me. His blue eyes were old and vacant over their hammocks of dark flesh. Then, suddenly, they cleared. 'Cheeky young devil,' he said. 'You cheeky young devil. You may not be my son, but you bloody well behave like it.'

I left him, and plunged into the boiled-lobster crowds of Malaga airport.

It was seven o'clock by the time I extricated myself from Heathrow. The aeroplane had given me time to work out where I was going, and I had an hour's sleep. The cool English air made me feel stronger and clearer-headed.

I rented a car from the Hertz desk, and drove across to the M3. On the outskirts of Basingstoke I stopped at a garage, and made a couple of purchases. Then I drove on into the green country around Winchester.

The evening was soft and springlike. There was young corn growing out of the chalk fields, and the hangers on the round hills were brilliant with new leaf in the low sun. The tyres of the hire car screamed on the tight bends of the lanes. At seven-thirty I turned in between the tall brick gate pillars of Philby Grange, residence of Paul Welsh.

An avenue of cypresses led up to the kind of house stock-brokers built in the 1930s after they had seen Hampton Court. It had timbered gables, barley-sugar chimneys, and an eruption of dormer windows. Paul's father had bought it, to convince the world that he had arrived.

Paul's BMW was on the gravel at the front. I came to a crunching halt by the front steps. The BMW's bonnet was still warm. It was quiet in the house except for distant watery noises. I walked quickly through, and into the back of the house. The noises grew louder.

There were two swimming pools at the Grange, one inside, one outside. The inside one was where the noise was coming from; a huge iron conservatory, with vomit-green tiles and indoor plants.

Paul had been washing off the dust of travel in the pool. He was naked, drying himself by the edge. He looked round sharply when he heard my footsteps, smoothing his dark curly hair back over his head. He said, 'Who let you in?'

I said, 'I just arrived.' I kept walking towards him, along the edge of the pool. He wrapped his towel round his waist.

He said, 'What do you want?'

I said, 'A chat.' I could see his face in great detail. A little square of skin was twitching at the corner of his mouth. I kept walking, right up to him. He decided not to give way. That was his mistake. As I took the last step, I pulled my arm back and hit him, hard as I could, in the solar plexus.

He made a revolting noise and leaned forward, all the way. I gave him my knee in the face. He rocked back. There were white wrought-iron chairs under a potted palm. I jerked one over, shoved it behind his knees. He sat down, hard. The towel fell away. I took out of my jacket the motorbike security chain I had bought at the garage. It had a padlock on it. Quickly, I looped it round his waist, under the chair's arms and round the back, clicked it shut. He was gasping for air now, the breaths booming in the vault of the glazing.

I said, 'Paul.'

He had recovered enough to glare at me. 'Let me go,' he said.

'Paul, I want to know about Deke.'

He said, 'You know as much about Deke as I do.'

I took something out of my pocket. I had bought it at the garage, too. His eyes followed my hand. 'All about Deke,' I said.

'What's that for?' he said.

The thing in my hand was a pair of garden secateurs. 'Cutting bits of you off,' I said. 'Fingers first. Then toes. Then anything else that sticks out. About Deke. From the beginning.'

He looked at my face. He was yellow and sweaty.

'Have you gone crazy?' he said.

226

I said, 'I found Henry MacFarlane half dead in a shed at Deke's. He told me that you organised the sabotage at South Creek. I want to know all about it.'

He looked at the secateurs, then at my face. He started to talk. 'It was James,' he said. 'I met him with James, in Spain. James said he had this bloke who wanted to make deals on beachfront land, for marina development. He said my face, my name would be useful, and I could make some money out of it. It was respectable, too. Honiton was with them. So I went in with them.' He shivered. 'I'm cold,' he said.

'Keep talking,' I said.

'So we did some deals,' he said. 'Straightforward deals. Then he asked me to keep an eye out for some sites in England. I thought of South Creek straight away. I told him about it, him and James. I said Henry'd never sell any of the land. Deke just laughed and said no problem. And things started to happen, at South Creek. You know about them.' He paused, ran his tongue round his lips.

'What about Raistrick?' I said.

'He was nobody. An errand boy.'

'Did he . . . make things happen at South Creek?'

'I don't know,' he said. 'They were nothing to do with me. I promise you they weren't. I was in Australia. So were you.'

I nodded. 'Yes,' I said. 'I remember. Vividly. Why did you buy the brokerage?'

He was chained to a chair, naked. Yet such was the vanity of the man that he managed to look smug. 'Investment,' he said. 'When MacFarlane sold, Sea Horse would have had to buy the goodwill off me.'

'So you had them coming and going.'

'Quite.'

'And what do you think Deke would have done when he found out?' His eyes shifted. 'Or didn't you know Deke so well, then?'

He shrugged. 'You could say that.'

'But you got to know him,' I said. 'Because you started to do things for him. You arranged to get that cash box stolen when he asked you to.'

'No,' said Paul. His eyes were wide, and he shook his head violently. 'Not me.'

'And you set the pontoon adrift.'

He said, 'I was at a dinner party that night. In Norfolk. You can check.' He was almost whimpering. 'Honestly,' he said. 'Honestly.'

I squatted on my heels, tapping the secateurs in my palm. His eyes followed them, to and fro, to and fro. 'So who gave you the box?' I said.

'Raistrick,' said Paul. 'There was a message from Deke. He wanted it delivered.'

I watched him hard. 'Did you know what was in *Aldebaran*'s cargo?'

'There wasn't any,' he said.

'Yes, there was,' I said. And I told him about the jewels.

His jaw hung slackly. He said, 'You're joking.'

I said, 'If you want to find out who is joking, you can go and look in my safe deposit box in the Banco de Bilbao in Marbella. And now, Deke is on his way to England.'

'Really?' he said. This time, he was not surprised. He knew.

'Yes,' I said. 'I think you had many interesting chats with Deke. I want to know how he is arriving, and when and where.'

'Would he tell me?' said Paul.

'Yes,' I said.

'Never,' said Paul again.

I went round behind him, until he could not see me any more. Stretching out my arm, I touched his right ear with the secateurs. His head jerked away. 'You wouldn't do it,' he said.

I thought of that lipstick scream in the bathroom cabinet. The pulses hammered in my skull. Quickly, before I had time to think about it, I opened the hand with the secateurs and shut it again. He yelled with shock. Blood ran from the little nick in his left earlobe.

'For God's sake, Martin,' he said.

'Twenty-five years,' I said. 'He'll go away for twenty-five years. He won't worry you, where he's going.'

He shook his head. His breath was coming in harsh sobs.

'On the knuckle,' I said. 'I'll start on the knuckle, on the joint. That's the easiest way. The blade goes in, levers the bones apart like a wedge. There's only a bit of cartilage in there. We'll pop it right out, easy as pie. It'll hurt, though.' I paused. There was silence. He was holding his breath. 'It'll hurt a *lot*. Even the first one.'

'You won't do it,' he said. 'You haven't got the bottle.'

I gripped the back of the chair and flung it sideways. He went over with a booming crash. There was a crack as his head hit the tiles. I went down beside him, and grabbed his left hand, which was uppermost, and jammed the wrist into the hard iron angle between the chair's arm and the back. He clenched his fist. But I burrowed the beak of the secateurs into the crook of his curled fingers, so the blade rested on the white skin on the outside of the knuckle. And I began to squeeze.

He screamed. It was a terrible scream, like a woman's; not pain, but fear. I stopped squeezing. There was blood, now. The blade had just penetrated the skin. I did not like to look.

'You filthy bastard,' he said.

I said, 'You're the bastard. Ever since we were kids, you've cheated and lied to get what you wanted, and damn everybody else. You're rotten, Paul. Now, where's Deke?'

I squeezed the secateurs. He screamed again. There was a gristly resistance, now. I felt sick. I thought of Helen being dragged out of her smashed house. I still felt sick.

'Tell me,' I said. 'Tell me.'

His voice was high and quick. 'His mother's ill. He's got a boat at Le Tréport. A pilot cutter. He's coming up the Horse Channel to the Medway.'

'How do you know?'

'He asked me for sailing directions.'

'Is Helen Gallagher with him?'

'Yes.'

'When?'

'Tomorrow. Let me go.'

I put the secateurs back in my pocket. 'That's all right, then,' I said. 'Thank you for your kind assistance.'

I dropped the keys to the padlock into the pool, pulled him a

229

safe distance away from the edge and left him there, keeled over on his vomit-green tiles, nude in the white iron chair.

It was dark outside. The hire car's lights made a yellow tube in the darkness. I went for the A303 on autopilot. Near Wilton, I threw the secateurs out of the window. Paul's housekeeper would find him in the morning.

At ten o'clock, I arrived at South Creek.

30

The gate was shut. A man in a black uniform with silver buttons and a peaked cap walked round to the car window, leading an Alsatian. I told him who I was, and he let me through. 'Mrs MacFarlane's left for Spain,' he said.

I went into the office and rang Emily, Mary's Tiger Moth-flying niece. When she arrived, round and brisk, I said, 'Do me a favour.'

'If I can,' said Emily.

'Get two of your planes to Kent tomorrow.' I pulled Reed's Almanac off the kitchen shelf. The tide off the North Foreland was low in the middle of the day. 'There's a boat coming in at about lunchtime from Le Tréport. Could you go up and look for it? Take up a radio each, marine channels.' I drew her a picture of a pilot cutter, and showed her the patrol area on the map.

'Can't fly in the dark,' she said.

'You won't have to. When you've finished, could you come back here and stand by?'

She looked at me with her shrewd green eyes. 'What's it all about?' she said.

'Can't say just now,' I said.

She said, 'Tell me afterwards.'

'Of course.'

I went in search of Tony. His house was dark, so I drove down the long red-brick streets of Marshcote to the Burnett

Arms. He was leaning on the end of the bar, reassuringly large and brown, a full pint in front of him, talking to a couple of fishermen. When he saw me, he got me a pint. I had a pie, too.

'Bloody terrible about Henry,' he said. 'Heart, is it?'

I nodded. 'He's OK now.' I did not want to explain. I said, 'I want you to come up to the North Foreland. We'll charter a boat. I've got a job on.'

'Racing?' said Tony.

'Just a day out on the water.'

'One of the charter boats is up Ramsgate,' he said. 'Any good to you?'

'Fine,' I said. 'Is she empty?'

'Bloke left today,' said Tony. 'Pillock got seasick. What's the job?'

'Tidying up something that happened in Spain.'

He sipped his pint. 'You got that *Aldebaran* there all right, then,' he said. 'Get on with Paul?'

'Bit iffy,' I said. 'He's got some nasty friends.'

'Wouldn't be surprised,' said Tony.

I finished my drink. 'I'm off,' I said. 'You coming?'

'I'll follow on,' said Tony. 'Nine o'clock OK? Boat's in Ramsgate Marina. *Opal*.'

I got into the hire car, told my eyes to stay open, and headed for Ramsgate.

Opal was a twenty-nine-foot Sadler. Her seasick charterer had left her jammed into a visitor's berth in the inner harbour. As I walked along the pontoon, a fresh westerly was rattling halyards. I climbed aboard, let myself in with the spare keys, and tumbled on to the settee berth in the saloon. I was exhausted. But every time I shut my eyes I saw a pilot cutter crabbing cross-Channel in the westerly with Deke at the tiller. And I wondered what someone like Deke did with an insurance policy once he did not need it any more.

I thrashed around on the bunk until the light came. Then I went up into the town and got a cup of tea and a bacon sandwich, and tried not to bite my fingernails. It was a pink and grey dawn; the forecast said westerlies, light with fog patches.

I went back to the Sadler, and cleaned her up, not because I was houseproud but because I desperately needed something to do. I was swabbing her decks for the third time when Tony came down the pontoon, towering above the people coming and going from the moored boats.

'Bastard of a drive,' he said, tossing his bag on to the deck. His fair hair hung lank and greasy, and there was a day's stubble on his big chin. The boat rocked as he heaved himself aboard on the shrouds. I started the engine and cast off the lines. Tony reversed off the berth, pivoted the boat with a hard yardman's kick of engine against rudder.

'Where to?' he said, as we motored through the lock gates into the outer harbour.

'North,' I said, and cranked out the roller genoa all the way.

We ghosted into the grey Channel seas. Over to port, the clutter of buildings round the North Foreland light came up above the low white cliffs. The tide was ebbing hard; it was low at two. I switched on the VHF, Channel 72. We moved slowly, pushing the tide.

'What's it all about?' said Tony.

'We're meeting someone,' I said. 'He's going up the estuary on the tide. He'll be using the Horse Channel.'

'Ah,' said Tony. He was beginning to look brighter.

The VHF said, 'Opal, Opal, this is Tiger One, Tiger One. Nobody coming, over.'

'Thank you, out,' I said. Suddenly my stomach was a hard knot. I had not allowed myself to think what would happen if they did not turn up. The tide runs fast through the banks and shallow channels of the Thames estuary. Plugging against the ebb is a futile business. It was eleven o'clock now, two hours to low water. If Deke was not within ten miles of the North Foreland, he was nowhere.

Tony said, 'Who is this bloke?'

'Guy who was giving us trouble at South Creek.'

'Ah,' said Tony. 'So why didn't you call the law?'

'He's got somebody with him,' I said. 'He'll hurt her if he sees anything like the law. We've got to be discreet.'

'Discreet,' said Tony. 'Yeah.'

An hour went by. We were an hour off low tide. Down to the west, the shore was splattered with Margate. Emily's friend went up, saw nothing. Then Emily went up. We were anchored now. I was smoking Tony's roll-ups in the Sadler's plastic cockpit. I had got it wrong. They were not coming.

At four o'clock, Tony said, 'They've missed the tide. I reckon we bugger off 'ome.'

'No,' I said, not because I thought he was wrong, but because I did not want to give up. 'He may be on the next tide.'

'So?' said Tony. 'It'll be black as your hat. You'll never see him.'

I went below, yanked the microphone out of its clips. We might not see him. But Emily would.

I took out the big English Channel chart, put the parallel rules on it, tracking the line from Le Tréport to the North Foreland. I squeezed the talk button, and said, 'Go sixty miles down track for Le Tréport, bearing 180 degrees true. He'll be making six knots over the ground.'

I heard the howl of her engine as she acknowledged. I rolled another of Tony's cigarettes, and we waited some more.

An hour passed. The sun was sinking, the tide high.

'We've had it,' I said.

'Thank Christ for that,' said Tony. 'Can we go home now?'

I was about to speak when the VHF crackled. 'Got a pilot cutter,' it said. 'Dark green. One man helming. He's twenty miles east-north-east of Dungeness, heading for you, over.'

It had to be Deke.

'Thank you,' I said. The relief was so intense it made me light-headed. 'We'll go looking for him. Can you stay up there, over?'

'Can do,' said Emily's small voice.

'Get the anchor up,' I said to Tony. 'We're off.'

The sun worked its way down towards the horizon as we sailed south. Its lower limb was grazing the blue hills of Kent when I saw, up ahead in a patch of blue sky, the tiny silver cross of an aeroplane. I thumbed the VHF mike, and said, 'Turn to starboard.'

The silver cross dipped a horizontal and flashed in the low sun.

'Got you,' I said.

'Snap,' said the VHF. 'Your friend is about ten miles away, bearing 178 degrees.'

He was coming up inside the Goodwin Sands. 'Thank you,' I said. 'Can you stay up there?'

'Twenty minutes' fuel,' said the voice. 'Then I'm off.'

The horizon was a clean curve under a sky of high cloud and patches of blue. Down to the south-west, a couple of yachts were heading in for Dover. Three container ships plugged along in the shipping lane to seaward. And far to the south, a whisker cut the smooth blue line. I focused the binoculars on it. In the disc of the glasses, it became a gaff peak and the top halves of two foresails.

'Got him,' I said. 'Ready about, and we'll heave-to.'

The sun sank behind the land. The clouds over in the west turned gold and red; the Calais hovercraft from Ebbsfleet whined astern. And the gaff peak came up out of the darkening sea, and grew a dark hull with a pram dinghy lashed bottom-up to the cabin top.

There was one head in the cockpit. Got you, you bastard, I thought. Helen would be below. She had to be below.

We pulled the jib in, turned the nose north and started trudging back up the Downs. We were catching the first of the ebb. We kept three miles ahead of them, our nose pointed as if we were heading for Ramsgate. The sky darkened. The cutter astern turned on her navigation lights. Very carefully and very gently, we followed her from in front towards the bulge of the North Foreland. When it was full dark, I turned off the running lights.

Tony said, 'What are you going to do?'

'Get into the South Channel,' I said. 'Follow him all the way home. Nail him as he goes ashore.'

The red-and-white flash of the North Foreland came abeam at ten-thirty. Tony was methodically chomping spam sandwiches. I was eating nothing at all. My stomach felt like a walnut. The black sea was full of lights; to port, the sodium glare and neon of the towns, and to starboard, the red and green jewels of big traffic moving in and out of the estuary.

At eleven, the red light over to starboard altered course to port. I altered with him. The wind had gone southerly, and light. We hung in the water, ghosting ahead. He was three-quarters of a mile away as we rounded the headland.

There was a different smell round there. It was not the clean, salty smell of the Channel, but the smell of all the muck that had come down the Thames, flushing the south of England. The red running light was still there to starboard, but the compass card had swung to 270 degrees, due west. Lights blinked ahead. The first of them was a quick-flashing white, the S.E. Margate, at the entrance to the South Channel, with beyond it the Gore Channel and the Horse Channel across the wide, black, shallow plain of the Kentish Flats.

The tide was still ebbing. He wanted to get well up the deep of the Gore Channel before it turned, to get as much flood as possible to push him up and through.

'Echo sounder,' I said.

The buoys stretched ahead, winking. On the port beam, Margate was a string of dirty jewels on the obsidian water, falling astern.

The port light started fading away northward. It left the white flash of the S.E. Margate buoy to port.

'What's 'e playing at?' said Tony.

The chart was spread on the seat. I flicked a red-shaded torch at it, and pointed.

The main channel runs along the shore of the north coast of Kent, cut off from the estuary by the long sandbank of Margate Hook. Margate Hook runs parallel to the coast, long and narrow. To its north there is another channel, slender and difficult, shoaling to a mere foot of water at spring tides. It is, understandably, a quiet place, a useful back door to the Horse Channel if you did not want anyone to see you coming.

We crept after them. We were moving very, very slowly. I was getting jumpy. It had clouded over, and visibility was decreasing. The white flicker of the S.E. Margate was three miles astern now. All around us yellow-brown banks of sand would be rising, invisible in the black. To the north, the only thing that was not black was the pinpoint of red light. If we lost it, I lost Helen. We needed a safety net.

'Take her,' I said to Tony. I went below, called up Thanet Radio and put a call through to South Creek. Emily must have got back soon after sunset. 'Listen,' I said. 'Get the police. Tell them to stand by to arrest Deke Blackah, wanted for armed robbery. He'll be coming in up the Thames estuary. I'll tell you where when I know.'

Emily said, 'Got you. The police have already been here.'

'Why?'

'Paul Welsh was found at the bottom of his swimming pool early this morning. Dead. Chained to a garden chair.'

I stared at the microphone for a moment. The speaker hissed like a snake. Then I said, 'Thank you,' and broke the connection.

When I had left Paul, he had been lying a good twelve feet away from the edge of the pool. There was no way he could have rolled in and drowned himself.

Someone must have pushed him.

I turned off the radio.

'Put your hands on your head,' said a voice from the companion hatch. 'Get up slowly, and come up here.'

A pair of hands appeared in the red-lit hatchway. They were holding a thick, blunt gun. There was an anchor tattooed on the back of the right hand. It belonged to Tony Fulton.

'Move,' said the voice. 'Or I'll blow you all over the fucking cabin.'

I put my hands on my head. As I did so, I caught sight of my watch. An hour to low water.

'Up,' said Tony.

I went out of the cabin, and into the cockpit. He was a black shadow standing by the tiller, steering with his hip. The gun was a dark bar between the two masses of his hands. Tony, I said to myself, and tried to feel surprised. But I could only feel numb.

'You killed Paul,' I said.

'Fucking right,' said Tony. 'Poxy little la-di-da.'

237

'Unlike you,' I said. 'A right little sleeper.' My tongue felt too big for my mouth. 'How long have you been at South Creek? Five years, is it?'

'That's right,' said Tony.

'Ever since the Walstein robbery,' I said.

'Very clever,' said Tony.

The numbness was fading. In its place came fear. I could see the chart in my mind. Must keep him talking, I thought. Must keep him talking.

'And you were doing a bit of moonlighting,' I said. 'What was on those charter boats you ran? A few more sparklers in the ballast?'

'Maybe,' said Tony.

'And *Aldebaran* took the last of it. Job done. Because old Deke was converting the Walstein's jewels into real estate, by then. A nice little earner for your retirement. But you're armed robbers, you and Deke. And you couldn't help using your old techniques when it came to negotiation deals. Pity about Dick.'

'That was an accident,' said Tony. 'He seen me. I had to.'

'Of course you did,' I said. 'Just like you had to drown Paul Welsh.'

'He had a big mouth.'

'I suppose it was you that stole the cash box. And you got Raistrick to clout you one in Southampton.' I sighed, theatrically. 'You've been a bloody nuisance, Tony.'

I saw the silhouette of his head nod. 'Yeah,' he said. 'I reckon I have.'

'What seems odd to me,' I said, 'is that you had all those jewels, if you wanted them. There was old Deke, living the life of Riley in Spain. And there was you, putting antifouling on boats at South Creek. Why?'

'I didn't want to get involved,' said Tony.

'So why did you do it?'

The silhouette of his head and shoulders was massive against the paler sky. He said, 'I done it because me old Mum told me to.'

I did not understand, immediately.

'But why?' I said. 'You liked Henry MacFarlane. And Mary.

238

We got on. Five years is a long time. So why stick with a bastard like Deke?'

'Do me a favour,' said Tony in a hard, flat voice. ''E's my brother. You're an all right geezer and everything, I will give you that. But 'e's my fucking brother, and I am taking him to see our old Mum before she passes on. And that's different.'

I looked down, remembering the portrait of the old woman with the savage eyes in the house near Marbella. The cabin door was open. The numbers on the echo sounder were flicking: 1.8, 1.6, 1.5. I knew I was going to die, unless I did something, now. But I could not think of anything to do.

So I simply said, 'You're going aground.'

'Oh, yeah?' said Tony. 'Well, I think this is about it.'

The deck under my foot hesitated, moved forward, tripped again.

The keel had touched bottom.

I took one step up on to the cockpit seat, and jumped over the side. As I went there was a huge explosion, and the night turned bright red, and something very hot seared my right ear. Then I hit the water.

It was freezing cold, with a flat, foul taste. I stayed under for as long as I could, cringing away from the blast of the gun. The tide was ebbing hard; when I came up, the pale semi-circle of *Opal*'s transom was already shrinking. I could hear the roar of the diesel. The transom moved. He had got her off the bottom. And over to the right was the red running light of the pilot cutter.

I felt sick. It was not the taste of the water; it was the feeling of struggling in the great black emptiness again, in a flume that wanted to fling me out into the Straits of Dover, suck me down, and turn me into fish food. While Tony and his brother had a good laugh; *not a mark on 'im*. And Helen was up there, half a mile away, ten feet from that red light —

The red light. It was still there, a tiny ruby hovering at the top of a long, gleaming slope of black water.

I started swimming for that light.

Of course, I made no headway. But as I swam, the current made me crab outwards until I was dead astern of the light. I could see the chart in my mind. *Not far now*, I told my freezing hands. *Not far now*.

The red light vanished behind its baffle. There was a white stern light now, and the dull, grassy shine of a starboard light on the black water. And as I saw the loom of the green, I grinned in the darkness. I had been right.

The lights should have been in line. They were not. The white was perceptibly higher than the green.

I grinned, and laughed as water ran between my teeth and into my mouth. And I swam until my shoulder muscles were on fire, and the muscles of my belly ached, towards the darkness to the right of that canted line of lights.

When I had been swimming for five minutes, I let my legs sink. My feet hit something under the water.

Sand. Hard, unyielding sand. The bottom.

31

I stood there for a moment, with the water shoving past my chest. The line of lights was a quarter of a mile away. The reason it was tilted was that the boat was sitting on the bottom. Aground. The channel here was no more than four hundred yards wide, bordered by drying banks, unmarked. Deke had got it wrong. Faintly down the wind there came the roar of an engine, and the smell of petrol. Deke had fired up the engine to try to get her off. But the ebb was still running. He was stuck for at least two hours.

Out in the channel, I heard a splash and a roar of chain. There was another set of lights out there. Tony in *Opal*. As I watched the navigation lights went out, and a single white popped out of the blackness. Anchor light. Everything done according to best cruising practice. There were splashings, the whirr of an outboard. Tony was coming to have a chat with his brother. I bent my knees, bringing my nose down to the water. The whirring travelled across the pilot cutter, stopped. *Yes, officer. My mate and I was cruising in company, waiting for the tide. Thought we'd have a nightcap.*

Very cautiously, I started to walk up the tide towards the lights.

It was hard going. The water was chest-deep, and running at more than a knot. On the third step my foot found no sand, only more water. Ridge, I thought. You've walked off the edge of a ridge. I let myself float back with the tide, and began to struggle along the crest of the ridge to the right.

The water shallowed to waist-deep, then knee-deep, then ankle-deep. Then I was on dry land.

I crouched on the sand, and wondered what the hell to do next. Four hundred yards away, the cutter had switched off her running lights, and switched on her anchor light. There was a dull glow from her cabin windows. There was none from the companion hatch. Tony and Deke were below. Helen was below.

I paused, shivering. There was no way back to *Opal*. The only way out was forward; get to the pilot cutter, steal the tender —

But now I was this close, I could not leave without Helen.

The air smelt raw and wet. The lights were growing haloes. Fog.

I set my teeth to stop them chattering, and began to walk quietly along the sandbank towards the lights. As I got closer I could see the pilot cutter's mast, heeled steeply over to starboard. The cabin lights were soft yellow squares. Forward of the square cabin windows were two round portholes, the yellow discs of their reflection wobbling on the water. They would be serving the forepeak. I waded into the black water, moving gently, so as not to make a disturbance, towards the black hulk of the grounded cutter. The inflatable bobbed astern. The water deepened; knee-high, waist-high. The current was slack, now. The tide was on the turn.

When I was up to my waist, the cutter loomed high above, her rail tilted down towards the water, the pale pine planking of her deck trending away uphill. Aft, the main hatch from the cockpit to the cabin was closed. My eyes travelled forward. Forward of the cabin top and the mast, I could dimly see another hatch. It would lead to the forepeak.

I stood still, holding my breath. Above the innocent clock of wavelets against the stranded hull, the murmur of voices came from the main cabin, and music: the James Last Orchestra.

I waded very carefully round to the bows.

The rail was a couple of feet above the water. I grasped it with both hands, pulled myself up like a man getting out of a

242

swimming pool. Water streamed from my legs. It seemed to make a noise like Niagara Falls. I hung there, waiting for the main hatch to burst open, the sawn-off shot-gun to blast a sleet of hot metal across the deck.

The voices kept up their murmur. James Last rattled on. Deke laughed, his empty, horrible laugh. Nothing happened.

Very quietly, I crawled up the deck to the hatch, ran my fingers round its edge. They found a hasp, secured by a loop of metal. My heart sank. A padlock. My fingers groped over it like pale spiders. No, not a padlock. A shackle.

A gust of wind came across the water. It moaned in the shrouds and set the halyards tapping against the wooden mast. I twisted the shackle pin. It gave, unscrewed. Slowly, I worked it round until it came free. The wind had dropped. The tiny clink of metal as I pulled the eye out of the hasp sounded like a gong banging. Cautiously, I wriggled my fingers under the rim of the hatch. James Last ground to a halt. The next track started. I waited for the noise to get going and lifted the hatch.

Light streamed out as I put my head down. It dazzled me. I whispered, 'Don't make a sound.' Down there in the dazzle, a voice said quietly, 'Martin.' A woman's voice. Helen's voice.

My eyes were getting accustomed to the light. She was pale, and her yellow-blonde hair was wild. I whispered, 'Can you lock your door?'

She stared at me for a moment with her grey-green eyes, as if she was trying to make herself believe what she was seeing. Then she shook her head. The voices in the next cabin were louder. 'Come out,' I said.

I laid the hatch cover back on the deck, stretched my right arm down. The bones of her wrist were slender as a bird's in my grasp. When I straightened, she came up the hatch without touching the sides. Then she was standing on the deck beside me.

I said, 'Wait until you can see. Then go over the side, get aft, and untie the tender. Take it away, and hang on to it.'

The shackle from the hatch's hasp was where I had left it. I screwed it up. There was the tiniest of splashes as Helen went overboard.

Down in the cabin, Deke laughed again. Laugh on, I thought, laugh on. I'll bottle you up and hand you over to the law. The whole package.

I twisted up the pin of the shackle. Then I padded aft. The mainsail was down. I felt with my hand until I found the shackle that held the halyard to the throat of the gaff, took the pin out. Then I went aft to the cockpit, picking my way through the tangle of ropes on deck.

The cockpit was a large one, full of dark, bulky objects. Very gently, I laid my hand on the companion hatch. It was a two-part hatch, with a slider on top, and louvred doors below. The louvres laid horizontal bars of light across the cockpit sole. My fingers crept across the top sill of the door, found what they were looking for: three rings, one on each door, one on the hatch slider. Slip a shackle through there, do up the pin, and nobody got out.

One of the voices below coughed. The music stopped, and there was a stirring. A shadow crossed the bars of light. I had the shackle through two of the rings. The pin was still in my right hand.

The hatch slammed back. The doors opened. A blaze of yellow lamplight poured into the foggy air. I jumped back to the far end of the cockpit. The head in the yellow hatchway was flat-eared, bull-necked. Deke's.

He said, '*Hello*,' in a nasty, quiet voice. His shoulders came out of the hatch.

I groped with my right hand over the lumpy objects on the cockpit sole. I found something. A can, with a handle. Deke's torso was rising from the hatch. From the cabin beyond, Tony's voice was shouting a question. I got a purchase on the can, and heaved it at Deke's head.

Something clattered on the deck. Suddenly the fog was full of the reek of spilt petrol. Deke roared and fell back down the hatch. I scrambled to my feet, found the rail, and tumbled over the edge and into three feet of water.

'I'm here,' said Helen's voice.

The light had blinded me. I could not tell where it was coming from.

Deke was roaring like an animal. 'My eyes!' he screamed. 'My eyes!'

I splashed round to the stern. There was a dark torpedo shape on the water. The tender. I lunged at it. My fingers hit smooth neoprene, skidded, and caught a bight of rope. An outboard roared next to my ear. I shouted, 'He's got a gun!' Then my arms were jerked forward, and my mouth filled with water. I rolled on to my back.

The cutter lay in a nimbus of light. There was a human figure standing on her side, black in silhouette, huge against the light. There was something in the hands. I knew what it was. I yelled, 'Swerve!' The outboard snarled in my ear.

Up on the side of the boat, the thing in the figure's hands roared and spat a long tongue of flame. The tender jumped in the water.

Tony's voice shouted, 'No! Put it down!'

I shouted, 'Swerve!' again.

'It won't steer,' shouted Helen.

The tube under my arm was shrinking. I yelled, 'Get down!' There were bubbles in the water by my head. The outboard went under, and stopped.

Helen screamed, 'It's sinking!'

'It won't sink,' I said. 'Get in the water.' She splashed in. I wrapped my free arm round her. We waited for the next barrel.

It came.

Tony was still shouting. It sounded as if they were fighting. Fighting over the gun.

A tongue of flame blasted into the night. I flinched. The shot went wide. But the flame of the gun did not go away. It spread, backwards.

Suddenly the pool of yellow light in the cutter's cockpit was very bright, with a bluish tinge, and there was a huge *whoomph* and a breath of air hot enough to burn my wet face. The mast and the rigging of the cutter were a brilliantly lit spider's web. Then there was an explosion; a real explosion this time, with a shock wave that pounded my kidneys and rolled me over like a dead fish. And the flames changed colour to dirty orange, and black smoke rolled low over the silky water, pressed down by the fog. In the smoke was the smell of burning wood.

The inflatable had two compartments. Only one of them was punctured. I unscrewed the engine, let it loose. We were drifting westward. The oars were still in the bottom. I climbed into the flooded boat, gave one oar to Helen, and took the other myself. Helen was shuddering with cold and shock.

'Paddle,' I said harshly.

Opal's anchor light hung in the mist ahead. We paddled. It took half an hour to get alongside. She was aground. The tide had turned. It was flowing strongly westward.

I climbed aboard, and pulled Helen in. She put her arms around me. The stink of burning passed over us. In the cockpit, we pressed our bodies together to pull warmth one to the other in the presence of the death glaring on the fog-wreathed sandbank a hundred yards down the tide.

Helen said, 'It's getting light.' It was true. The fog was greying overhead. In the pale glimmer of the dawn I could see lines of exhaustion bitten into her face.

She lifted her hand and pointed. 'There.'

There were two dark figures on the bank by the burning cutter. They were standing still, watching. They looked small on the great whaleback of the sandbar. One of them moved. He walked down to the water's edge, and seemed to be peering out across the channel.

Helen's hair stirred in a breath of wind. The fog to the westward rolled, and became transparent. In the grey light, a great stretch of metallic water opened out. It had no far side, that we could see. The Kentish Flats.

I said, 'Put some dry clothes on.' She went below. I followed her, called Channel 16, emergency.

When we came back on deck, the two figures were still at the water's edge. One of them turned to his brother, and shouted something. The voice was harsh, the cry of a bass gull. There was a flat patch of sand beside them. A tongue of water ran across its lowest point, shining and sinuous as a snake. Two minutes later, the patch was covered with water.

Still the two figures stood at the water's edge, retreating with little steps as the water rose.

They started to walk.

It was light enough to tell one from the other, now. Tony went first, wading, shoving the water aside with big, purposeful movements of his long arms. Deke went after him.

Their wake made an untidy V of ripple on the glassy water. They did not look round. They walked straight out until they could walk no further, and stood, two black heads in the metal shield. Then they started to swim for the other side of the channel.

It was less than a quarter of a mile. But there was a two-knot tide running in the channel. We were fast aground. There was nothing we could do but watch.

The heads began to veer to the right, up towards the red flash of the Hook Spit buoy. They travelled quickly, snatched away from the far bank of the channel by the tide. The fog had lifted all the way, now. The Kentish Flats stretched miles away to the Isle of Sheppey: a plain laced with torrents of tide, two metres deep at low water.

Only a giant can keep his head above two metres of water.

Helen was sitting up, watching. There was more wind now. It blew her hair back. Tears were running down her face. She hid it in her hands.

The little black heads were two full stops on a great grey page. Then there was only one. And then there was none at all.

Helen took my hand. *Opal* stirred to the tide, bumped and floated. I pulled up the anchor, and we turned the bow for the far pencil-line of the land.

All Sphere Books are available at your bookshop or newsagent, or can be ordered from the following address: Sphere Books, Cash Sales Department, P.O. Box 11, Falmouth, Cornwall TR10 9EN.

Please send cheque or postal order (no currency), and allow 60p for postage and packing for the first book plus 25p for the second book and 15p for each additional book ordered up to a maximum charge of £1.90 in U.K.

B.F.P.O. customers please allow 60p for the first book, 25p for the second book plus 15p per copy for the next 7 books, thereafter 9p per book.

Overseas customers, including Eire, please allow £1.25 for postage and packing for the first book, 75p for the second book and 28p for each subsequent title ordered.